FLYING SAUCER
ROCK & ROLL

Richard Blandford was born in 1975. He lives in Brighton. His first novel, *Hound Dog*, was published by Jonathan Cape in 2006.

By the same author

Hound Dog

Richard Blandford

Flying Saucer
Rock & Roll

JONATHAN CAPE
LONDON

Published by Jonathan Cape 2008

2 4 6 8 10 9 7 5 3 1

The author is grateful for permission to reprint material from the following: 'Music'
(John Miles) – Orange Songs (Velvet Music). Reproduced by kind permission of RAK
Publishing Ltd. 'Doctor! Doctor!' (Bailey/Currie/Leeway) – Universal Music Publishing
MGB Ltd. Used by permission of Music Sales Ltd. All rights reserved. International
copyright secured. 'Foxey Lady' written by Jimi Hendrix © Experience Hendrix, L.L.C.
Used by Permission/All Rights Reserved. 'Flying Saucer Rock 'n' Roll' by Ray Scott.
Used by permission of Ridgetop Music.

First published in Great Britain in 2008 by
Jonathan Cape
Random House, 20 Vauxhall Bridge Road,
London SW1V 2SA

www.rbooks.co.uk

Addresses for companies within The Random House Group Limited can be found at:
www.randomhouse.co.uk/offices.htm

The Random House Group Limited Reg. No. 954009

A CIP catalogue record for this book is available from the British Library

ISBN 9780224081894

The Random House Group Limited supports The Forest Stewardship
Council (FSC), the leading international forest certification organisation. All our
titles that are printed on Greenpeace approved FSC certified paper carry
the FSC logo. Our paper procurement policy can be found at
www.rbooks.co.uk/environment

Mixed Sources

Product group from well-managed
forests and other controlled sources
www.fsc.org Cert no. TT-COC-2139
© 1996 Forest Stewardship Council

Typeset in Galliard by Palimpsest Book Production Ltd
Grangemouth, Stirlingshire

Printed and bound in Great Britain by
CPI Mackays, Chatham, Kent ME5 8TD

TO THE SKYMAN

I

The Golden Age

1

I heard a song on the radio the other day. I don't listen to the radio very often, but right then I wanted a bit of company, or at least the sound of another voice. I'd just had something weird turn up on my doorstep and it was freaking me out a bit. Anyway, this song, about seven minutes long it was, or seemed like it, kept on changing all the way through, like it would start out as a slushy ballad, and then it would be rocky, then all classical, then it would do another thing, like go funky or something. The song hardly had any words, though. It just went, 'Music was my first love, and it will be my last. Music of the future, and music of the past.' And that was pretty much it.

It's a silly song. This guy says he loves the music of the future as well as the past, but how does he know what the music of the future's going to sound like, let alone that he's going to love it? I mean, that song was probably written in the mid-seventies or something. What music of the future was he expecting to love? Rap? Industrial? Gabba? I don't think so, somehow.

But anyway, there I was, sorting through this weird shit inside the big fuck-off box that the Parcelforce man had woken me up to sign for at eight o'clock in the morning, and which was so heavy it had taken both of us to carry it into the flat, when that song came on the radio. And the strange thing was, even though I'd never heard it before, and it's crap and everything, it got about halfway through and I thought I was going to cry. I really did, until the weather report came on and snapped me out of it. I don't need to think that hard about why. It's obvious, to me anyway. The reason is that, and I suppose this will make me look pretty fucking stupid, I can kind of identify with that song. Not that music was my first love, because that would probably be *Star Wars* or trains, but it was a major part of my life for about ten years, and it affected nearly every single thing I did back then in some way. So yeah, I can understand where he's coming from. I loved it once too, so much. And then gradually, without really noticing, I stopped. It was a golden age, back when I loved music, and music, I thought, loved me. I remember how it began. But when and why did it end? Maybe it's time to find out.

I suppose hearing that song the other day must have started the train of thought that led me to want to do this, to – I nearly said make my confession. But that's not quite it, or not all of it. I do want to tell my story, though; not just to make sense of it all for myself, but also because I think people should know what happened. Maybe it might even help a few people to not make the same mistakes that I did. Fuck, who am I kidding? You can only really learn from the ones you make yourself. What happened to me will happen to somebody else tomorrow. In fact it's probably happening to hundreds, no, thousands of people, right now, up and down the country. Then a hundred times more around the world. A hundred thousand dreams, all smashed.

But I can't pretend that I don't feel a bit guilty about how some of it turned out. Mostly, I feel bad about Neil. There's so much of that shit still floating about in my head, every day, however much I try to ignore it. Now's the time to face up to it, I guess, try and make sense of it properly once and for all, get out of this

4

rut I've ended up in. Typical Neil: you're getting along, doing your own thing, and he comes and screws your head up just by sending you something through the post. Even now, after all this time. It's a skill he has, I suppose.

So here I go. Back to the golden age.

Where did it all start for me? Music, I mean. In the womb probably, because they've proved you can hear music there, and seeing as I was born in 1976 that means I was most likely hearing Abba and Wings and Brotherhood of Man. But the first music I remember listening to, other than nursery rhymes and the theme tune to *Trumpton* and stuff, was 'Raindrops Keep Falling on My Head'. I had a Fisher-Price music box made to look like a radio that used to play it. You'd turn the dial to make it work, and it had the words written on the back – although I couldn't really read them, I was too young – along with a picture of two seventies kids with umbrellas splashing about in puddles. My mum used to sing it to me as it played. Burt Bacharach. What do they call music like that? Loungecore. I was into loungecore long before everyone else.

But other than that, I didn't listen to music much as a little kid. Actually, I tell a lie. I really liked John Williams. Not the classical guitarist; I mean the guy who wrote the theme tunes for *Star Wars* and *Jaws*, *Indiana Jones* and *ET* and stuff. Top tunes. If you asked me to hum any of them I could, right on the spot, as well as all the love themes and villains' tunes or whatever. Someone told me once he nicked all his ideas from classical composers like Stravinsky, and played me some to prove it. I could see what he was saying, but you can't hum Stravinsky five minutes after hearing it. John Williams, on the other hand, you can hum a good twenty years later.

5

And then I can't remember what music I liked after that. I was aware there was this thing called pop music, and some of it certainly had a catchy tune, but I couldn't really say I liked it. I was much more interested in my Commodore 64. Most of it I just thought was stupid, or at least I did when Neil made me laugh about it. 'Doctor, doctor, can't you see I'm burning, burning?' I mean, what's wrong with this doctor – is he blind? I remember Neil saying that. He was as sharp as fuck when he wanted to be, even though he was away with the fairies. Aside from that, I got a few albums on cassette as Christmas presents, like *Now That's What I Call Music* and UB40 and things, though I can't say I was particularly into them. But sometime around the age of twelve, that was when I began to get it. It all started then really, with Christian heavy metal.

Now, don't get me wrong, I was never a Bible-basher, but hearing Stryper for the first time, it was the door to something. 'To Hell With the Devil'! 'Come to the Everlife!' 'Rock the Hell Out of You'! Those were some of their song titles. I got into them through Barry. He was my older sister's boyfriend back then. I liked him, he was a good bloke. I thought so at the time, anyway. He was quite shy and quiet, but nice to be around. He looked pretty weedy, wore big glasses with thick blue frames, like you used to get in the eighties, though they didn't really go with the heavy metal gear he wore, with the logos of his favourite Christian bands sewn onto everything and drawn on the back of his fake leather jacket. Barry had a mullet, a classic one, but he usually tied it back into a ponytail. He was interested in computers, I mean knowing how to program them and stuff. And he was a God-botherer, obviously. Anyway, one time he was round and he played me his Christian heavy metal,

6

and I just went mad over it. He lent me a load of his records
– Petra, Sacred Reign and Stryper, of course, and others – but
made me promise not to tape them, because that was stealing
and stealing was a sin. I taped them anyway. He told me that
he used to be into normal heavy metal before he became a
Christian, but then God told him that it was the Devil's music,
so he didn't listen to it any more. He still had all his old records,
though, for some reason. I begged him to let me hear some,
but he wouldn't for ages.

Then one day he finally said yes, because he'd decided I ought
to know what to guard myself against in the future. He played
me Metallica, . . . *And Justice For All*, and oh my fucking god. I
mean, it was just fucking unbelievable. This was music with the
power of John Williams's Darth Vader theme, but with guitars.
Really fucking loud fucking amazing guitars. And they looked like
gods. Screaming, hairy gods, their thick muscular arms pounding
down on their instruments in the photos from the magazines Barry
showed me, which he'd guiltily stashed in a drawer like they were
pornography. Christ, they made Stryper look stupid all of a sudden,
with their matching yellow and black uniforms like fucking
Christian metal-playing bees. All the while, Barry was telling me
how the music glorified Satan, and how I should keep this in mind
if I ever heard it again, but his argument didn't make sense and
anyway I couldn't care less. I remember him saying that even
bands like Fleetwood Mac were glorifying Satan in their music, I
think because they wrote a song about a witch or something.

Next time I saw Barry, he said it had been wrong of him to
play me that kind of music, that he was very sorry, and God had
told him to go into the garage and smash up all his old records
with a sledgehammer. He started getting a bit weird round about

then and my sister broke up with him. I bumped into him in the street a few times, then I never saw him again. My sister heard that he'd ended up losing his faith and having a mental break-down. Sad really.

Anyway, after hearing that Metallica album I got myself a paper round, so I had money to buy my own copy, plus a lot of their back catalogue. I listened to my records every day after school and drew the Metallica logo on my pencil case and all my folders. Pretty soon, kids would just come up to me and sort of say, 'Oi, mush. Didn't know you were into Metallica.' Then they'd say, 'Have you heard such and such?' and I'd say no, and they'd say they'd do me a tape. It was like a secret society, and you'd never know for sure who was a member because school rules meant you couldn't grow your hair over the collar. But every so often you'd see a kid pass round a copy of *Kerrang!* and then you'd know they were one of 'us' too. Soon I was being lent loads of stuff. The softer bands like Poison, Queensrÿche and Bon Jovi reminded me of Stryper, but with decent non-religious lyrics, and I liked that, but it was really the harder stuff that I got into. Iron Maiden, Megadeth, Anthrax, Slayer. Thrash metal, mostly. Then one day this kid, John, told me I had to listen to someone called Joe Satriani. He said that he was a great guitar player and he'd do me a tape. He'd want it back at the end of the week, though.

I hung on to that tape all through the Christmas holiday, and by the end of it Joe Satriani was even more exciting for me than Metallica. It was all instrumental. Hard-rock guitar solos played very fast. It all sounded complex and very, very hard. I was obsessed with the music and, I suppose, the man. When I wasn't listening to him, I was thinking about him, fantasising about what Joe Satriani was like, and how it would feel to be able to play guitar that well, what it would be like, in fact, to be him. And while I was listening to that album, over and over again in my bedroom until my sister burst in to tell me to stop bloody playing it, I realised I had to learn to play guitar, and get really, really good. Then maybe, one day, I might even be good enough for Joe to want to jam with me. And then maybe he'd want us to form a band together, him and me both taking solos. Why not? If I could play as well as he could, then it would be only right, he'd have to let me, wouldn't he? And we'd be mates, and hang out together all the time, playing pool and discussing technique, and maybe even snogging ladies occasionally, although that was something I hadn't begun to get my head round yet. It was all just a silly little boy's daydream, but it wouldn't leave my mind. Not only that, it had a power most things that pass through a kid's head don't have. The power to actually make me get off my Commodore 64-playing arse and do something about it.

Now wouldn't you know it, I found out from another metaller kid that you could take guitar lessons at school, beginning straight after the Christmas holidays, and they'd even lend you an instrument to practise on. The lifelong comradeship of Joe Satriani was surely within my grasp. I don't think anybody's been as excited about their first music lesson with a peripatetic teacher as I was that Tuesday, and not just because it got me out of German with the terrifying Miss Rand, who stank of cigarettes and could make the hardest lads break down into an uncontrollable stutter just by looking at them.

I had imagined rows of metaller kids, hunched over their guitars as a cool long-haired guy in leather took them through 'Master of Puppets'. It didn't turn out like that. Firstly, we all had to play on folk guitars with nylon strings wound so tightly you couldn't bend them even if you had a crowbar. Also, we were learning from a book called *The Complete Guitar Player*, by some bloke called Russ something-or-other. There weren't any Metallica songs in that book, just songs by people my mum liked, like Cat Stevens and John Denver. The guitar teacher was called Mr McDiarmid, and was from Yorkshire or the West Country or somewhere. He had bales of hay for sideburns, and used to go on about how 'Streets of London' was a really great song that we just had to learn so we could entertain our friends at parties and impress the girls, who he called 'lasses', that were all waiting just round the corner for us when we started 'wooing' in a few years. We couldn't get him to realise we wouldn't have any friends, let alone 'lasses', if we played that old crap.

There were four of us in the class to start with, and by the second week there were two. Me and a lanky boy called Ben, who had sandy hair and a centre parting, metaller-style. He used to walk in, slouch down and put his feet up on another chair and stretch out, sighing at the effort of it all. Then he'd yawn constantly, until his guitar distracted him and he came to life. He was good. Better than the rest of us. He could play stuff he'd worked out for himself and everything. He wasn't exactly communicative, but by the third week, we were just about on speaking terms. I think it's fair to say that Ben was one of those people who just have something about them, and you know that they're special in some way, despite the fact that, guitar-playing aside, he was obviously very lazy. I realise now that Neil had that too, in some weird way.

Anyway, after three weeks of these bloody guitar lessons, I was almost ready to go back to Miss Rand and take my chances.

Already, our spirits were nearly broken and dreams shattered by the constant down-strumming on nylon strings without even a plectrum for protection. I mean, it was almost like we were in a folk-guitar concentration camp. We had to find an escape route.

Well, we found one. Ben told me his older brother could play rock guitar, and he knew about something called a power chord. Instead of having to learn all the different shapes for the different chords, you just learned one, and ran your hand up and down the fretboard to get all the different chords. He said that his brother would be willing to show us both how it was done. If I went round his house on Saturday afternoon, he said, his brother would be there then. 'OK,' I said, and we went to tell Mr McDiarmid we wouldn't be coming to guitar lessons any more.

'Oh well,' he sighed, 'that'll be another thirty quid a month sup money I'll be doing wi'out.' He said we had to give the guitars back to the school, but we never did, and no one ever asked for them again.

So that's how it began, the golden age. With Christian heavy metal, a borrowed tape of Joe Satriani and nylon guitar strings. If only I'd realised, I would have treasured every second, bottled the air. But the best times rarely announce themselves as such, and it's rarer still for them to let you know that they're over.

A beginning. Now I must pick through all the threads of my memory, all the paths through the knotted jumble of thoughts and sensations that make up my life, and find those that might lead me through. Out of all of them, it is the path marked 'Neil' that beckons.

2

'Chris! Chris!'

A voice from the school gates called to me. There, a boy was waiting, gangly, blond and pale, almost albino. Neil. As always, he'd got there ahead of me, to make sure we walked home together. This being a Friday, he was no doubt also hoping that I'd invite him round for an hour or so before tea and, if my mum was in a good mood, which she usually was when Neil was there, that he'd be allowed to stay and eat with us and spend the evening. Sometimes, I admit, I wished he wasn't waiting for me, so I could be free to invite someone else round for once, or even actually go round theirs. But I never minded too much because, for all his awkwardness and occasional inconvenience, Neil was responsible for some of my happiest memories. Not so much actual specific events I could pin down, but little fleeting moments of remembered pleasure that came with Neil's face attached when they popped into my head.

Neil waved to me as I got near, beaming his usual goofy grin. 'Hi, Neil.'

'Chris, you'll never guess what!' he said, as we swung through the gates to freedom.

'Dunno, what?'

'I heard the new Morrissey single on the radio last night!'

'Really?'

'Yes! It's called "Piccadilly Palare"! It's mega!'

'Sounds . . . good.'

This was a lie. Aged thirteen, someone like Morrissey meant nothing to me other than a thing to be avoided. His music, like all that featured on the 'indie' rundown on *The Chart Show*, seemed either wet or poofy. Unlike metal, which was impenetrable, hard, masculine. There lay certainty and truth. But Neil loved all that indie stuff, which made me think that he might be bent, so I might not want him around so much. Especially as he seemed so desperate to hang out with me, which was beginning to strike me as a bit homo. Even though he had been my best friend for all those years, right then there were things about him that were making me uncomfortable.

'Yeah, it is,' said Neil. 'Apparently, "palare" is a secret language that gay people used to use, and that's what the song's about.'

God help me, I thought, it's definitely time for a new best friend. Still, Neil and I went way back. We were probably about six when we met. He was the new kid in school and the teacher gave me the job of looking after him and being his pretend friend while he was settling in and making proper friends for himself. But Neil never really did settle in and make proper friends. It was pretty much just me, and I guess I had that job for the next seven years, although I stopped thinking of it like that after a while. He never fitted in at school, or anywhere else, for that matter. It was as if he'd just beamed down from space, or something. Neil was plain at odds with the world. A tetrahedron in a round hole, was how he put it in one of his more reflective moments. People generally didn't like him, and he had a unique gift for getting on the wrong side of people without trying. But if you got to know him, then you'd realise he was the sweetest, most caring person you could ever meet, without a malicious bone in his body. He was just very, very odd and a bit annoying.

One time, for instance, we were in my garden, and my cousin Jo was there. It was the summer, and my mum had brought us out a jug of fizzy squash. Jo was a couple of years older than us, and mouthy, the way some girls are at that age. When Neil was in the toilet she told me that she was finding him a bit creepy, thinking that he fancied her and was trying to impress her with all the weird things he was saying. Neil was just being Neil, and at that age probably hadn't even started thinking about girls, but back then Jo thought that all boys were trying to get off with her. After he came back from the toilet, Neil said something really odd about the leaves on the trees being fish, and you could tell they were fish because you could see them wriggling about. In those days, Neil always went on about fish, thinking it was really surreal. And Jo just says, can she pour her glass of squash over Neil's head? And Neil says, sure, all right, he'd be delighted. So she picks up her glass and literally pours it all over his head. Then he's just sitting there with sticky orange squash in his hair for the rest of the afternoon, until my mum finds him and makes him wash under the tap before he goes home.

I could go on. Every so often, something that strange would happen, and half the stuff he said you could tell he thought was clever, but it was just rubbish. And it would wind you up and you'd want him to fuck off. But sometimes it would all click, and he would be really funny, and everything he said actually would be as clever as he thought it was. And that made it all worthwhile, because those moments were priceless, they really were. But right then, attending a boys' school and having your best friend get really excited about the next single by a gay pop star that was

14

all about how gay people talked was not priceless. And to be honest, I just wasn't in the mood, and certainly didn't want a whole evening of it, especially not a Friday evening. At thirteen, I was just becoming aware of the specialness of that night, and the idea that it was meant to be spent in the pursuit of thrills of one form or another. Problem was none were currently on offer. At least not for me. As for Neil . . .

'Chris, I'm afraid I won't be able to hang out with you this evening.'

'No problem. Don't worry about it.' It was a problem, of course. If I didn't have anywhere better to be, then why should Neil, especially since the fact that I didn't was obviously his fault?

'Yeah, sorry. It's just that Scott and that lot have asked me to go round and play Dungeons and Dragons after tea.'

'Really? Didn't know you were into that sort of thing.'

'I'm not really, but I just wanted to check it out. 'Course, I know it's going to be wizards and elves and that, but I like the idea of having a game where you get to make things up. I just think it's a shame you can't have one where instead of fighting orcs and wizards, you go to the shops and get a part-time job in Sainsbury's and stuff.'

'I guess. Don't think it would catch on, though.'

'Well, it should. Then maybe people would learn to think a bit harder about the choices they make in life, that they don't have to go to work and just buy stuff all the time, that there are other things to do.'

'Everybody's got to go to work, Neil,' I said.

'Not if they're an artist or a musician or something – then their work is play.'

'Yeah, well, in the real world, not everyone gets to be one,' I

15

snapped back. I was probably feeling a bit defensive because I still wasn't playing onstage with Joe Satriani.

'Everybody's an artist.'

'No, they're not!'

'They are, they just don't know it.'

Jesus, looking back on it, he was only thirteen and he was saying stuff like that! Incredible. Maybe he'd read it somewhere, or heard it on *The Late Show* or something – I don't know.

'Chris, I've just had a thought! Why don't you come and play Dungeons and Dragons tonight?'

'Oh, I can't. I've got things to do.'

'Oh, that's too bad. What are you up to?'

'Uhh . . . family meal.'

'Sounds like fun.'

'No, not really, but I've got to go.'

'Well, I'll give you a ring over the weekend sometime, yeah?'

'Yeah, sure.'

'OK, seeya!' And with that, he sprinted across the road, closer to the oncoming traffic than was sensible, and off in the direction of his house. I looked around for someone else to walk with, but there was no one I knew, just anonymous older boys in the white shirts and black jumpers of our school uniform. So I walked home alone.

The sun was low in the sky on the late January afternoon as I followed the soft bends of the suburban streets of Sholeham. Quireley, that's the suburb where I lived. Can you think of a softer, less threatening name for a place? Quireley. Quire-t-ley. Not posh or anything, lower middle class. But safe. Very, very safe, or at least that's how it felt. I'd been allowed to walk to school by myself since I was eight, my childhood pretty much free of any fear of

16

paedophiles snatching me away into the woods, pre-teen drug addiction or drive-by shootings. A couple of videos in school about staying away from men in Ford Escorts who wanted me to eat their sweets and see their puppies, and that was it. Maybe we were the last generation whose parents weren't scared into locking us up in our homes for our entire childhoods to be dulled into obesity by PlayStation. Well, I suppose there was the Commodore 64.

I remember the sky as blue blending to gold as the sun went down. No doubt I could see my breath in front of me on that winter day as I made my way through the various Cresstons that made up much of Quireley. Cresston Road, Cresston Gardens, Cresston Crescent, where I lived. The safest, most suburban of all the streets in Sholeham, and therefore the world, or so it seemed.

You know, the funny thing about Sholeham is – well, there's nothing funny or even unusual about it, that's the thing. It's a relatively large place that isn't particularly notable in any way, even though it dates back to Roman times or something. I mean, name three famous people who come from Sholeham. Or one big rock band that started here. A famous landmark. Anything at all. The football team does all right, second division, but that's it. Well, you see my point, don't you? For a town of this size, it's remarkable in that it's spawned virtually nothing of note, nobody who's achieved anything at all in any field. Not even a decent serial killer.

So I suppose it's only fitting that all this stuff with me and Neil and music and the band started here in Sholeham, exactly because it could have happened anywhere in England. Anywhere that's nowhere, that is. And Sholeham is the capital of nowhere. Most of this country is made up of nowhere, or nowheres. What I mean is have you ever been on a slow train, on a journey that seemed to go on for ever, and watched all the stops go by, towns you've

17

never heard of, and wondered about them? Well, from my experience, for what it is, whenever I've had to step off the train into one of these places, I've found they're all the same. They have a small, pedestrianised shopping centre, where there's a Woolworths, and that's where everybody buys their music, or at least the music that Woolworths lets you buy. There's a nightclub that everyone goes to, even though it's shit. And there are houses, lots of houses, that young couples move into, then breed, and grow families, and the children of these families grow into teenagers, and a proportion of these teenagers one day decide that they want to make music just like the music they bought in Woolworths, and so they learn instruments, and form bands, and get ideas, and have their hearts broken. Sholeham's just like all these places, except it's bigger: there's an HMV, which has a wider selection than Woolworths, and an Our Price, though that's gone now, of course, and there's a range of shit nightclubs you can choose from. Other than that, it's really just the same.

Now, running my fingers through my knot of memories, looking for more threads, I find myself coming home to an empty house. Empty other than our old beagle, Bess, who gets off the chair she's sneaked onto long enough to wag her tail 'hello' before skulking off again for more illicit furniture squatting. Named after a dog in a book, I think. Now that my sister's going to sixth-form college, that's the way it usually is after school. Mum won't be home until half five, Dad not until half six. What do I do between coming home and tea? I don't know, probably watch some kids' TV that I'm beginning to feel too old for and eat crisps. What am I watching? I can't remember; what was on back then? *Masters of the Universe*? No, I think that was earlier. *Grange Hill*, no doubt. That's always on.

18

Shit, I don't know what I was watching, and of course it doesn't matter, but the point is that with a lot of this stuff, I'll say it happened in such and such a month and one event followed another, but I'm going to get a lot of it wrong, I expect. Things I say happened on the same day probably didn't at all. Maybe I'm even getting my years mixed up on some things. Some places probably aren't quite the way I remember them. But I'm pretty sure I'll get the gist of it all, I mean the spirit in which things were done, or at least how I perceived them at the time. Or maybe I'll get a whole load of stuff wrong, maybe nothing I have to say really means anything or is any use to me or anybody else. But this knotted bundle that clogs up my head is driving me crazy. I've got to sort it out. Separate all the threads. Find the ones I need. Throw the rest away.

I pick up the thread I'm following. It vibrates with the sound of footsteps on the path. Soon my sister will open the door, not eat her tea, get changed and go out clubbing, to my mum and dad's dismay. But they can't do anything about it really; she has a part-time job, it's her money she's spending. And they secretly both understand it's all part of growing up, it's inevitable; she's got her head on straight, and deep down they know nothing bad is going to happen to her. It's all going to be OK. But they wouldn't be good parents if they didn't pretend it wasn't and worry that she was wrecking her life in some vague, unspecified way. And me, I'll sit on my own, playing my records, dreaming of Joe Satriani and missing Neil a little bit. Wishing it was Thursday, Scouts on Thursday.

My sister pops her head round the door. 'All right,' she says, without affection. 'Mum not back yet?'

'No, not yet.' It'll be several years before I think of her as a person, with a name, Nicki, instead of just as this vague blur of bleached-blonde hair and make-up called my sister.

'I'll be wanting to watch *Neighbours* in a minute,' she says.

'All right,' I mumble, as all teenage boys should.

Neighbours. Now who was in it back then? Scott and Charlene would have left. Dorothy Burke. No, before her, surely? Bouncer.

Forget it. That thread ends there.

3

I met Ben at eleven o'clock, Saturday morning outside McDonald's in the High Street. Like me, he was wearing the teenage metaller's uniform of a denim jacket – an affordable substitute for the leather jackets we could only dream about. He had more patches sewn onto his, though, and most of them were for bands I'd only vaguely heard of – Black Sabbath, Led Zeppelin, Deep Purple.

'Wotcha,' he said, the established metaller greeting at our school.

'Wotcha.'

It was funny, up until this point I wasn't even sure he was one of us – a metaller, I mean – but just looking at him, I could tell that he had tasted of metal's goodness to a level I had previously not known to be possible. I felt rather puny in his presence, like a novice confronting a master wizard in one of Scott and his spazzy mates' Dungeons and Dragons games.

'So what's the plan then?' asked the wizard of his pupil.

'Dunno, really. Um, what time's your brother going to be round?'

'Dunno, mate. Probably about two.'

'Um, well, we could get something to eat, then go round the record shops for a bit,' I said, hoping that would satisfy the wise one to whom I had become apprenticed.

'You mean down St Anne's?'

21

'Yeah.' I hadn't meant that at all, of course. I'd meant HMV and Our Price in the High Street. I'd never even been to St Anne's, much less heard about any record shops that might be down there. The suburban roads of Quireley and the High Street were practically all I knew of the town I'd spent my entire life in, apart from occasional visits to the sports centre and the swimming baths. But the wizard knew more. He knew about the other record shops, and I would have to follow him, without letting on that I really knew nothing.

'Sounds good,' he said. 'Shall we go in then, or what?'

'Yeah, course.'

We went under the golden arches, and for only the second time in my life I bought fast food with my own money. It was that bygone time – the end of childhood, when fast-food restaurants were bright, magical places, before you had started to notice the food on the floor, and the surliness of the staff, and the never-ending screaming of the babies, or had been so zealously informed about their role in the destruction of the rainforest, what their food did to poor people's health, or the sparseness of the wages they paid. In those days you could eat there and feel good, instead of guilty and worried someone will see you when you leave.

'So what bands you into, then?' asked Ben as we sat down. Obviously I did not have enough patches on my denim for him to glean that information, and for that I felt ashamed.

'Oh, thrash metal mostly,' I said. 'Pantera, Megadeth, Slayer. Also Metallica, Iron Maiden . . .'

'Yeah, they're good bands,' said Ben. 'Do you like any of the older stuff, like Sabbath, Led Zep?'

'Yeah, I like them too.'

'Have you heard *Physical Graffiti*? That's a fucking amazing album.'

'Not sure,' I said. 'I think I have but not all the way through.'

'Jimmy Page's guitar playing is fucking mental on that album.'

'Yeah, yeah,' I said, nodding my head like a toy dog in a car window.

'Do you like Hendrix?'

'Yeah, they're good. I like their earlier stuff, anyway. Good band.'

Ben looked at me with his eyes wide. 'Hendrix aren't a band, you monger – he's a bloke!'

I sank about a thousand feet inside. 'Oh, Hendrix! I thought you meant someone else. Yeah, I thought you meant . . .'

'Yeah, like fuck you did.'

I felt still more ashamed. I'd failed my master already, and he'd caught me trying to deceive him. I was also curious as to what a monger was, although already I was pretty certain that I did not want to be thought of as one, especially by Ben.

'I've got to educate you, man,' said Ben.

God, yes you have, I cried inwardly, tell me everything.

'Come on, let's get a move on,' he said, standing up from the padded seat of the McDonald's booth. I hadn't finished, and was going to make an issue of it, before thinking better of it. That wouldn't be cool. It would be babyish.

'Wanna get my hands on some vinyl,' said Ben, apparently to himself, as I followed him out.

I walked beside Ben down the High Street, trying to give the impression of knowing where we were going, until he took a sudden and unexpected right that left me waiting by myself by the traffic lights.

23

'This way, you monger!' he called out to me, waving sarcastically from some feet away.

'Sorry,' I replied, smiling a silly apologetic smile.

'You will be. Jesus. What's wrong with you?' he said as I caught up. 'Do you like Hawkwind?'

'Uh, yeah, they're good.'

'You haven't heard them, have you?'

'Yeah, well . . . no.'

'They've got an album of theirs I want in Weasel's. *In Search of Space*. It's got "Master of the Universe" on it.'

That made me think of something funny. Maybe Ben would also think it was funny. 'You mean, like He-Man?'

'No, not like fucking He-Man!' Ben slapped me round the back of the head. I looked for affection in the gesture but could find none. 'The song came first. It's been around for bloody ages.'

'Sorry, I don't know it.'

'Right, here's a trivia test for you. What famous bassist and lead singer of another band started out in Hawkwind?'

'Ummm . . . I don't know, who?'

'Come on, think!'

'I really don't know, sorry.'

'Lemmy!'

'Oh right.'

'And what band's Lemmy in?'

'Hawkwind.'

'No, you monger, what band's he in now?'

'Umm . . . I don't know, sorry.'

'Motörhead, stupid!'

'Oh, yeah, I knew that,' I said, in a small voice I couldn't will to be any bigger.

'No you didn't,' Ben said gruffly. I knew he was irritated with me now. I had to find a way to please him somehow, but I was feeling too ashamed to think of anything right then.

Ben led me further down the strange road, at the end of which was a dual carriageway. On the other side was a strange construction of metal pillars and a corrugated roof. It had the words 'Queensbury Market' written in bright green metal letters on the side. There seemed no way to get to it across the road, as the traffic was fast and thick, and of course a barrier in the middle blocked the way. Did the council or whoever was in charge of these things expect us to jump over it?

I must have looked confused, because Ben elbowed me in the ribs and pointed to our left. 'Down there, come on,' he said, sighing at me in frustration. It was something I'd never encountered before, a tunnel, going underneath the road, with an unsettling mixture of dank urine-tainted air and sodium glow. I didn't like the look of it, and it seemed exactly the sort of place you could expect to be stabbed, but there was no way I was going to let Ben know I was afraid. So I went down the slope after him and into the tunnel, certain that we were being watched and followed as I entered a subway for the first time. It may sound bizarre, but it really was something I'd never come across before. This was simply a thing they did not have or need in Quireley. Even by the standards of the time I suppose I was a sheltered child. Ben walked ahead, taking giant strides with his long pipe-cleaner legs that I could not hope to match. Silhouetted against the light from the other side, he turned. 'Are you coming or what?' he said over his shoulder. I scurried along, my dignity trailing far behind me, until we emerged onto another slope leading up, taking us into what turned out to be the market car park.

'We'll go through the market, it's quicker,' said Ben, who now seemed resigned to the fact that I clearly didn't know where I was, and had apparently never been outside ever, and that he had to lead the way completely.

It was another world. Spoilt cabbages and oranges were at our feet as Ben took us through the market. It was bustling with trade on this grey January Saturday, a forest of anoraks and pacamacs and shell suits, with the smell of fruit and clothing damp from the drizzle. Shouts about things I didn't understand, market stuff, jokes I didn't get ricocheted off the corrugated roof. 'Ron is a coppers nark,' read some graffiti on the wall. I had never had cabbages at my feet before, and I had never come across any mention of narks except on the telly. That graffiti was the closest I'd ever got to real criminality. But what I found really strange was, well, the people. They didn't look like the sort of people you'd find in Sholeham High Street. I mean, I'd seen the working classes before, I hadn't lived totally in a shoebox, even though I hadn't seen a subway, but here in the market, en masse, they all seemed – I suppose 'damaged' is the word. The young, the old, trader or customer – there was a strange look in their eyes I hadn't ever seen, something I couldn't pin down back then, but I suppose I would describe now as a kind of matter-of-factness. I mean, and this is hard to describe, not visibly enjoying where they were, and not obviously hoping for something better, but just being. But I remember them smiling and laughing too, loud working-class laughing. It's confusing.

I don't know, I'm probably talking rubbish, I'm just trying to articulate how they appeared to me at the time, that's all. If you showed me the same people today, maybe it wouldn't seem that way. Anyway, the market's been totally redeveloped since then, probably looks and feels completely different. And I'm a lower-middle-class arse and that probably accounts for everything. But that's what places like Quireley do to you. However much you experience, wherever else you go, it will always seem a bit alien. Anything that's not suburban, anywhere that's not quiet, won't feel quite right. The only places that will sit right with you are places that are like where you came from. Places that are nowhere.

Ben led me over a zebra crossing. I could see that we were somewhere dark and scary, but very, very exciting. This was something new, I remember telling myself, something necessary and good. We walked past shops that had boards for windows, and signs on them indicating that they were for over-18s only, and that there was a back entrance for discretion. Along with the discovery that a copper's nark had been in the vicinity, the mere sight of these shops made me feel that I was a man. 'This way,' said Ben. 'We'll go to Underground first.'

I can only remember a few things about Underground Music now. Dark and dank, with the smell of second-hand merchandise in the air, it's long since gone, but I remember that it had posters of the type of bands that meant nothing to me on the walls, the sort of music that Neil liked, probably. I didn't really know how to behave or what to do, so I just copied Ben as he flicked through the records nonchalantly. Even though I didn't recognise half the stuff I was looking at, I picked up the records the way Ben did, slipping the inner sleeve out, then the vinyl out of that, and inspecting it for scratches. The guy behind the counter didn't pay us any attention. He just read his *Melody Maker*. I prayed that Ben wouldn't spot me looking at a record he didn't approve of and have a go at me. To prevent it I always looked at the rack he'd just looked at, and sometimes even the same record.

'What are those tapes in that box?' I asked, pointing to a collection of D60 cassettes with home-made photocopied covers.

'They're bootlegs.'

'They're what?'

'Never mind. Come on,' said Ben, 'let's go to Ferret's and Weasel's.' Then he walked out of the shop, not bothering to hold the door for me.

Ferrets and Weasels? Was he suggesting we go to a pub? But we were too young! Still, I'd learned from the 'Masters of the Universe' incident not to question anything Ben said, and so I followed his gigantic stride as best I could, down the street, past the porn shops, bookies and haberdasheries, until we approached another record shop. 'Ferret's', it was called. Now I was really confused. Ferret's, yes, that made sense, but why had Ben mentioned weasels?

'All right, we'll spend a few minutes in here,' said Ben. 'Then we'll go across the road.'

'What's across the road?' I asked, stupidly forgetting that I wasn't meant to ask questions.

'Weasel's, of course! For fuck's sake.' Ben grabbed me by the neck and pushed my head up to the glass of Ferret's, so that all I could see were picture sleeves on display. 'This is Ferret's!' he snapped. Then he swung me round to face the other way. 'And that's Weasel's!' There, across the road was still another record shop. 'Weasel's' said the hand-painted sign.

'Ferret's sells singles! Weasel's sells albums! They're both run by the same people! Is that fucking clear, you stupid monger?'

And something inside of me stirred. I knew at that moment that I was not as soft as Ben thought I was, or indeed as I was acting. Yes, I had not been in a tunnel under the road before, or

28

seen many working-class people, but I knew I could cope with both and more. If I was going to survive in this new world that was opening up for me that day like a strange and exotic flower, then I was going to have to toughen up. I knew then that I didn't have anything to fear from Ben, and neither would he desert me. I could taste his loneliness in his anger and saw that he desperately needed my company, despite his unpleasantness.

'Look!' I said, as I elbowed Ben squarely in the stomach, winding him. 'Don't ever grab me like that again, OK? I know I don't know as much about these places as you do, but that's because I don't live round here, innit? Now get off my back and let's go to Weasel's cos I'm not interested in buying singles.'

Ben shifted from one foot to the other and looked to the side of him. 'No need to elbow me so fucking hard,' he mumbled. 'OK, let's fucking go, then.'

So Ben and I crossed the road, dodging the traffic that travelled so much faster than any of the cars I'd had to deal with in Quireley, to Weasel's, a record shop that would prove to be in possession of even greater magical beauty than Underground. Turned out neither of us had the money to buy anything after McDonald's, but it didn't matter. To be near the music was enough.

4

When we got to Ben's house in Latham, it wasn't as bad as I thought it'd be. OK, it wasn't nearly as good a neighbourhood as Quireley, but the houses were mostly the same type, semi-detached, although more likely products of the sixties than the forties, which was when they built most of Quireley. The people loitering on the streets looked a bit scummier to me, though. Still, it felt a darn sight safer than the route through St Anne's we'd just taken.

Two things surprised me about Ben's house on that first visit. The first was the thick smell of tobacco smoke. None of my other friends' parents smoked, or if they did, they took great care to make sure their house didn't reek of it. The other surprise being, despite the overwhelming smell, how nice it all was. I mean, it wasn't in particularly good taste, but the furniture looked quite new, and their sofa was puffier, and would turn out to be more comfortable, than any I could remember sitting in before. Also, they had a nice big television and hi-fi system. CD player and everything. But what was really impressive was the computer, an Atari ST. The Commodore 64 was totally on the way out by then, and kids in school were switching to games consoles, Sega mostly, but no one else I knew had managed to upgrade to one of the new generation of computers like the Atari or the Amiga. I don't know, I just presumed that, what with Ben's dad being a taxi driver, they'd be living in squalor in a bare room with rats or something. But no, it must have been bringing in some OK money. That and maybe credit, I should imagine.

As Ben let us in, I heard activity coming from a quite futuristic-looking kitchen. 'Benjamin, is that you?' a woman's voice called as we stood in the hallway.

'Yeah, it's me,' he shouted back, at a volume no one would consider using in Quireley.

A plump woman, over fifty, with sandy-grey hair flowing loose over her shoulders and a fluffy pink dressing gown, appeared in the kitchen doorway, cigarette in hand. 'Oh, hi there,' she said upon seeing me.

'Hello,' I said back.

'Is this your friend, Benjamin?'

'Yeah,' he said, the word short and low, given reluctantly.

'Kenneth said to say he's still coming, but he won't be here till later. Why don't the both of you sit down and I'll fix you a snack? Would you like that, Christopher, is it?'

'Uh, yes please. That would be very nice.' I didn't know if it would be, as I hadn't eaten in the house of somebody whose dad didn't have an office job like my dad's before, let alone in a house in which all the air seemed to have been replaced by cigarette fog. All I could think of, for some reason, was a plateful of the jelly from pork pies, which gave me an impulse to gag I had to suppress. But when Ben led me into the living room and I saw the sofa, I thought it might be all right, which it was, of course. Ben's mum came in a couple of minutes later with two plates piled with processed-cheese sandwiches, crisps and chocolate biscuits, and two glasses of lemonade.

'Here you go,' she said. 'Put the telly on or something, Benjamin.' Ben had been awkwardly showing me some recent copies of *2000 AD* while we waited, telling me about the characters and the artists, but the TV made us both feel a lot more comfortable.

'Do you want to watch *The Young Ones*? I've got it on video,' asked Ben.

'Yeah!' My parents had never let me watch it when it was on telly, and I couldn't believe that Ben was allowed to watch it in the afternoon, with his mum in the next room and without any cloak-and-dagger operation to hide it. Meanwhile, a black poodle scuttled in on tiny legs and sniffed our ankles before daintily sitting on its own plush cushion in the corner. We could never train Bess to stay on anything that was meant for her, be it a blanket or a basket.

Of course, *The Young Ones* was hysterically funny. I was laughing so much I was in pain. Waiting for Kenneth, we got through the first two episodes of season one, and halfway through episode three. It was strange hearing Ben laugh so unguardedly after his tough-guy act of the morning, and then his quiet sheepishness following the window incident. His voice was getting lower, but had not yet fully broken, and had a strange quality, like the sound of blowing through a pipe. His laughter was that of a child, and like his need to share his comics, it undermined all his efforts to appear grown up.

Sometimes his mum would wander in, and she would laugh at *The Young Ones* too. This was odd for me. Toilet humour, mild swearing and people hitting each other were not things any parents I'd encountered before approved of. Here, a new, freer order prevailed, it seemed.

There was the sound of a key in the front door.

'That'll be Kenneth now, I expect,' she said.

32

Kenneth walked in, wearing motorcycle leathers and carrying his helmet. About thirty-five, balding, with weathered face and hands, like an aged version of Ben after putting on a stone or two. Thick neck. Small eyes hiding far back in his face. Hard like stone. Way too old to be anybody's brother.

'Hi, Mum. Hi, Ben,' he said, kissing his mum on the cheek.

'All right, Ken,' Ben said. I could tell he was pleased to see him, although I don't think I was meant to see it.

'Ah, brilliant, *The Young Ones*,' said Ken. He watched it with us for a few minutes, sitting on the armrest of the sofa. All of us, me, Ben, Kenneth and their mum, leaning in the doorway, were laughing unreservedly. Ken's laugh was a low chugging sound, while his mum's was a piercing whoop, both utterly unlike the softer, considered laughs of my parents and their friends.

Madness appeared in the mid-episode musical interlude, to Ken's excitement. 'Ah, Madness, brilliant,' he said.

'You said you'd show us how to play power chords today,' said Ben, oblivious to his brother's enjoyment.

'Yeah, OK,' said Ken softly. Then he clapped his hands, and said much louder, 'Right, I'm going to go upstairs and change, and then I'll show you.'

'Shall we come up in five minutes or something?' asked Ben.

'Make it ten, yeah?'

'OK.'

We watched the episode to the end, then almost reluctantly, because there was a whole other tape with another three episodes, we went upstairs. Past the pink lavatory and along the landing, we came to Ken's room. The door had posters all over it. Ben knocked, and a voice from inside shouted for us to come in. Inside, it was a shrine to what I would learn was called the New Wave of British Heavy Metal from the early eighties, with tattered glossy fold-out posters of bands like Judas Priest, Motörhead, Diamond Head, Saxon and Tygers of Pan Tang covering the walls and ceiling. A large picture of Iron Maiden's mascot Eddie hung in an antique gilt frame next to the wardrobe, which itself was plastered with magazine cut-outs. It was strange, you could have almost imagined it being the bedroom of a twelve-year-old girl, if the pictures had been of New Kids on the Block and Big Fun. But this room was the work of a grown man.

The floor was a tip, covered in collapsing piles of magazines, empty cassette boxes and disembodied pieces of electrical equipment – circuit boards and wires that led nowhere. Ken was on the bed, his leathers in a heap to his left, next to his helmet. 'Right, lads,' he said, 'take a pew.'

Ben sat on the bed next to his brother. I realised that under a pile of faded and suspiciously smelling band T-shirts, there was a chair. 'Oh, just chuck 'em on the floor,' said Ken, which I did.

'Right, could you pass me my geetar, please, Ben?' he asked, and Ben dutifully unearthed a guitar case from behind half a television. Kenneth clicked open the locks and took out a Fender Stratocaster, spray-painted black with various band names stickered all over it. A beautiful thing, nevertheless, or so it looked at the time. Indeed, in that moment, just looking at it and the anticipation of holding it filled me with a rare excitement.

'OK,' he said, putting the strap round his neck and hunching over the guitar, 'to play a basic power chord, you need two fingers – this one,' holding up his index finger, 'and this one.' He forced his other fingers down with his thumb so only his ring finger was up. For a moment, I thought it might be rude but then realised it wasn't. 'Now, what you do with this first finger is place it on the bottom string on any fret, it doesn't matter. Except if you want to play E. Then you just leave the string open. Now with this one, you put it here, two frets up from the other one, over the fourth and fifth strings.' He demonstrated the shape, and then deftly carried out a downward strike on the bottom three strings of his guitar. I was expecting an almighty blast of rock greatness, so was a little disappointed by the tinny sound that it made. Then I remembered that there was no amp. It would sound better with an amp, I reasoned.

'So, with this shape,' Kenneth continued, 'you can play any chord just by running your hand up and down the fretboard, like this.' He did just that, playing a dark, satanic riff very fast.

'Wow,' I said, in a stage whisper.

'How do you play minor chords, then?' asked Ben.

'Ah, that's the beauty of it. In a power chord, you're playing your root note, the same note an octave above, and a fifth. You're leaving out the third note of the triad, so the chord is neither major nor minor. So you can use them instead of either.'

'Wow,' said Ben. I didn't know what either of them was talking about, but it sounded very exciting and useful.

'OK, do you want to try it?' said Ken, passing the guitar to Ben. Ben took it, and after shuffling his long fingers about for a few seconds, got them in position, and there and then struck a perfect power chord. First time. He ran his hand up and down the fretboard for a full five minutes or so, sometimes linking chords that clearly didn't flow, other times hinting at potential riffs. It was as if that guitar and him, that chord shape, belonged together. It was meant to be. Ken just looked on in admiration. 'Yeah, you've got it,' he said.

'Want a go?' Ben said to me, after what seemed an age.

'Yeah, sure.'

He passed me the guitar and I struggled to get the strap over my head. The Stratocaster seemed to sit much lower in my lap than the school folk acoustic, and it felt like it was in danger of slipping off my leg completely. The strings were insanely loose compared with the cheese-cutter tightness of the school guitar, and I found it hard to get a grip on the thin neck. Finally, I tried to get my fingers in the right position, and though I thought I had it, when I gingerly hit down on them, the strings made a horrible scraping sound that, even amplified, wouldn't have sounded any good.

'Um,' said Ken, his hand rubbing his chin. 'Um. That's all I can say really. Um.'

I tried again, but it just got more scrapy and clanging the more I stabbed at it.

'No, what you want to do is only hit the bottom three strings. And you really need to push down with your ring finger on those two strings so you get a good sound. You'll need to learn how to do that with the other finger as well. Pass it back here and I'll show you why.' I did what I was told, and Ken played a riff I would later learn was 'Smoke on the Water'.

Ken went on to play us lots of different things on the guitar, most of which I didn't recognise, except some Iron Maiden stuff. Ben knew most of it, though. As well as riffs, Ken could solo too, although nowhere near as well as Joe Satriani or Kirk Hammett of Metallica. Watching him play was my first experience of that strange fascination you get watching someone messing about on an instrument, riffs mutating into other riffs, songs half-started, songs abandoned halfway. It made me nervous too. Was this the same song as before? Or a different one? Was I expected to know?

After a while, Ken stood up and stretched and said, 'Right, I've got to shoot off soon, so you two had better scarper.' He shooed us downstairs while he got on with whatever he was up to in that tip of a bedroom.

I would learn later that he didn't live there at all – he had a girlfriend and a little boy who he lived with on the other side of town. That was his old bedroom, which he used for storage, a place to keep all the electronic junk he liked to fiddle with. At some point I would hear about his musical journey: a hard rock and prog kid in the seventies, a brief flirtation with punk, then a switch to heavy metal when he grew dissatisfied with punk's low level of musicianship. Apart from heavy metal, he also liked music that made him laugh, like the songs from *Monty Python* and *Spitting Image*, 'Star Trekkin', 'The Winker's Song' by Ivor Biggun. He'd been a bit of a social misfit during his twenties, hence the room full of posters and clippings, but at some point in the last few years had got his act together, finally moving out of his parents' house at the age of thirty-one. He'd given a lot of his old records from the seventies to Ben, which explained Ben's thorough knowledge of music made several years before he was born.

It was still a while before I was expected home, so Ben suggested we watch the second *Young Ones* tape. But I wasn't finding it as funny as before. Maybe because even the funniest things wear thin after three hours, but mostly because I was hacked off I couldn't play that fucking chord and had ended up looking so useless in front of Ben and Ken. That might also explain why suddenly, and without reason, I kicked my leg out and sent a half-full glass of lemonade across the room, soaking the carpet in froth.

'You stupid monger!' Ben snapped at me. I couldn't argue with him on this one.

'Benjamin, don't talk to your friends like that,' his mum said, running into the room, still in her dressing gown. 'What's happened? Oh dear.'

'I'm really, really sorry,' I said, doubling up in embarrassment.

'That's OK,' she said. 'Could have happened to anybody.'

'Yeah, if they're a spastic,' said Ben.

'Benjamin, do not use words like that!' said his mum.

She fetched a cloth and bent over to clean it. As she did so – and there was no way I could avoid it – I saw down her dressing gown and caught a glimpse of most of her tit. It felt funny, nearly seeing my first real-life tit, a combination of excitement over the fact of it, and disgust at the strange crêpe-paper quality of the skin of the middle-aged breast and the blueness of the veins. That night, I would try and talk myself into believing I had seen a nipple, but I knew I hadn't.

Ben looked at me when she'd left the room, his voice covered by the sound of the TV and the washing machine. 'You looked at my mum's tits,' he said.

'No I didn't,' I said, now feeling terrible at not only defiling the loveliness of this proletarian home with spilt lemonade, but also being caught trying to catch a sneaky eyeful of my host's knockers.

'You did,' said Ben.

I had to think quick. 'Well, if I did, so did you.'

'Don't be stupid.'

'You must have been looking to know I was looking. Which means you're a dirty pervert, cos you just stared at your own mum's tits.'

'Just shut it, all right.' I let Ben get the last word, because I knew I'd won.

5

That evening the phone rang for me. It was Neil.

'Hi, Chris,' he said, enthusiastic as ever. 'How was your family meal?'

'Ah . . . it was OK, pretty boring. What's up?'

'Oh nothing, just thought I'd give you a ring.'

'Right. So, um, how was your Dungeons and Dragons thing?'

'Not that great, to be honest with you.'

'No? Shame.'

'Well, I spent ages creating my character, rolling the dice for my various strengths and things, then five minutes into the game I came across a troll and because I was new and hadn't any special powers I was dead almost straight away. Scott and that lot survived because they'd accumulated loads of spells and protection and stuff over previous games. So I just had to sit there and watch them play for the next two hours. Pretty boring really.'

'That's a bit crap. Yeah, sorry I couldn't make it. Not.' Did I really say that then? Where's that from? *Wayne's World*. I think it was a bit before then. So I didn't say it.

'So,' said Neil, 'what are you up to tomorrow?'

'Oh, homework, probably. Got a lot to catch up on.'

'Have you done that thing for French yet?'

'No, I don't really get it.'

'Well, I could come round and we could do it together if you like. I think I know how to do it.'

'Ah, I'm not sure that – yeah, why not? Yeah, come round in the afternoon.'

'One o'clock OK?'

'Make it two. But yeah, come round. Listen, I've got to go, got stuff that needs doing, but I'll see you tomorrow, yeah?'

'OK, bye.'

Neil always ended phone conversations abruptly. As soon as the business of the call was finished, he saw no need for further pleasantries and just hung up.

To be honest, I don't know if I'm remembering this sort of thing that well. I mean, the way I recall it, we always more or less talked like adults, but we couldn't have done, could we? We were only thirteen. I must have filtered out so much: childish things we talked about, silly phrases we would have used, impressions of people on telly, little in-jokes, stupid noises probably. But if it was there, it's mostly been edited away. Now pretty much only the barest of facts remain, and the underlying emotions of all these situations. You can never blot them out completely, I've discovered.

The strange thing is, after that evening, my memory skims over a whole period of time. Almost a year, in fact. There are hardly any threads that lead through there at all. Where has it all gone? Who knows why some things stick with you while other things, it's as if they may as well never have happened. Maybe what gets remembered is remembered for a reason, even if the reason is not immediately clear. Maybe there's a lesson in all our memories. Maybe.

So what can I remember about that year, other than World

Cup '90? Well, I remember more trips to St Anne's with Ben, some second-hand vinyl purchased and more visits to his home, with the occasional guitar-playing tip from Ken, either from the maestro himself or passed on via Ben. It wasn't long before I'd got the hang of that initial power-chord shape, although I found an easier way of playing it, using my middle and ring finger instead of making a barre with just the ring. Ben said it wasn't proper, but it made the same sound, so I didn't see the problem. I think it was because it didn't hurt as much that Ben didn't like it. Besides that, I began to piece together a basic vocabulary of the guitar, some from Ken and Ben, some from the trusty *Complete Guitar Player* by Russ what's-his-name, which turned out to be not so bad after all, now I didn't have to play from it within earshot of other schoolkids. At other times, I just tried to play what was on a record, and to my surprise got it right, more or less. I wasn't actually that bad after a couple of months. Ben was better, though. Loads better. He could solo by the spring, it was ridiculous. Whereas I had to break everything down to work out how to do it, he just seemed to know how to without really trying, or at least that's how it appeared. I'm sure he was practising like mad at home.

As to Neil, yeah, I still let him come round and stuff, and not just because he was loads cleverer than me and could help me with my homework, although I guess that's the way it might have seemed sometimes. I still enjoyed his company, but I did manage to distance myself from him a bit – got him out of the habit of coming round every Friday anyway. But the time was coming, here at the dawn of my teenage years, when I would be expected to be seen hanging outside the gates of the nearby girls' school. Indeed, soon, very soon, I would be expected to have a girlfriend. The pressure was already on. 'Get a girlfriend, mate' was entering the playground vocabulary as a put-down. I had never had a girlfriend, nor had any real desire to have one. I still didn't, but what I did have was a need to be seen as part of the crowd. I estimated that not ever having had a girlfriend was going to seriously marginalise me within a year. Time was of the essence, and one way of ensuring my success was to position myself at the most advantageous point in the secondary-school social hierarchy. Having Neil as my best friend would not help me there.

This is the way things were at our school. Although real class differences were covered up by the levelling burr of our county accent, and really rich kids had been shipped off to the public school down the road, there was still a definite social hierarchy, although one in an inverse relation to economic privilege. At the very top were the kids who were cool. They obviously wouldn't have called themselves cool, they'd have had their own word for it that you wouldn't have learnt until it was too late and it was embarrassing to be caught saying it. I think the rest of us said 'cool', though. Sometimes it's not cool to say 'cool', but I think it was cool when I was at school. Anyway, these kids always came in on the bus from areas on the other side of town I'd never been to, strange, forbidden places where everybody was cool – well, not cool but mega, or wicked, or champion or whatever their word for it was – and had great trainers. Tottern Park, Tottern Manor, Raneleigh Park. These kids usually listened to house, which was despised by us metallers because it required no skill, and could be made just by pressing a button on a computer. They were always either hard and ugly, and to be avoided, or good-looking and flash. They were all called Wayne, Shane or Dean. Great at football and running. Untouchable. Now, of course, I realise they were most probably shagging like bunny rabbits while the rest of us were still dreaming about one day touching a girl's tit.

Down at the bottom of the heap were the spazzers. Politically incorrect to call them that these days, I know, but that's how they were thought of, although Ben called them mongers. I would later learn that he'd got that off Ken, who'd got it from a record from his punk days, 'Mongoloid' by Devo. But whether it's spazzer or monger, I hate to admit this, but I still get a guilty thrill out of saying it. If you went to an all-boys school, it doesn't really leave you, it's been encoded into your genes. Spaz. It just feels good saying it, I can't deny that. And I know it's wrong, but I'm going to use it, because if I don't I won't be telling you how it really was. Anyway, the Spazzers were Quireley all over. Weak and wet, terrible at sport, and likely to be accused of being gay most days, they stuck together, more for survival than out of any genuine affection. Generally unattractive, with moles, acne and corrected harelips, they'd be very good at maths, but not so good at science, as that involved holding things without dropping them. They were suburban and mollycoddled, the sickly children who in the olden days would never have made it to adulthood. Scott and his mates, the Dungeons and Dragons wizards, safely belonged in this category.

In between the high and the low, the cool and the spazzy, was the great bulging middle. Here the boys were somewhat anonymous, destined never to reach the heights of cool of the kids from the other side of town, across the Tottern River bridge, but generally not in too much danger of slipping into the Quireley spazzy zone. This was a diverse pool, in which you could find metallers and indie-kids, the extrovert and the quietly confident, the lesser-spazzed Quireley boy, as well as the Asian kids from St Anne's, who were too academically driven to be as cool as the Tottern Parkers, but too street ever to be spazzy. Here in the middle, you'd probably never get to be best at football, but you'd never find yourself being too good at chess either.

And it was in the upper section of this middle that I sought to establish myself. I felt it was a realistic goal. Getting to know Ben helped. He was probably only middle of the middle, but helped my cause much better than Neil, who was lower-middle and in more and more danger of toppling right over into spazzland as his behaviour got weirder. Ben's friends were mostly other metallers, who apart from a few spazzers were as a breed generally middle-middle or upper-middle.

Another thing that helped was that I was quite good, although not excellent, at basketball. I was still good enough to make the team for my year, though, and got to spend time with some of the flash kids. Even though they must have sensed my inherent Quireleyness too much to let me get that close, just to have them know who I was and call me by my first name was enough. More than most middle kids could lay claim to.

Anyway, thanks to basketball, Ben, and my general ability to blend in, I managed to establish myself in what was probably the upper-middle-middle, maybe even verging on lower-upper-middle. As spring became summer, I received various invitations to play football on the fields with some pretty OK kids, and even got to hang out round their house and stuff at the weekend. I had escaped the curse of Neil, although I still saw him occasionally. And then, thanks to my clever social manoeuvring, in the last weeks of that summer term, all the hard work paid off. I got my first girlfriend.

It only lasted a couple of months, and we never did much more than hold hands and kiss with our mouths closed, but it served its purpose, which was, of course, to be known as one of the kids who'd had a girlfriend. Her name was Karen. She had blonde hair, blue eyes and a grey tracksuit. I remember very little else, except that I met her through hanging out with another of the good, but not excellent, basketball kids. It's funny, isn't it – I remember so much more about meeting Ben for the first time than I do her, but then in the long run Ben turned out to be more important, I guess. The same with Neil: I can remember nearly whole conversations we had, but I can barely remember anything I said to Karen, or anything she said to me, other than her telling me that we shouldn't see each other any more because Paula Abdul was wrong, opposites don't attract, but that I would always have a special place in her heart. A few months later I saw her in town and she pretended she didn't recognise me.

But looking back, it's the music I really remember. That was the summer I fell in love with Napalm Death and their thirty-five-second-long songs. If I ever hear thrash metal like that now, it still brings to mind endless summer days in suburbia, and the evening glow over Sholeham Fields. Ben played me a lot of his seventies metal, but it still didn't register that much with me, not like the newer stuff. He'd always lend me far more albums than I could listen to, then ask for them back a few days afterwards. I'd usually have to lie about having listened to them.

Then summer became September, and the new term began. The return of homework and the nights drawing in made free time seem more valuable, to be devoted to something more fruitful than just football in the park or girls in tracksuits. Ben and I spent a lot of time playing together, me getting better gradually, Ben faster than seemed humanly possible. His abrasiveness was more or less gone now, towards me anyway. I'd worn him down, except for when he felt threatened by something I said or did, which usually involved refusing to admit to the supremacy of Zep, Purple and Hendrix. I just thought Joe Satriani and Metallica were better. Steve Vai too now; in fact, I was feeling guilty about thinking he might be even better than Satriani.

It was around this time that we first started talking about the band. We didn't have much of a plan, but at some now forgotten point in those autumn months, we stopped being two teenage boys learning guitar. We were the band. We were the only members of this band, and did not have any real instruments, equipment or material to play, but some great mental shift had subtly taken place, and a band we were. We'd both asked our parents for electric guitars and amps as joint Christmas and birthday presents for that year. Ben's parents said yes, and ended up buying him a separate birthday present anyway. Mine said, 'We'll see.'

Christmas would come too late, however, for what I felt should be the band's first gig – the school talent show. Held each year, the talent show gave students the chance to prove themselves either too cool for school, or too spazzy for living. Most of the acts were spaz acts, lone trumpet players, choirboy singers, comedy routines with no discernible jokes. They would be met with indifference, then abuse after the performance when no teachers were about. But also every year, some boys would distinguish themselves with something spectacular – break-dancing to Vanilla Ice, or a particularly lengthy and violent solo by the school brass band drummer. In my mind, the talent show was where the band would claim its place in music history legend, elevating us to the level of gods in the playground.

Ben felt otherwise.

'There's no fucking point,' he said. 'We're nowhere near ready.'

46

'We could get ready,' I argued, 'if we just practised.'

'No we couldn't. Anyway, we'd look stupid, playing on those bloody school guitars.'

'Well, so what? People would still see how good we are.'

'I'm not doing it, Chris.'

'Well, maybe I'll do it by myself then.'

'OK, your funeral.'

I didn't, of course. I'd never have gone onstage without Ben. I barely had the confidence to play in front of my family.

Not long after Ben and I had this conversation, Neil came bounding up to me with some news. Outside the science block, just coming out of a lesson. Mild, grey day.

'Chris, guess what!' he said.

'Dunno, what? You've finally kissed a girl.'

'No, better. I've entered the talent show!'

'Ah, OK. Doing what exactly?'

'I'm going to be playing the synthesiser, an old one without a keyboard or anything, just knobs you turn to make a sound. I found it at the back of the cupboard in the music room. No one's used it in years. And I'm going to be singing!'

'At the same time?'

'Yeah!'

'That sounds . . . interesting.'

'Yeah, and I've decided not to prepare anything. I'm just going to make it up as I go along.'

God help us. 'Right. Listen, Neil, are you sure that sort of thing's right for the school talent show?'

He looked puzzled. 'Why wouldn't it be?'

'Well, people might not like it.'

'So? That's not the point.'

47

'Well, what is the point, if no one likes it?'

'Just doing it. Doing it is the point.'

'Yeah, but why, though?'

'If I could tell you that I wouldn't be doing it.'

I didn't get it, and that's what I told him. In fact, I told him that he was talking crap and he was going to make himself look stupid and I'd be embarrassed to be seen with him afterwards. That seemed to hurt, but I felt he needed to be hurt for his own good. But also I felt jealous because his balls were a hundred times bigger than mine.

I could tell Ben was worried, although he was trying hard to hide it.

'There's a band playing the talent show,' he said.

Shit. It should have been us. We both knew it.

'Oh right,' I said, as if it didn't matter. 'Who is it?'

'Dunno. Think they're in the top set.'

At our school, years were divided into sets: upper, middle and lower. I was in the middle set, where it was safe. Best place to be. Not too clever and not too divvy.

'Are they a proper band, with a drummer and stuff?'

'Yeah. They play crappy indie rubbish, though.'

'How do you know?'

'I heard them practising in the music room.'

'Did you go in?'

'No, but you could hear them outside for miles.'

The bell rang and we went to our respective lessons. Ben was in the lower set. Not that he was thick, I think he just couldn't be bothered to try any harder. Neil was in the upper set this year; he'd moved up and I didn't have lessons with him any more. My homework suffered as a consequence.

About a week later, I was playing football on the sports field at lunchtime, getting my trousers muddy, when I saw Ben waving at me from the playground. I kicked the ball towards the goal, hit a jumper and held up my hand to pause the game.

'That band are playing,' said Ben as I got closer to him. 'Do you want to go and check them out?'

'Yeah, why not,' I replied.

'Hurry up, Hurry!' someone shouted.

That's my surname, 'Hurry'. Nothing better than being blessed with a comedy surname at a boys' school. Even the teachers had fun with it when they did the register. 'Hurry.'

'Pre—'

'Hurry up, Hurry, are you here or not?'

'Pre—'

'Quickly, boy, quickly! Hurry!'

And so on.

I shook my head and went to collect my jumper. The game had carried on without me anyway.

We made our way to the music room, which was a prefab hut on metal stilts isolated from the rest of the school at the other end of the playground. Every so often someone would kick their ball underneath it and have to crawl among the rusty crap that was dumped there to fetch it. A small crowd of boys were huddled around it now, all black jumpers, white shirts, grey trousers. Spiky bog-brush hair. Yellow and black ties with the thin part showing, the kipper tucked away.

There was a clatter of drums coming from inside. This wasn't uncommon, as the school brass band drummer often filled time before rehearsals with his interminable solos, but this was different. It was a solid, unfussy rock beat, clearly recognisable as proper music, and if you put your hand on the wooden banister of the stairs leading to the door, you could feel its pulse. Every so often a deep bass note would resonate like a sonic boom, sending a ripple of excitement through the gathering. Then a loud buzzing, followed by a feedback squeal that made some of the spazzy kids put their fingers in their ears. And after that a bluesy twiddle on the top strings of the guitar. For a few minutes, the drums, bass and guitar were playing at the same time, although not together. The guitar and bass stopped. But the drums carried on. 'Shut it!' someone was screaming, again and again, until the drums very slowly died away in a series of cymbal crashes. 'OK, a one, a two, a one two three four,' a muffled nasal voice counted. And the music started.

It was hard to make out at first, the playing wasn't very tight, and mostly all you could hear was the drums, but gradually something recognisable emerged. Although very rough around the edges, it was, undeniably, 'Need You Tonight' by INXS. Hardly indie, but Ben was even more militant than me in some things back then. There were no vocals, just that funk-rock riff, repeated over and over again, admittedly devoid of any of the funkiness it might have once possessed. Bluntly, it wasn't very good, and that cheered me up a bit, but it didn't really matter. The fact was, they were doing it, and I wasn't. Plus, they already had an audience, eager to listen to them lumpenly and endlessly play that one riff. It should have been me. Should be me. One day one day.

'Good, aren't they?' said a spazzer, bopping his head.

'Shit,' said Ben, 'utter fucking bollocks. Why can't they play some Motörhead? "Ace of Spades" or "Overkill" or something.'

'Well, I think they're good,' said the spaz kid, 'but then I like INXS.'

'INXS are indie bollocks,' Ben scowled.

'INXS aren't indie,' said the kid. 'They're a rock band.'

'They're fucking not! They're fucking poofter indie music. Rock's what Led Zeppelin and Black Sabbath do, not fucking music for queers.'

The kid shook his head and left it. Rather than coming across as a hard nut, Ben was just embarrassing. This was something I had discovered over the last few months. No one could stay scared of him for long; he always ended up looking more tragic than hard. Even the spazzers weren't scared of him; you could see them grinning and giggling. Now, back then I was no gay lover, although I knew fuck all about them really, except for those two they had in *EastEnders*, and I don't have a problem with them now obviously. But even I knew that there was something a mite extreme in Ben's attitude that was far from appealing, and for that minute it was worse than being out with Neil. But metallers didn't break ranks over such things, at least not at our school in those days, so I just stood there nodding in agreement, like a total idiot.

Still, Ben had left a bad taste in my mouth, and that may be why I found myself climbing those wooden steps, and pressing my face to the square mesh of the reinforced glass of the door and looking in. I couldn't see much, they didn't have the light on, but I recognised the guitar player as being one of the kids who had dropped out of the lessons after the first week. On the drums was a large boy, large in a muscular sense, that is, not fat, who I'd seen about the playground but didn't know. And on bass, well . . . you could hardly not know who Thomas Depper was. He stood out a mile in the playground. Blind as a bat, but he was no speccy monger who was going to have his glasses stepped on. And yes, he was curly and ginger, but this was no freckleface to be bundled behind the bike sheds. Because you didn't mess with

Thomas Depper. He buzzed with a dangerous energy that kept any potential predator away. His reputation for apparently random acts of cruelty, both verbal and physical, preceded him. He'd been dragged up in assembly several times for fighting, but he'd never been caught or punished for most of the things he'd done. There are boys, grown men now, who still bear the scars of what he did back in those days. And not just spazzers either, but pretty savvy lads. Depper had a chip on his shoulder about something, all right, although exactly what wasn't clear. Perhaps his dad used to slap him about, or maybe he was a spoilt mummy's boy gone rotten. I never really found out. I'm not sure if anybody knew what the problem was. Maybe Jase did, I don't know. Jase was the drummer. But I'll talk more about him later.

I'd only ever spoken to Thomas Depper a couple of times, and he'd just looked at me with contempt, muttering insults under his breath, but then he did that to almost everybody. Strange thing was, he did have friends, a small bunch of kids like Jase who'd probably known him all his life and knew exactly where the boundaries were. They all used to hang about on the grass verge leading down to the playground from the fences that backed onto people's gardens. No one else dared go anywhere near them when they were up there. And because he was so exclusive, it meant of course that actually getting to be his friend, or just getting away with not being insulted, seemed quite attractive, even though he himself plainly wasn't. On a physical level, if he hadn't been so mean, there'd have been nothing to distinguish him from your average spazzer. It was attitude, pure and simple. Mean, surly attitude that made half the school, I don't know, fall in love with him, in a way. I don't mean we were all gay, although maybe some of the boys were, who can say? But there was definitely a hold that he had, a fascination that everybody tuned into to some degree or other.

I had been unaware that he had any musical interests up until this point, but the very fact he could play and apparently owned a bass guitar was remarkable, as none of the kids in school ever aspired to play or own a bass. Loads of kids wanted to play drums, but no one could ever persuade their parents to buy a kit. Everybody wanted a guitar, and there were just a few kids who had one, and some even had an amp, although usually just a practice one. But a bass? That was unheard of.

The repeated riff finally disintegrated into sustained drum rolls and guitar fiddling. The bass was not playing and I should have taken that as a sign of bad things to come. You see, I'd been stupid enough to break the cardinal rule of dealing with Thomas Depper. Never take your eyes off him. But he had his eyes on me. Too late, I saw those jam jars pointing my way. He laid his bass down, walked over and opened the door. I wonder to this day why it didn't occur to me to move.

'Yeah, what you fucking want?' he snarled.

'Uh, nothing, I was just watching, that's all.'

'Well, don't, all right, you little twat. Now fuck off before I thump you one.'

He gave me a prod in the chest, which to my surprise sent me back nearly a foot, and tumbling down the wooden steps. As he did so he caught sight of the assembled spaz kids. 'And you lot can fuck off too!'

Most of them took flight immediately, disappearing into the playground masses. Only the foolhardy few and Ben remained.

'Well,' I said, trying to hide the fact I was slightly shaken, 'he seemed a nice chap, didn't he?'

'Bollocks did he,' said Ben. 'Fucking wanker. Probably a queer.'

As we walked off, drum clatter and guitar fiddle were again silenced with shouting and the sound of something being thrown, before the riff began again. I could still hear them playing it half an hour later when the whistle went.

7

The weeks leading up to the talent show dissolved in a soup of home-work, basketball games and the usual playground stuff – five-a-side, bundles, throwing someone's bag over the fence. Ben was good at the last one, and it actually gave the spazzers a reason to be wary of him, which was probably why he did it with such regularity, though usually to the same three or four boys. Every so often, the riff to 'Need You Tonight' would blast out of the music hut, and it gradu-ally began to sound a bit less lumpy, but not by much. From time to time I'd see Thomas Depper in the playground, either playing footy with his circle, or carrying his bass and amp to or from his practice sessions. Sometimes he'd see me looking at him, and scowl.

I even tried to strike up a conversation with him a couple of times. The first time, I'd barely even managed to say 'Hello' before I was cut short by his customary 'Fuck off', but the second time I was more lucky. Well, slightly anyway. 'All right, Tom,' I said, passing him after the home bell had rung.

'Yeah, what?'

'Oh, nothing much, I was just wondering how it's going, with the practising and that.'

'Fucking shit. I'm playing my bollocks off, but the other two can't get anything right at all.' I knew from listening that though he wasn't as good as he said, his band-mates weren't as bad either. The drummer had it down pretty much, I reckoned.

'Sounds all right to me,' I said. He grunted. I continued, 'So do you think you stand a chance, then?'

'Chance of what?' He had a way of saying the word 'what' that could destroy you. It was as if your very existence was a gross inconvenience to him, and if you had any sense you'd jump off a cliff just to avoid the possibility of ever being a nuisance again.

'Winning the talent show.'

'We'd better bloody do.'

'Well, I think you're good.'

'Yeah, I am.'

'Well, all of you are, I meant.'

'Yeah, except for that wanker on guitar and that other wanker on drums, we are.'

'Your drummer's OK.'

'If you think that, you obviously know fuck all about music. Now you've got to piss off. I've things to do.'

With that he walked off to the bike sheds. He passed me a minute later, cycling out of the school gates, his bass in its case strapped to his back, his sports bag hanging to one side and pulling him dangerously off-balance.

And then pretty soon after that was the day of the talent show. Cold winter again, chill penetrating thin grey trousers. I saw Neil on the morning of the show, I think, maybe even the lunch break just before. I asked him if he was still going to do it, hoping against hope that he wasn't.

'Absolutely,' he said. 'Why wouldn't I be?'

'And you're still playing the synthesiser and singing?'

'And harmonica. I decided it needed something else.'

'Since when have you known how to play the harmonica?'

'Well, that depends what you mean by knowing how to play.'

'Listen, Neil,' I said, 'I'm sure what you're going to do is fine, but are you really convinced it's right for the talent show? I mean, it's not too late to drop out. It's just I'm not sure anyone's going to get it.'

'Well, maybe they're not meant to get it.'

'What?'

'Maybe them not getting it is part of the point. Maybe by showing them something they don't get, I'm trying to tell them something.'

'Like what?'

'That what you know is not all there is.'

'Yeah, well . . . who cares?' I wasn't going to get into a conceptual argument with Neil, partly because at that age I hadn't learned how to, but mainly because I just didn't see the point of thinking like that. Total waste of time. Just got you laughed at and called a ponce.

'I do,' said Neil defiantly as I walked away to hang out with some less cerebral and therefore less embarrassing kids.

When showtime finally arrived, they rounded up the whole school and sat us down in the hall – row upon row of seats, crammed too tightly together, from the closed dinner hatch right to the other end where the piano was. Youngest boys at the front, oldest at the back, a mile away. Together in tutor groups, we had little say in who we sat next to. I found myself sandwiched between two of the least spazzy of the spazzers I could manage under the circumstances. Fortunately, I was spared having to pay attention to them when a gruff voice behind me, only recently fully broken, mumbled, 'All right, Chris.' It was Ben. 'Should be a laugh, shouldn't it,' he said.

'Yeah,' I replied. At least it would be that, I hoped, even though

58

it was now clear it would mean the certain end of me and Neil's friendship. Sitting there, I felt a tightness in my chest, partly because Thomas Depper's band were about to steal my place in music history, but also because I was nervous about just how badly Neil was going to go down. I didn't understand why he had to do this. More to the point, I didn't understand why he had to do this to me. He was hurting me, and he didn't seem to care. Fuck him.

The mass babble of the whole school talking in unison continued for a few minutes. Then the deputy head appeared from behind the curtain on the stage that was normally used for assembly, brass band concerts and the end-of-year play. Shiny bald head and a gaze that said, We're going to have a laugh, but don't take the piss. 'OK, lads, quiet now!' he shouted, waving his arms at us. He would be the compère. He was well liked and a funny guy, or at least we all thought so at the time. Don't know if he'd make me laugh now. Think I'd probably hate him.

Once he'd got everybody's attention, he told some jokes to get us warmed up, which I can't remember at all. I think he nicked all his stuff off Frank Carson or people like that. I just recall the strange sense of unease created by a teacher seeking the approval of his pupils. Most of the time they went out of their way to make sure we weren't entertained, so to have one working to keep us happy felt peculiar. I was bored already, even though I was laughing. Still the tightness in my chest. Then I remember he said something like this: 'OK, gentlemen, on with the show. We have comedians, we have jugglers, we have break-dancing, we have two bands and we have one lad playing the spoons. And much, much more.' The 'much, much more' was most likely Neil, but wait, did he say two bands? I turned round to Ben, and mouthed 'Two?' He shrugged his shoulders.

59

The curtains parted. The show opened with some kids jumping over a vaulting horse or something. After that some first-year spazzers did a shit comedy routine about a farmer, then came the spoons player, and some other stuff which, luckily, has slipped from my mind. But with each act, my unease deepened. It was like when a storm is on its way. You can feel it in the wind. Then it was the deputy head again. 'Gentlemen,' he said, 'are you ready to rock? Are you ready to roll? Are you ready to go oooba-joooba-joooba?' Everyone laughed. 'Are you ready for . . . the Horned Gods?' Was that Thomas Depper's lot? I waited for the riff to 'Need You Tonight' to ring out, played slightly below competence level. The curtain opened. A guitar riff. But not the clean, crisp, funky riff of 'Need You Tonight'. This one was dirty. Not too familiar, but I knew it. Then it clicked: 'Foxey Lady'. And there, onstage, were a bunch of little kids. Really little, from the first year. A full band, drums, two guitars, bass, and really decent equipment. Shit, I thought, no one knew about them, no one. What the hell was this? I mean, they looked the part, sort of. Their hair was still just about school-regulation length, but half of them had it tied back in tiny ponytails. And they wore proper metaller denim and band T-shirts, although it was all very clean. But still, they were good, very good. So good it hurt. Until one of them started singing.

You know you're a cute little heart-breaker. Foxey!
You know you're a sweet little love-maker. Foxey!

It wasn't that he was bad, just that his voice hadn't broken. And not only that, but two of the other kids were going 'Foxey, foxey lady' in similarly high-pitched tones. Ben and I looked at each other and smirked. As long as they were doing something wrong, it just about made it bearable.

Not that anyone else cared. Everyone's attention had been wandering during the shit farmer sketch and the other stuff, but this got them. Obviously no one could stand up and rock out, that wasn't allowed, and no one would want to with the whole school there, but quite a few heads were bobbing. This was the biggest sign of enjoyment allowable with all the teachers in the school prowling down the rows, looking for the first sign of trouble to stamp on. The lead guitarist copied the solo pretty damn well. He was probably as good as Ben, or nearly.

And then it was over. There was an enormous round of applause, along with the strange mixed cheer of broken and unbroken voices, like the cheer you used to get on *Crackerjack*. Even the kids from the other side of town were cheering, and they all hated rock music. Shit, I thought. Shit. Shit. Shit. Not only were they doing it, they were great, and they were younger than me. I had a lot of catching up to do.

'What do you think?' I said to Ben.

'Fucking rubbish,' he said.

'Yeah,' I said.

Some spaz kid came out and read some humorous poetry he'd written and got jeered. The teachers snapped 'Quiet!' up and down the hall. I zoned out for a bit, still thinking about those kids. They'd made me forget about Thomas Depper's lot, and not only that, they'd made me forget about Neil.

Then the deputy head came back on. 'And now we have, well, some more music, I suppose,' he said, embarrassed, almost murmuring, before quickly disappearing offstage, as if not wanting to be caught at the scene of a crime.

Neil walked out. I felt sick. He was the only kid performing to whom it hadn't occurred to change out of his school uniform. Hadn't even got his equipment set up, and had to wheel his synthesiser on an old TV stand to where he could find a plug, which was right on the lip of the stage, a long way from the curtain. People were already sniggering. The teachers weren't seeing fit to hush them either.

He asked someone for a microphone, and one, complete with stand, was stretched to him from behind the curtain. He fumbled about trying to get it at the right height, but couldn't quite manage it, finally leaving it at chest level, where it had stuck and now refused to move. He took a harmonica from his pocket, and stooping down into the microphone, began to blow in and out of it, making a hee-haw noise like a siren. As he did so, he twiddled with the knobs on the synthesiser with his other hand, which began to emit a low rumble through the PA that made the light-fittings rattle. Then he started to, well, sing, I guess you'd call it.

'I'm your receiver, your golden retriever, the only believer . . .'

I'd never heard him sing before. His voice was like a honk, and refused to settle on any note in particular while it made unpredictable jumps up and down the scale, never quite hitting whatever was presumably intended. It was a horrible sound. Boys were putting their hands over their ears as the synthesiser rumble got louder and harsher in tone as he turned the knobs, finally resulting in a sheer white noise that he seemed quite pleased with. He played his harmonica again, the same siren pattern, before singing some more: 'Night light, beat band, try to scale my wall . . .'

It was all nonsense, obviously made up off the top of his head. Then he started screaming. A high, intense scream, like a woman's, straight out of a horror movie. It just went on and on. Mixed with the high frequencies coming from the synthesiser, it was actually becoming unbearable. People had stopped laughing now. They were just in pain and upset.

Finally, the deputy headmaster took matters in his own hands and motioned to the kids working the PA to kill the sound. The synthesiser cut out, but the screaming carried on. The deputy head tapped him on the shoulder, but Neil just wouldn't give him his attention. In the end, he had to literally pull him off stage, his legs flailing. There was a round of applause. It was for the deputy head.

'Right, ah, and now for something completely different,' said the deputy head when he came back on. There was some very nervous laughter. Meanwhile, you could hear Neil having a coughing fit offstage, a result, no doubt, of all the screaming.

Some kids came on and break-danced to EMF's 'Unbelievable'. They were all wearing baseball caps and cycling shorts, and were careful to avoid Neil's synthesiser, which still sat confrontationally near the lip of the stage. But no one was paying attention. Everyone was still recovering from Neil. Despite the teachers' best efforts, we were all either mumbling or laughing about it, although the laughter was still nervous. Something very disturbing had just happened to all of us, and although no one would admit it, it could not be hidden. And me, right then, I knew. Neil was on to something. There was something in all of that which was important. Something I needed to confront. He'd opened a door in me, and invited me to look inside. And through that door, I would finally see the secret, I would discover the meaning of Neil. And once I'd seen it, I would never be the same again. And maybe for that reason, I chose not to look. If only I'd had the guts to take a peek, maybe I wouldn't have fallen through that door, head first, all those years later.

Perhaps others were wrestling with something similar, or maybe they were just feeling the after-effects of an encounter with the weird. I don't know. All I know is, when Thomas Depper and his friends came out and played their lumpy instrumental version of 'Need You Tonight', most failed to notice, and no one really cared, not even me and Ben. Neil had stolen the show.

Not that he won it. That would have been madness. That accolade went to the little kids who played 'Foxey Lady'.

8

As expected, there was considerable fallout in the wake of the talent show. Firstly, the 'Foxey Lady' kids – or the Horned Gods as they called themselves, which was a *2000 AD* reference, as pointed out by Ben, obviously disgruntled that they were into his special thing – became instant school celebrities, which was very unusual for little kids. It went to their heads pretty quickly, because by the time I got round to talking to a couple of them a few days later, they were arrogant little shits.

I made a point of crossing the playground to talk to them, one the singer and rhythm guitar player, dark, nearly black hair, the other, the lead guitarist, fairer-headed, both metaller centre partings, both of them way shorter than me. It's funny, in that moment I wasn't checking out the competition, I was genuinely star-struck. I wanted a piece of them.

'All right,' I said.

'Yeah,' one of them said, a look of amused condescension on both their faces. It said to me that I had one chance of proving myself worthy of their attention, and that I was already boring them slightly.

'You were good at the talent show the other day,' I said.

'Yeah,' they said.

'It was good that you won,' I said.

'Yeah, it was,' they said.

'I can play guitar too,' I said. 'Well, a bit anyway.'

'Yeah?' they said. 'Big deal.'

'Do you like Joe Satriani?' I asked.

'No, of course not,' they replied, smirking.

'Well, I think he's good,' I said.

'Yeah, so?'

'Well, I'll see you around then,' I said.

'Hope not,' they said, and made wanker gestures to each other as I walked away.

Over the next few days they alienated their entire fan base in a similar manner.

There were even fewer good vibes being sent out by the losers. I swear this is true, the break-dancers staged a sit-in in the deputy head's office in protest at their defeat, doing back-spins on his desk to an audience that had assembled outside, peeking their heads through the window. They got weeks of detention for it, but they simply break-danced their way through it, to the delight of the other assorted troublemakers. In the end it was cancelled, as it was just providing them with a platform.

Similarly, Thomas Depper was not best pleased. I bumped into him in the toilets, using the long communal urinal that never quite managed to contain all the boys' piss that passed through it.

'Don't look at my cock, you queer,' he snapped as he caught me in his peripheral vision.

'All right, Thomas,' I said.

'I was until you turned up.'

'You did all right at the talent show.'

'No I didn't. Well, I was all right, but my band was fucking rubbish. Last time I play with those two spastics.'

He zipped himself up and made his way to the door without

washing his hands. I'm ashamed to say I didn't either, as I wanted to keep up with him.

'I play guitar,' I said, 'a bit anyway.'

'Do you?' he said, sounding almost as bored as the Horned Gods.

'Yeah, maybe we could get together sometime and jam or something?'

'Yeah, maybe. Probably not, though.'

He walked out without saying goodbye, but, and this made me tingle inside, he held the door open long enough for me to catch hold of it before it swung shut. With Thomas Depper, this was an act of some significance.

But what of the real star of the talent show, Neil? I didn't know all the details at the time, because like half the school I would cross the playground in the opposite direction rather than get anywhere near him, but what I later found out was this. Immediately after the end of the talent show, the deputy head had practically dragged Neil to his office, where he demanded to know what the hell he thought he was playing at. When Neil told him that it didn't matter what he himself thought he was playing at, it was everybody else's idea of what he was playing at that counted, the deputy told him not to act all smart and superior with him and gave him indefinite detention. But before Neil could attend his first session, he was saved by a furious intercession on his behalf by Miss Millachip, his art teacher. You know the sort, middle-aged hippy, beads, lots of hand-dyed orange and purple, probably a lesbian. Apparently, when she overheard the deputy head boasting about the punishment he'd doled out in the staff room, she ripped him apart on the spot, and could be heard right into the canteen, bellowing away in her posh north London accent, voice lowered by years of herbal cigarette smoking. She informed the deputy head that Neil was working in the confrontational tradition of performance art, an internationally recognised and celebrated art form, and just because it did not fit into his small-minded idea of what constituted worthy forms of expression, this was no justification for punishing Neil. To do so, she declared, was nothing more than cultural fascism.

The deputy head relented, not because he understood the argument, he was overheard referring to Miss Millachip as 'a mad old bat' not long afterwards, but more likely because he just wanted her to leave him alone. Anyway, the end result was, Neil was free. Scarily so, in fact. Literally, he had become untouchable. All the kids either pretended not to see him, and darted in the opposite direction like I did, or nervously shouted 'Loony!' or 'Freak!' or stuff like 'Know any good songs, Neil? Don't fucking sing 'em.' But really all we were doing was covering up how much he'd stirred everyone up.

Christmas was round the corner, and I didn't speak to Neil in the last days of the autumn term at all. He phoned my house several times, but I got Nicki, who always answered the telephone in the hall in those far-off, lost days of the pre-mobile teenager, to say I wasn't in. I spent more time with Ben, both of us excited about our imminent Christmas gifts of electric guitars and amps. Of course, in the event, while Ben got a Fender Strat like his brother and a big fuck-off Marshall amp, my ostensibly socially higher parents could only stretch to a crappy pink Argos catalogue job, and a little practice amp. I made an effort to look pleased on Christmas morning, but truthfully I felt a bit shafted. I pledged to get an evening as well as morning paper round to save up enough to get a proper amp at least. I could always spray-paint the guitar black to disguise its crappiness. When I showed it to Ben he laughed and called it 'shit', which made me nervous as I'm pretty sure my dad, who was in the next room, could hear. I think it was round about this time that Ben went to his first concert, Motörhead at the Hammersmith Odeon. He went with Ken. He said they both went right down the front and it was mental, everyone was head-banging and you couldn't move, you just got swept along with the way everyone else was going. He said that if you'd fallen over you'd have died, and that his ears were ringing for a week afterwards. I had asked my parents if I could go and they'd said no.

Back to school too soon, and the New Year brought in strange, invisible changes, like a cold wind that blew through us. I bumped into Thomas Depper again, this time on the stairs, his Head sports bag hitting me in the back as he pushed his way past me.

'All right, Thomas,' I said.

'Oh fucking hell, not you again,' he said, but not in a harsh way, and slowed from taking two steps at a time to let me catch up.

'Have a good Christmas?'

'Fucking shit, mate. What about you?'

'Not bad, not bad. Got a guitar and amp actually, well, a practice amp anyway.'

'Did you really? Well, I was meaning to talk to you about that sort of thing.'

'Oh right.'

We reached the bottom of the stairs. He stopped before the swing doors and faced me.

'Listen, I was wondering . . .' His gaze began to wander, sometimes on me, sometimes around me, his eyes little balls bouncing around in the transparent containers of his glasses.

'Yeah, you see, the thing is, I don't want to play with those twats I was playing with any more, but I've got to keep the drummer cos no one else owns a kit, but, well, do you want to play guitar with us?'

'Yeah, sure, that would be great.' There was no real way I could express to him how amazingly happy he had just made me, in case he took it as a sign of weakness, but I was elated. This was simply the best thing ever. I suddenly had a proper, functioning band, and not only that, but Thomas Depper had effectively just asked me to be part of his circle, or at least a satellite of it. I don't think he'd asked anyone before, not that I knew of, anyway. But, wait a minute, what about Ben? Weren't we meant to be the band . . .

'Um, Thomas, I've got a friend, who plays guitar too, really well. Maybe he could be in the band as well . . .'

'Oh, fucking hell, not that lanky twat you hang around with.'

'Yeah, it is, sorry.'

'Oh well, bring him along if you must. We can always kick him out later if he's shit.'

'OK, so when's our first practice?'

'Dunno, get back to you on that one. But we'll go in the music hut after school sometime. Got to talk to the Queer about it.'

The Queer was the flamboyant music teacher, Mr Evans. Not in any way gay, but his taste in frilly shirts and velvet jackets and the bouffant quality of his hair were enough to mark him out as an object of ridicule. Even the staff thought he was fruity, and he was a constant thorn in their side, taking kids out of lessons for brass band and choir practice and afternoon concerts in old people's homes. But he didn't care what anyone thought, he really didn't; all he cared about was the music.

'OK,' I said, 'I'll talk to my mate, Ben, and see what he says.

But he should be OK with it. What type of music do you generally play, anyway?'

'Oh,' said Thomas, 'stuff like Guns N' Roses, Quireboys, INXS obviously. Like to do some Def Leppard at some point. Hard rock mainly.'

'Cool,' I said. 'What about Metallica, Iron Maiden, that sort of thing?'

'We don't really go that heavy, to tell you the truth. What about you?'

'Yeah, I'm more into that sort of thing. But it doesn't matter. I like the stuff you're into too.'

'Yeah, well, I'll get back to you on that one. Right, see you.'

Thomas took a left. I went right and headed for the lavs. I tracked down Ben as soon as I could and told him about the opportunity.

'Fucking hell,' he said, grumpily, 'why would we want to play with those cunts? They play fucking gay indie music.'

'No they don't,' I said. 'They play hard rock. OK, it's not metal, and some of it's shit, like INXS, but it's something. We can always make them play the music we like once we're properly in the band.'

'Yeah, I s'pose,' he said, quietly, miserably, but with an air of resignation that signalled he was about to say yes. 'OK then, I'll fucking do it. But I'm not sticking with it if it's shit.'

''Course,' I said. 'I won't either. It'll be our band anyway.'

'Better bloody be,' he said, and though I could tell he didn't want to, and he definitely didn't want me to see it, he smiled.

9

What did we get up to at that first rehearsal? I don't know, I think there's a tape somewhere. Jase used to tape everything we did. Not just the songs, but all the talking and messing about as well. I'd like to hear it sometime, if he's still got it, and all the others. But we don't know each other any more, so I doubt I'll ever get to. It's funny, I was never really introduced to Jase, he was just there waiting for us in the music room, beating seven shades of shit out of the brass band drums, until Thomas made him stop by holding his cymbals while he tried to hit them. Turns out that was the only way to shut him up. I don't think we even spoke to each other until the next rehearsal.

Me and Ben got there after school. We had the room until the caretaker locked everything up at five. Thomas and Jase were there already. Thomas eyed up Ben with suspicion. 'All right,' he said, more a statement than a greeting. Ben just grunted back.

Jase was banging on the drums. Steady, not flashy. Not too difficult, maybe not that talented, but solid, good. As I said, I never really talked to him at that first rehearsal. Thomas talked to him, or more to the point ordered him to do things, usually without result. I talked to Thomas. Ben did not talk to Thomas or Jase. I talked to Ben. And that's the way it worked at first.

It's weird, even though a band was exactly what we'd been fantasising about for ages, neither me nor Ben got that excited about the first rehearsal. I mean, we should have been, we desperately wanted a band, and I'd gone as far as trying to engage Thomas Depper in friendly conversation to get in. But in between then and the first rehearsal, my enthusiasm had ebbed to the point where it almost seemed a bit of a chore, getting all my stuff up to the school and everything. I don't know what it was, maybe we just knew this was not really it. Wherever we were trying to get to, it wasn't going to be achieved in that music hut playing INXS covers. The key lay elsewhere. The key lay in the very place we could not look. Still, we had fun. Just more low-key fun than the ecstasy of group interplay we'd anticipated.

What songs did we do? Well, we didn't do anything properly as none of us sang, but we did 'Need You Tonight', which didn't make Ben very happy, 'Sweet Child O' Mine', 'Johnny B. Goode'. I only knew it from *Back to the Future*. Each one about seven times or something.

Were we any good? No, we were rubbish. I was struggling to get the hang of the chords Thomas had scribbled down for me, and even though they'd been playing together for ages, Thomas wasn't really clicking into Jason's drum patterns. Well, when I say we weren't any good, as a band we weren't, we were all over the place, but Ben, Ben was something else. He'd never played any of these songs before, and had hardly ever heard them, but by ear, he could pretty much replicate the riffs and general feel of the solos. I mean, it wasn't perfect, he fumbled changes like the rest of us and played the odd clanger of a wrong note. But he always recovered. Ben was good, all right. Although he didn't say anything, I could tell by the way he looked at him that Thomas had noticed just how good he was.

So that was our first practice, although what we were practising for hadn't really been discussed. In fact, very little was said. Just the odd bit of direction from Thomas to me, direction and abuse from Thomas to Jase, and no attempt at direction at all in regard to Ben. It wasn't a momentous occasion; it didn't feel like we were making history; it was what it was, a start. But when the practice was over, and we were making a small and half-hearted effort to return the music room to normality, something else happened.

You see, while we tidied up, Ben had rested his guitar, which was out of its case, against a table that had been moved to the side of the room. Thomas, either not seeing or not caring, it was impossible to tell, decided to move the table back to where it came from. The guitar fell face first onto the floor. It was a horrible sound, that thud of wood on floorboard, which was, incidentally, coated in trumpeters' spit from the brass band practice earlier that day. A thud and a tinny jangle of unamplified strings. Ben leaped with his grasshopper legs across the room in a panic. 'You fucking monger,' he snapped, as he held his guitar closely, looking for any damage.

Thomas Depper just stood there, his gaze fixed firmly on Ben. 'I'm going to make you sorry you said that,' he said.

Ben looked up at him. Their eyes locked. Neither of them said or did anything else. They just looked at each other. Little did we know how much was being determined in that meeting of wills. Ben's eyes were seething, but ultimately his gaze was weak. Because for all his surliness, he wasn't mean, he was merely grumpy. But Depper, Depper was mean, really mean. Behind those jam jars, there was something that would sting you, you could see it clearly then. He had venom in his eyes, and Ben was no match. He looked down at his guitar, and pretended that the chip in the body wasn't there, and just mumbled, 'Well, it looks OK.'

We went our separate ways. Jase and Thomas, who had permission to leave his amp in the band instrument cupboard, cycled away, while I waited with Ben for his dad to pick us up in his taxi. But before any of us went anywhere, we all agreed to meet again, same time next week. Which we did, and then most weeks after that, when the brass band wasn't doing extra practice after school for a concert. Our repertoire never got much bigger, and we never got much better, except for Ben, and there was really no hope of catching up with him. He didn't even seem to want to be in the group that much, but he kept on turning up anyway. Privately he used to tell me that all we played was 'soft-rock bollocks'. He'd moved on from calling it 'indie', but it was still 'fucking poofs' music'. As for me, it wasn't really what I wanted either. But I couldn't quite envisage what that was precisely, as it was becoming pretty clear I was never going to be Joe Satriani. So, like Ben, I just kept on turning up, really because it was the only show in town. And besides, even though it wasn't my thing, I honestly quite enjoyed it. So did Ben secretly, I think. Still, I'm sure we both felt the pinch of the gap between our dreams and the hard reality. We both knew we should be more excited than we were. In any case, group relations weren't improving much at first, which put a downer on developing any team spirit. I tried to talk to Jase, but he didn't seem that interested. Thomas and Ben talked civilly, just about, for a few seconds every week. But really, our strange rules of communication didn't get broken very often.

I think it was the week before the Easter break. Ben was at my house one day, at the weekend, I expect. We were listening to records and working out guitar parts when he said, out of the blue, 'I was, uh, round Thomas's the other day.'

I tried not to sound surprised, but how could I not be? 'Really?' I said.

'Yeah.' He carried on fiddling at a speed that was completely beyond me.

'What were you up to?'

'Oh nothing, really, just listening to music and stuff. Why'd you ask?'

'No reason.' For the same reason you mentioned it, Ben. To establish where we both stood now.

In the days before we broke up, it was all change in the playground. Coming out of a CDT lesson, I saw Ben with Thomas and his gang on the grassy verge. All of a sudden, Ben was in the inner circle, it seemed. Even though I'd been asked to be in his band, Thomas had always managed to maintain a distance, which meant it would never have occurred to me to ever stand up there like I was his mate. But there Ben was, up there, with Thomas and Jason. I didn't feel confident enough to go up and say hello.

To my surprise, it was Jase who ended up coming to me. I was playing football with the cool kids I chose to call my mates when it happened.

'Chris,' he said, tapping me on the arm.

'Hi, Jase,' I said, hoping the ball wouldn't come down my end in a hurry. Couldn't these musicians ever understand that you're not meant to just drop out of a game of footy like this? Made me look a right spaz.

'Yeah, just came over to say that we're going to be rehearsing at my house over the holidays.'

'At your house? Won't your parents mind?'

'No, not really. They'll both be at work anyway.'

'You must have very understanding neighbours.'

'No, but fuck 'em. Tuesdays all right for you?'

'Yeah, sure.'

The next Tuesday I was round Jase's house, deep in suburban territory, in his bedroom. Quite nice, tidy, flat-pack bed and table from Homebase. I remember it being different shades of blue. Anyway, we had to crouch in strange places to fit us all in with our amps and stuff. I was stuck between the bed and the wall, Ben was over by the door, Thomas was sat on the bed, complaining that he could feel the vibrations from the amps in his arse. It was funny, maybe because Ben was in his gang now, or maybe because he was in a different environment, but Thomas's tone had changed. The way he talked was a lot less direct and cutting, and there was almost a sing-song quality to his voice. Not only that, but it was as if he spoke in his own language, with his own special words for things, which Jase seemed to understand and sometimes used himself. I suppose it was because they'd known each other so long. For instance, if he wanted someone to move out of his way while he lifted his amp, he'd say, 'Schnoo, schnoo!' Or, if he wanted Ben to have a dirty sound through his amp, he'd say, 'Make it all gurgly-wurgly', or if he wanted a clean one, 'Shiny-winy'. It was weird, it should have been childish and embarrassing, but there was something almost magical about it all. As if knowing his language was an entry to something – a protected space. It gave you power.

So we met at Jase's a couple of times over the Easter break, and then back in the music hut when school restarted. But not for long, because one day we didn't bother to put the room back to normal for some reason, and Mr Evans went mental. It was terrifying and funny at the same time. He cornered Thomas, Jase and Ben the next morning on the grass verge, waving his arms in his velvet jacket and screaming his head off about us abusing his good nature. He was carrying his baton, even, and as I watched from the football pitch, I really thought he was going to throw it at them, like a Ninja dagger or something. And that was the end of that, no more music hut. We tried to put a brave face on it, and made fun of Mr Evans and called him a queer, and joked about how he liked to bum all the boys in his band, but it was no good really, it was a fucking blow. It meant we wouldn't be able to play again until half-term, and then after that, not until summer. And that was the way it turned out. One practice at Jase's, then not another for six weeks, which, when you're fourteen, is for ever.

Not that the band was the only thing occupying my time back then. Other things were happening too. I would have a couple more short-lived relationships with girls I didn't really care that much about over the summer, more basketball, Scouts on Thursdays during term-time. Still, I never did get that evening paper round because it got in the way of too much else, and so it took me right until October to save up for a proper amp. My family bought their first CD player, which was exciting, but I couldn't buy anything to listen to while I was saving, so the only thing to play on it was my mum's Cat Stevens, which I hated. Metallica's 'black album', officially known as just *Metallica*, came out at the end of the summer, and that was the first CD I bought, putting my amp purchase back by a couple of weeks or so. Me and Ben and other metallers used to listen to it over and over again. We even got Thomas and Jase into it. It was just so fucking great, 'Enter Sandman' and all. In fact, the only person I can remember not liking it was Neil. He said that the black cover was funny because it was just like the album in *Spinal Tap*. I didn't know what the fuck he was talking about. But I didn't care what Neil thought about anything by then. I hardly ever spoke to him, and I don't think I saw him at all over the summer. His only friends now were total spazzers. Always talking about that *Twin Peaks* programme that was on back then that made no sense. In fact, Neil had slipped right down from lower-middle to the very bottom of the whole school hierarchy, if not virtually outside it completely. You could say he'd screamed his way out at the talent show. As for me, the band were my friends now. My real friends anyway.

After school ended, and the summer holidays began, we went back to practising at Jase's during the day. But the funny thing was, at that first practice after the lay-off it didn't feel quite right. We were all sitting there, waiting to get started, but none of us wanted to, we were embarrassed. The lay-off had made us self-conscious. Already, the fragile spell had been broken. 'Are we going to play anything or what?' said Thomas, but he didn't look as if he could be bothered either. It seemed stupid all of a sudden, like when you wake up and know you're too old for *Star Wars* figures. We weren't saying anything to each other, but the same thoughts were going through our minds. What was the point of learning all these songs? Who were we ever going to play to? And nobody would say it, but it was what all of us had been thinking in the time out of action: what was the point of a band that played songs which didn't have a singer? We could never just make instru-mental music like Steve Vai or Joe Satriani because Thomas didn't like instrumental music. He only liked songs. On the other hand, none of us wanted to sing, as there seemed to be something deeply

79

homosexual about standing up in front of people and doing that. And the idea of bringing into the group anyone so bent that they'd want to do it wasn't something any of us could stomach back then either. But a change of some kind had to be made. We all felt that.

'Let's just fucking play something,' said Thomas, probably trying to justify in his mind having just lugged all his equipment down the road. 'Right, "Sweet Child O' Mine", go.'

We got through a verse and a half, badly and painfully, when Jase just stopped playing and threw his drumsticks at his feet. Thomas looked daggers at him and motioned to me and Ben to stop too.

'What the fuck are you playing at?' snarled Thomas.

'I've written a song,' said Jase.

10

'You what?'

'I've written a song,' said Jase.

'That's nice for you,' said Thomas. 'Now why did you stop fucking playing?'

'I think we should play it,' said Jase.

'Play what?' said Thomas.

'My new song,' said Jase.

'Do you now?' said Thomas.

'Yeah.'

'What did you write it on?' I asked.

'His cock,' sneered Thomas.

'Guitar,' said Jase.

'Didn't know you could play,' I said.

'Well, I can play chords.'

'Yeah, fucking badly,' said Thomas.

'So what have you written, just chords?' I asked.

'Yeah,' he said, then adding in a barely audible voice, 'and words.'

'I'd like to hear it,' I said.

'Don't bother,' said Thomas. 'It'll be fucking shit. I've heard his songs before. Crap, the lot of them.'

'I want to hear it too,' said Ben, out of nowhere. Bit of a surprise.

Thomas, knowing that a king can only rule with the consent

of his subjects, and sensing that his power could one day slip if he didn't give a little, raised his hands. 'OK,' he said, 'play the fucking song. But I'm warning you, it'll be a complete fucking waste of time.'

Jase made us lift up our legs as he pulled out a hitherto concealed acoustic guitar from under the bed, where it was kept like a dirty secret, nestling next to his porn mags, most likely. He rested it on his knee as he hid behind his drum kit, a great big barrier between him and his audience. Then after several minutes of tuning away imaginary discordances, he started awkwardly forming chord shapes and strumming softly, stopping and starting, stalling for time, postponing the moment when he had to reveal his tormented soul as promised.

'Just play if you're fucking playing!' shouted Thomas from the other side of the drum kit.

Goaded, he began, in a manner of speaking. 'OK, this is a sort of an intro,' he mumbled, and played some minor chords, folk fingering, not barre, Am to Em I think, two bars each, probably about eight times in a row.

'Fucking long intro,' sniggered Thomas.

'Yeah, well, there'll be a guitar part over the top, so it won't seem too long then,' said Jase. 'And then it goes into a verse, which goes like this.'

I think there was quite an awkward leap to Emaj, then G, back to Am, then repeated. It didn't make that much musical sense, even at the time I could see that, but it held together, just about.

'And then it's the chorus, which is the same as the intro, and you've heard that, so you don't need me to play it.' He turned his guitar upright and clutched it to himself, his face hidden behind the neck.

'Right,' said Thomas. 'That's it, is it?'

'Yeah,' said Jase softly. 'Well, there are words too.'

'Really? And what might they be? Or do we have to fucking guess?'

Jase got up and opened a drawer in his desk and took out a school notebook. In fact, I think it was his science rough book. He found a page at the back and looked as if he was going to give it to Thomas, but then he hesitated, before handing it to me, both of us stretching over the drum kit.

I looked at his blockish handwriting, obviously written slowly and with effort. A whole page of lines, the shape resembling that of the poetry we were occasionally forced to dissect in English lessons. Nervously, I made it form words. I remember some of it, about half of it anyway. It went like this.

> Feel the misery of searing pain
> Burning through me like an evil flame
> Nothing can ever save me from this
> Not even the taste of your kiss
>
> I'm a soul in torment
> I'm a soul in torment
> Unhappiness flowing like electrical current
> I'm a soul in torment

As I read it, Thomas stuck his head over my shoulder.

'"Feel the misery of searing pain, burning through me like an evil flame,"' he read in a cruelly mocking voice. 'Not up to your usual standard, Jase.' Jase shrank further behind his guitar, as he turned deep red, bordering on purple.

'Let's see,' said Ben. I passed the sheet over to him. He looked through it, mouthing the words to himself as he read. 'I like it,' he said when he got to the end. 'I think we should do it.'

'Well, I don't,' said Thomas.

'Why not?' asked Ben.

''Cos it's shit and it would be a waste of our time.'

'I'd like to see you do better,' said Ben.

'I could do if I could be bothered,' said Thomas.

'Well, why don't you then?' said Jase.

'I can't be fucking bothered, can I?' Thomas said, laughing.

'Let's put it to a vote,' said Ben.

'I vote that we don't do it,' said Thomas immediately.

'I vote that we do,' said Jase.

'And me,' said Ben.

Thomas turned to me. 'So what do you want to do then, Chris?' he said. His eyes told me what answer I was meant to give.

'I think we should . . .' I paused, partly for dramatic effect, partly because I'd started my sentence without really knowing what I was going to say. But ultimately my answer was '. . . do it.'

'Oh fucking hell,' said Thomas.

'OK, that's settled, we're doing it,' said Ben.

Jase couldn't contain his beaming smile at his triumph and the validation of baring his soul in torment. But what made me say yes? It's not that I actually thought the song was that great. Though I wasn't yet familiar with decent lyrics, I hadn't heard any Dylan or anything, even then I knew that Jase's weren't that good. Not only that, but I could see the chords didn't really hang together. Still, I knew this could be the start of something. This was a way towards being a band that people gave a shit about, instead of just being a bunch of teenagers covering Guns N' Roses songs without any vocals.

Jase ran us through the chords one more time and we were ready to play. It wasn't exactly challenging and we picked it up in a few goes. Ben had a lead part all worked out in practically five minutes. After half an hour, it was sounding pretty good. We were pleased with ourselves by the end of it, even Thomas, and no one was thoughtless enough to break the mood by pointing out that we had a whole set of lyrics with no one to sing them. After we'd played it about seven or eight times, we decided to give it a rest for a bit and went back to 'Sweet Child O' Mine'.

Jase revealed other songs to us over the summer. Each time he got a little less shy about it, even daring to play his guitar in front of the drum kit rather than behind it. But though his confidence grew, he would never consider actually singing the melodies that were so clearly in his head. Always the chords, followed by the passing of the notebook. None of the songs were that good, and they were all on the themes of eternal pain and suffering, but we learned them anyway, to the point that by the end of the summer holidays we had a good half-dozen.

As we prepared to go back to school, we were getting quite cocky, even though we no longer had a place to rehearse, now that we couldn't practise at Jase's house on weekdays. So much so, in fact, that we wanted to present what we'd done to other people, play a gig of some sort. At least that was the discussion we were having as we packed up after our final practice of the summer, until Jase said the unsayable.

'We need a singer.'

'Oh fucking hell,' said Thomas.

'He's right, we do,' said Ben.

'Yeah, I guess,' I said, trying to stay neutral, as usual, or at least noncommittal.

'Well, we're not going to get one, are we? At least not one who's not a total bender,' said Thomas.

'Yeah, well, we still need one,' said Jase.

'Fucking who, though?' said Thomas.

'I have to say I can't think of anybody,' I said.

'Neither can I,' muttered Ben.

'Chris, what about your friend, the one who did the talent show?' asked Jase.

'Fuck no,' said Thomas. Ben shook his head and looked down. Christ, Neil in the band was the last thing I wanted.

'Ah, I don't think Neil would really be right for us,' I said.

'But he's the only person any of us know who's not afraid to sing in public,' said Jase. 'And as well as that, he can play the harmonica.'

'He didn't sing, he screamed,' cried Thomas, 'and made a right tit of himself. And I don't think he knows one end of a harmonica from his arse.'

'Well, I didn't think he made a tit of himself,' said Jase. 'I think he'd do OK.'

'Yeah, might do,' said Ben.

'I just don't know if he'd be right for what we're trying to do,' I said.

'No, he won't be,' Thomas said, 'but . . . we'll give him a try, I suppose. And if he's shit like I know he's going to be, we can have a fucking laugh at him.'

And so it was agreed that I should ask Neil if he would be our singer. Which I did, later that day. It was awkward, of course, having not spoken to him all summer, but for the good of the band and all, I picked up the phone, dialled that number I knew off by heart and asked his mum, who was mad, if I could speak to him.

'It's Chris, is it?' she said. 'Lovely to hear from you again!' She started laughing hysterically at absolutely nothing and went to fetch Neil.

I heard the sound of him bounding down the stairs like a herd of gazelles, before picking up the receiver in the hallway. 'Hi, Chris,' he said, what I took to be fake nonchalance not quite covering his excitement.

'Yeah, hi. Listen, Neil, the reason I'm phoning is that, well, you know that I'm in this band? Well, the thing is, I was wondering if . . . We need a singer, and the only person we could think of who would do it is you.'

'Wow, I don't know really. Yeah, OK.'

'You'll do it?'

'Yeah, it'll be fun. Don't know if I'm really what you're looking for, though.'

'Um, well, we'll see. We're still looking for a new place to prac-tise now we're back in school, but we'll give you a ring when we've found somewhere, yeah?'

'OK, bye then.'

With the typical phone manner of Neil, the line had gone dead. My heart sank. Now Neil was actually in the band. It was a night-mare come true.

11

Neil was a problem, not just because he couldn't sing, but because I had so much to lose. That summer had been glorious. Me and Ben had both made it onto the verge. Ben was cagey about telling me how he'd got up there at first, but eventually I dragged it out of him that he had been helping Thomas learn to play proper six-string guitar. He'd earned the rare pleasure of going round Thomas's house a couple of times to do so and this, it seems, had given him a magical pass onto the verge. I got up there because of a girl, just before school broke up for summer.

One lunchtime, I was walking across the playground to the football field, when I heard someone call, 'Oi! Mush!' One of Thomas's friends was beckoning me from the verge. I went over.

'Didn't you go out with that Karen bird a year or so ago?' he said.

'Yeah,' I said.

'Give us her phone number,' he said.

'Well, I don't know if I still have it, but I'll look for it.'

'Yeah, do that.'

'Ask nicely, or you don't get,' I said.

'Fuck off,' he said.

'Right, no number then.'

'OK, OK,' he said. 'But if you could bring it in tomorrow that'd be wicked.'

'We'll see.'

I knew that Thomas and Ben could see me from their position several feet away, but they said nothing. I felt Ben's discomfort, knowing he wanted to say hello, but that it wouldn't be a good idea with Thomas watching him. Ah, the mysterious etiquette of the grass verge. With no more business there, I went back to my mates from basketball in the playground.

So, the next day, during morning break, I went over and I said hello to the bloke who wanted Karen's number, but I didn't give it to him straight away. I made him wait, and made him talk to me, which he did because he wanted the number obviously, but then some of the other boys were talking to me too. It wasn't until about ten minutes before the bell went that the boy decided he'd waited long enough to ask for it, and I held off for another five before I finally stopped stalling and gave it to him. I didn't go back there at lunch that day, but at break the next day I went up again, and no one told me to fuck off. Or more importantly, Thomas didn't tell me to fuck off. I was there practically every break and lunch from then on, except when I was playing football, and I pretty much stopped doing that after a bit.

So I was now officially in Thomas's circle of friends. I was allowed on the grass verge. Pretty soon I knew them quite well, although I've forgotten most of them now. I can remember a few faces, and some names, Ewan, Ashley, Alex, two Jameses. But really, not much else. I think I went round some of their houses a few times after the school term had finished. And we played football down the Fields too, but Thomas wasn't really into football, so that was never a big thing. Still, we used to hang out together quite a lot over that summer holiday, all of us in the band and the others. Down on the Fields or outside the sports centre, spending time with girls for the first time properly. But as with everything else, it's the band I remember most. It's as if the band's in Technicolor, with nearly every detail in focus, but everything else is in black and white, and vague, blurry even.

I remember that bloke did end up going out with Karen, although at first she was freaked out that he'd got her phone number. It meant I had to talk to her again, and it was quite funny watching her pretend to be pleased to see me, even though she'd ignored me that time before. She was actually quite grumpy I'd given her phone number away, but she didn't care really because she'd got a boyfriend out of it. She didn't wear her grey tracksuit any more, though. That guy made her wear a denim jacket and stretch jeans and spike-heeled boots, the usual metaller girl outfit.

Well, she had to really, it was the gang uniform. I say gang, although we didn't do anything like commit crimes or get into fights with rival gangs or anything. We just hung out together, a big blanket of black and blue on the green of the Fields. But still, we had a uniform. Even though Thomas was more hard rock than metal, and it was his gang, we still all had to wear metaller gear. It was what he wanted, for some reason. Jeans, boots or trainers, stud wristbands and belts, skull buckles, that sort of thing. And if you could afford a leather jacket you had to have one, because it gave you automatic superiority over those who couldn't and had to make do with denim. I wouldn't have enough money to get a leather jacket for another year, so that put me pretty low on the totem pole that summer, I can tell you. Not that they were nasty to me or anything, but it was obvious me and Ben and the other denim-jacket boys weren't on an equal footing with the leather boys. Not even being in the band helped us. Then later on, when Ben had his birthday in August, Ben's supposedly working-class dad bought him a bloody great leather jacket and that left me right in the fucking cold, socially speaking.

Now here was the weird thing. Obviously, Thomas had a leather jacket; it wasn't the coolest one in the world because he'd gone and drawn the INXS logo on the back of it, though no one was going to argue about that. But Jason didn't have one – and he didn't have a denim one either. He had a bloody townie Puffa jacket. He didn't look like a metaller at all. And he didn't even listen to metal. By rights he shouldn't have been in the gang. But he'd known Thomas since they were three or something, so he was. But he didn't give a crap. Didn't even try to fit in, at least not in that way. He had balls, really, looking back on it.

That summer, the first summer of the gang, at least as far as I was concerned, was pretty innocent. We were too young to be out late. We'd play football sometimes, but mostly we'd just sit on the grass. I didn't smoke – I didn't want to die, whatever anyone said. But some of the other guys would, if they could get a shopkeeper to sell them any. Jason and Thomas smoked, and Ben did eventually. It was quite funny, Ben would always be wussy about things like that, even though he was trying to come across as a hard man. I mean, I wouldn't smoke because I knew it was stupid, but Ben just didn't because he thought he might get into trouble. It was only after he had the piss taken out of him about it that he started lighting up.

Idyllic as it was, there was something eating away at us boys. Something we knew we had to deal with. An itch to be scratched. The girl itch. Girls, tits and shagging. Now, this is a thread I need to follow. So much of what would happen I know is tangled up in it. So much of the, well, pain, I guess. You see, we were fifteen, some of us were going to be sixteen soon, and we knew that any boy who wasn't doing it at sixteen was a complete sad spastic. God help anyone who held on to their virginity after their seventeenth birthday. I wasn't in as much shit as a few of the others because I wasn't going to be sixteen until the following June, but some of those guys would be hitting it in September. Now, if we'd been less suburban, and come from Raneleigh Park or whatever, then we'd have probably done it loads already. But being from Quireley, well, I suppose there was a bit less pressure. Also, as we went to an all-boys school, we just came into contact with girls less, so in a way they weren't so much of an issue. At the time, many of the boys still spent far more time thinking and talking about military hardware than they did about girls, because there were no girls around to tell them they were losers for being so interested in military hardware. But still, as the magical and dreaded sixteen appeared on the horizon, the whole girls, tits and shagging issue began to consume us all, that first summer, out there on the grass at the sports centre.

We'd all been wankers for years, of course. Two or three or maybe even four years, some of us. Ben was a real wanker, professional standard. Some boys lied and said they didn't, and at the time I even believed them, but looking back on it, they must have been, mustn't they? Or else it would just be shooting out in their sleep. But Ben didn't lie about it. On the contrary, he was proud of his wanking prowess. He'd go on about it constantly.

How many times a week or even a day, how long he managed to hold it in, how quickly he managed to get it out. No one was really asking him about it, but he didn't care. Once, as a kind of trophy, he brought his own spunk to school, in one of those plastic canisters rolls of film come in. It backfired, however, because instead of being impressed, everyone just thought it was hilarious and teased him, saying that his dad had wanked him off in the back of his taxi. Christ, he got grumpy about that one.

Me, I was a wanker too, of course. Not nearly on the scale of Ben, no one was, but, yeah, I was doing it. Usually in the bath. I mean, sometimes I'd do it and sometimes I wouldn't. It wasn't as if I just couldn't help myself. And actually, though I did want to see a girl naked, I didn't have that much of a desire to have sex with one. Well, I did in a way, but that's because I knew I'd soon be expected to. But I didn't have an urge to do it for its own sake, if you see what I mean. Maybe the whole social pressure blocked out the physical aspect of it. Having said that, on balance, I would say I am, overall, a tit man. Yeah, I like tits.

With all this in mind, our main objective for that summer was to get girls and go as far as we could with them. Unfortunately, for the most part, we were naive enough to think that you had to go out with them before you could do anything. That probably hindered our progress a bit. But still, we attracted a lot of attention out there that summer. Word got around and girls would actually come to us. We were pretty good-looking for the most part and pretty cool, so why not? Like I said, I had two girlfriends that summer, and got to kiss both of them with tongues. Now, this was OK, because none of the other boys ever boasted of anything more than a feel of tit through clothing. Well, they did,

93

but no one believed them. And besides, some boys – like Ben, most of the denim jacket lot except me and a couple of others, in fact – never got lucky at all, so two girlfriends meant I was safe. For the time being.

But the truth was that everyone would escape serious ridicule as long as Thomas Depper had yet to announce that he'd done it. He'd never actually said that he hadn't done it, and he liked to keep an air of mystery about it all, but it was a fair bet that if he hadn't said he'd done it, he hadn't. He had a few girlfriends too that summer, and he was the first of us who worked out you could get off with girls without actually going out with them. That they really didn't mind. Liked it even. He got his tongue down the throat of a couple of girls other boys had their eye on, which pissed them off a bit, but they weren't going to say anything. Like mine, his relationships seemed to last about a fortnight, but back then a fortnight was a lifetime. Girls would usually break it off first, giving some deep complex reason they'd got off the telly. But we were never that sad about it. It just meant we were free to go after another girl who might actually let us cop a decent feel.

So that was the summer. A smaller golden age within the larger. Sunny days on the grass, sitting on denim jackets, kissing with tongues. Beautiful. I didn't want it to end. But of course, with the autumn term and the return of Neil into my life it did end. Little did I know that another golden age in miniature was just around the corner.

12

Here's a little loose memory I found from that summer. A tiny thread, and not a knot in it. This one's even in colour.

I'm lying on the grass by the sports centre, and I can see the basketball court and the mini-golf course and the little amusement place where they have the tiny go-karts for kids and the swingboats. It's a really beautiful summer's day, the sky's a deep blue, the grass is the greenest green, and there's one of the gang, Alex, and a girl called . . . I forget. Anyway, Alex has a rugby ball, and he throws it to me, and then we pass it to each other, the way you do in rugby, always throwing behind you, so one of us throws it, then the other catches it and has to run ahead before he can throw it back. We're doing that, and then the ground begins to slope down, and we end up going faster, until we're going really fast, and then Alex doesn't catch it, and the ball rolls off down the slope. At the bottom of the slope is this path, and the ball goes on the path, right in front of this cyclist, who nearly hits it and has to swerve to avoid it, but then he skids and falls off his bike. He's OK, but he's probably grazed himself pretty badly. And he's saying 'fuck' over and over again, and he looks up, really pissed off, and we're thinking we'd better say sorry, but he's just some weedy guy wearing bloody cycling shorts, and a helmet, and nobody wore cycling helmets in those days, and he sees that we're metallers and that Alex has a leather jacket, which he wore even when it was fucking hot and he was running about. And this guy just gets on his bike and cycles off, wobbling from side to side like he's bricking it. He must have thought we were going to do him over or something.

So then me and Alex go back up the slope, just laughing at this bloke, and then that girl whose name I can't remember, she's sitting on her denim jacket in the shade under a tree, wearing a Def Leppard T-shirt, I think, red hair, well developed, very well developed actually, pretty, freckles, and she calls out to me to rugby-tackle Alex for dropping the ball and I do, and we both roll down the slope, and we do that loads of times and then . . . and then . . . that's where it ends.

13

Three weeks into the new term and we still hadn't found anywhere to practise. It was frustrating, no one's parents would have us round their house, and we were all too young to afford a proper rehearsal space. When I say we, I mean the band as was, not Neil. Because even though Neil was now technically in the band, I was still doing my best not to speak to him. I was delaying the inevitable, obviously, but I just wanted to enjoy those few extra weeks of not being associated with him. I'd worked hard to maintain my playground cred, even to the extent of being allowed on Thomas's grass verge, but a hell of a lot of that would disappear as soon as I was spotted in Neil's company again, I was sure.

Not that it stopped Neil trying to talk to me. Every so often he'd spot me across the playground or in the corridor and sprint over before I'd had a chance to find a reason for turning the opposite way, and once he'd cornered me, he'd always say the same thing. 'Chris, do you know when we're practising yet?'

And I'd say, 'No, not really. I'll give you a ring when we know, yeah?'

'OK,' he'd say, his goofy grin no doubt hiding his disappointment.

Except finally he didn't do that. Instead, he asked, 'Is there a problem? You haven't practised for weeks.'

'Oh, nothing, really,' I said. 'We're still looking for a new place to practise in. But we'll probably have somewhere very soon, so we'll ring you then.'

Then he said, and I don't know why it hadn't occurred to us before, but he said, 'Why don't we practise round my house?'

Yeah, why not? I thought to myself. His mum wouldn't mind, because she was mad, and neither would his dad, because he didn't live there. No one knew where or who he was, probably not even his mum. It was a perfect set-up.

'Well,' I said, 'we probably won't have to, but I'll put it to the guys, and if our other leads fall through, which they probably won't, then I'll get back to you about that, OK?'

'Yeah, sure,' he said, before realising his company was no longer welcomed, and scarpering.

So that Saturday, two o'clock, me and Ben were in Neil's front room, with Neil, sitting in ancient armchairs that were falling apart, awkwardly quiet, waiting for Thomas and Jase. Oh Christ, that house. That house smelt. It was because they had that big stupid dog, I expect, that St Bernard, which mercifully his mum took for a walk when we practised. It just stank the place out – the smell of wet blankets and dog food everywhere. Disgusting. And you'd always feel what were probably fleas. Not only that, but all the furniture was literally falling apart; the chairs and the sofa were torn, with stuffing coming out, and you could feel the springs in some of them. I mean, it was dirty. Or was it? It felt dirty, that was the thing. I don't have an actual memory of there being dirt as such, and at that age why would I care? But it felt dirty. You felt like being sick when you went there. Besides the crumbling furniture, it was decor-ated with stuff from the seventies that everybody else's family

98

had thrown out years ago. Lurid wallpaper, horrible paintings of sunsets over mountains in Switzerland. Just crap she'd brought back from holiday years ago. There were so many clashing colours in that place it looked radioactive. I'd never liked going round there when we were growing up, and I don't think Neil could have liked it that much, seeing as he was always trying to spend so much time round mine. But you never heard him complaining. He never said anything bad about it or his mum. Not outright.

God, his mum. Absolutely fucking hatstand. I mean totally barking. She had the loudest voice in the world, and she laughed a deep booming mad laugh. 'Har, har, har, har,' it went. Uncombed corkscrew hair, and wonky teeth. She worked as a dinner lady at the primary school we'd gone to. And she'd always say totally mad things, like she'd say out of the blue that she always thought I looked a bit Chinese, but then she looked at me again and decided I didn't look Chinese after all, more Spanish. And seeing as I'm quite fair-haired and light-skinned, they're both pretty fucking bizarre conclusions to come to. Or if it was raining and you didn't have a hood, she'd offer you a plastic bag to put on your head. Nobody took one, not ever. And she always bought Neil's clothes from charity shops. Once, someone's mum gave their jeans away to Oxfam and Neil turned up wearing them on non-uniform day.

Yeah, she was a fucking nightmare. No wonder Neil ended up such an outcast. But Neil didn't seem to mind, he always acted as if he really loved her, far more than a teenage boy should be seen loving his mum. Embarrassingly so, in fact. At least it was like that most of the time, but every so often, very rarely, she'd be being her usual weirdo self, and Neil would say something back

99

that, if you took it a certain way, could be making fun of her. Or she'd make a stupid point and he'd say, 'Mum, if you went on *Mastermind*, the chair would win.' It would throw you. She didn't appear to notice, but, I don't know, it seemed to signal, to me, anyway, that Neil's away-with-the-fairies routine was covering some stuff up, a bit.

So there we all were, in Neil's front room. It hadn't got off to a great start. As soon as he'd walked in, lugging his amp, Thomas had taken a big sniff and exclaimed, 'Jesus! What's that smell?' Neil didn't answer. He didn't look bothered, though. Not even when Ben mumbled, 'Yeah, fucking stinks in here,' from his armchair.

Me and Ben had got there first, followed by Thomas about a quarter of an hour later. Neither Ben nor Thomas granted Neil a 'hello' or any other form of communication except vaguely hostile body language, leaving it to me to fill the awkward silence while we waited for Jase to turn up. Every so often, Neil would get excited about some band or other we'd never heard of, and he'd just be met with silence or an 'Oh, right' from me. Not that it dissuaded him from having another go a few minutes later with a different band we were bound not to know about.

But then Jase arrived. 'Hi there!' he said to Neil as he opened the door for him. 'I'm Jason. I'd shake your hand but I'm carrying all these drums.'

'That's OK,' said Neil, obviously a bit surprised. I doubt anyone had acted pleased to see him in months. 'We're through here.'

Jase followed him into the front room, and set his drums down where we'd left a space for him. His dad appeared out of nowhere, with his beard, trainers and tracksuit bottoms, carrying the cymbals and a drum stool. 'All right, lads,' he said. He made a face in our direction, fortunately away from Neil, that was obviously meant to say, 'What is that smell?'

Jase and his dad went in and out a few times fetching stuff from the car before his dad left, agreeing to pick Jase up at four. Neil waited patiently at the mike that Ben's brother had lent us. We'd plugged it into my practice guitar amp because it was the only thing we had to put it through, seeing as we couldn't afford a PA on our pocket money and paper-round wages. It distorted the mike input like fuck, and wasn't that loud. Neil would have to do some serious bloody screaming to be heard over the rest of us.

So Jase was setting up his drum kit, and he was talking to Neil. 'Really liked what you did at the talent show,' he said.

'Really?' said Neil. The only other person who'd said they'd liked it, out of an audience of one thousand two hundred, was Miss Millachip, the lesbian art teacher.

'Yeah,' said Jase, 'totally fucking mental. Great stuff.' Thomas threw daggers at him from across the room out of his jam-jar glasses.

'Thanks,' said Neil, quietly.

Jason finished setting up and started beating the shit out of his drums. Immediately Thomas shouted at him to shut up, and after a few minutes of standing by his head, miming hitting a punching bag, he succeeded.

'Right,' said Thomas, 'what shall we do, then?'

'"Johnny B. Goode"?' suggested Ben.

'Nah, let's do "Soul in Torment",' said Jase.

'OK, if we must,' said Thomas.

Jase handed Neil a sheaf of lyrics. 'It's this one here,' he said.

101

'This is the verse, and this is the chorus. There's a bit of an intro, but watch me, yeah, and I'll nod when it's time for you to come in.'

'Um, what's the tune?' asked Neil.

'Well, it doesn't really have one,' said Jase. We all knew he did write tunes secretly and sing them to himself in his bedroom. But the only way he was going to preserve them was by singing in front of us, and as he wasn't about to do that, they were doomed to be lost for ever. 'You can make up your own.'

'Right,' said Thomas. 'I'll count us in, shall I? One, two, three, four.'

We started playing the dirge-like and frankly overlong intro. It seemed to last even longer than normal, as we all waited apprehensively to hear what Neil was going to do, that is, if we could hear him through the tiny amp. Jase nodded.

And the most out-of-tune, out-of-time honk of a vocal you could ever imagine cut through everything, loud and unfortunately clear. God, it was dreadful. I mean, really, really bad. It just didn't seem to bear any relation to what the rest of us were playing at all. Ben shot me a despairing glance. We got through verse one, the chorus and the second verse, and it wasn't sounding any better. I was dreading finishing because, looking at Thomas's face, I could tell he wasn't impressed. In fact, he was seething. By that point, I knew that Depper seethe only too well.

Then, on the second chorus, Neil started doing something different. Not that he sang in tune, precisely, or even in time, but he started doing something with the words that meant that it didn't really matter. It was as if he was hiccupping, almost. Like he'd go, 'Soul in,' and do it low, then up high for 'tor', and then down again for 'ment'. And then he'd start doing it really fast: 'Soul in TORment! Soul in TORment! Soul in TORment!' Then he'd just go, 'TorMENT! TorMENT! TorMENT!' And then, 'TorMENT-MENT-MENT-MENT!' Followed by, 'F-F-F-flowing through me like elec-lec-lec-lectrical c-current.' And back to 'Soul in TORment! TORment! TOR-TOR-TORment!' It was all very strange. I didn't like it very much.

We took that as a good place to end the song. There was a moment of quiet, filled only with the buzzing of the amps and the last resonations of the high-hat. Neil blew his nose. We all looked at each other. Then we looked at Thomas. We needed to know what he thought before any of us would ever dare to venture our own opinion. At least I felt like that. 'What?' he said, aware he was being stared at. Neil carried on blowing his nose, a sound not unlike his singing, to my mind.

'Well,' said Jase, 'what do you think?'

'Yeah,' said Thomas, turning to Neil. 'Well, you started out shit, but towards the end, that was . . . OK actually.'

'Thank you,' said Neil, from his tissue.

'Well, I thought it was absolutely excellent,' said Jase. 'Bloody brilliant, in fact.'

'And thank you,' said Neil.

So what did I say? Well, I said the thing that seemed most sensible at that moment. 'Yeah, I . . . liked it too,' I said. 'What did you think, Ben?'

He shrugged. ''S'all right,' he mumbled, pretending to be looking at some tourist trinket on the wall.

'What shall we do next?' said Jase.

'"Johnny B. Goode",' murmured Ben from his armchair.

103

'OK,' said Jase, with enthusiasm, as Neil hastily leafed through the paper for the words. 'Let's go. One, two, three, four.'

Ben played the riff. He hadn't even got to the end before Neil made his entrance. 'WAY down! WAY down! WAY down! In the WOODS! WOODS! WOODS . . .'

14

It was after the practice. Ben's dad had picked us up in his taxi and we were back at his house, up in his bedroom listening to AC/DC.

'How'd you think it went?' I asked him.

'Fucking shit,' he said.

'Yeah, me too.'

'He can't sing for shit,' said Ben.

'Too fucking right.'

'I mean, listen to this, right, this is fucking proper singing right here. Bon Scott doing "Highway to Hell".' And then, with his guard down, Ben ripped into the most uncanny Bon Scott impersonation. It was the first time I'd heard him sing. He'd obviously been practising in his bedroom too. Startled, it didn't occur to me that it might actually be significant, other than fleetingly suggesting to me that Ben might be slightly gay, or offer any alternative to the problem of Neil. '"I'm on the hiiiighwaay to Helllll!"' sang Ben. 'And not the "HighWAY! HighWAY! HighWAY!"'

We both cracked up laughing at Ben's wicked impression of Neil. Soon we were both going 'HighWAY! HighWAY! To HE-e-e-e-E-ell!' We were in hysterics for ages.

And then Ben said, 'Why'd you say you liked it when you fucking didn't? We're fucking stuck with him now.'

'Well,' I replied, 'I didn't exactly hear you giving your opinion.'

'Yeah, but I didn't say I liked it, did I?' said Ben, grumpy now. 'I just didn't say I fucking didn't.'

'Well, that's a fucking fat lot of fucking good.'

'Yeah, well, at least I didn't fucking lie and say I liked it, did I?'

'No, I guess not,' I said. 'Look, I just didn't want to piss off Thomas right now.'

'S'pose.' That was Ben's new word. He'd say it to practically everything. 'Do you want a can of Lilt, Ben?' 'S'pose.' 'Ben, do you fancy that girl you were talking to just now, the one with the gorgeous tits?' 'S'pose.' 'Do you want to join Motörhead, Ben? There's a vacancy going for lead guitarist.' 'S'pose.' Soon Thomas was saying it all the time too just to take the piss, then he forgot that he was meant to be taking the piss, and he just ended up saying it to everything too.

As for my lying about Neil, I didn't need to explain it to Ben because I knew that he understood. As long as the band was safe, then we both had our place on the grass verge. But more important, now that the summer was over, was the youth club. This was the new hanging-out place for Thomas and his gang. And it was working out very well for us, in regard to girls and stuff. The club was in some church hall in Quireley, the other side from the Fields and the sports centre. Baptist or Pentecostal or something, not C of E. It's not there any more, got burnt down a couple of years ago. No one knows why. So this youth club was on Friday nights, and it was run by a bunch of young God-botherers, but it wasn't religious in nature – I mean, they didn't make you pray or anything. I think the idea was to keep us off the streets on a Friday night, so we didn't wreck bus shelters or smoke crack or whatever. Really, all we did, or were meant to do, was play badminton or kick a sponge ball about. But that's not what we were all there for. We were there to meet girls.

We weren't the only ones. There was a bunch of Quireley spazzers there trying to get some action too. Obviously they didn't get any because they were spazzers, or mongers I should say, because round about that time, probably during the summer, at the sports centre or the Fields, Ben's phrase had caught on, and we all used it – well, all the boys anyway. Some of the girls thought it was cruel and nasty, and didn't like it when we said it, either 'spaz' or 'monger'. If girls wanted to label someone like that, they'd just say they were 'sad', which was crueller in a way. But the fact that the girls didn't like it couldn't stop us saying it among ourselves. It was addictive. You just had to say it, you were compelled to. Monger.

So there were some mongers there, hiding in corners and every so often nervously shuffling up and trying to start a conversation with us, only to be told to fuck off. Or they'd hit on a girl and just get slapped down, and we'd all have a good laugh. But not only were there mongers, but would you believe, the Horned Gods. They'd always stand at the opposite end of the hall to us, in the leather jackets their rich dads had bought them. It was like two magnetic poles, us and them, with girls and mongers being pulled one way or the other. The mongers would get pushed away again, but the girls we'd try and keep hold of, as long as they weren't plain or ugly, or at least as long as Thomas didn't think they were. Then we just left them for the Horned Gods or the mongers.

The Horned Gods hated us, naturally. Every time they saw any of us, they'd just nod and smirk. The mongers wouldn't even get a nod. Once one of them, too young and stupid to know better, the lead guitarist I think, tried it on with Thomas, calling him 'ginger' or 'specky-boy' or something. Thomas just kneed him in the bollocks while the God-botherers were looking the other way at a stained-glass window or something, and said, 'That'll stop 'em dropping for another year,' before walking off.

I must admit, the Horned Gods did get their fair share of girls, even though they were younger than us. Having said that, a lot of the ones they got didn't really have tits yet. But other than the fact our voices had broken, we had another advantage. At our end of the hall was a piano. And some of us could play the piano. Not too well, obviously, and you wouldn't want to play too well because that would send out the message that you'd spent your childhood practising rather than going out playing football and stuff, but a few of the guys – Alex could, I think – knew how to play some chords, and 'Axel F' and stuff. And if you had someone playing the piano, then the girls would hang around. That was the strange law of the piano in the youth club.

Things were going very well for us with the girls there. We all got off with somebody in the first few weeks, even Ben, for the first time probably. We'd all now worked out you could get off with them without even going out with them first. We felt this made us men. The God-botherers would just stand around looking worried, not quite sure if it was all right or not – whether to enforce the word of God or let the kids do their thing, man. Jase said he'd even felt a girl's tits in the alley by the side of the church, or her norks, as we called them. Said they were spotty. But other kids were going further.

We were all in the last year of school by then. But kids from the local sixth-form college started to come to the youth club as well. And Christ, that opened our eyes to stuff. Because these kids, who seemed about ten years older than us, rather than just the year they actually were, were blatantly doing it. Not there in the club, obviously. But the boys had girlfriends, and they'd be shagging, and everybody would know they were, and the boys would even talk about it and what it was like and stuff. We'd nod as if we knew what they were talking about, but they could see straight through us. I mean, some of the things they talked about I still don't know what they are. And they'd even talk about the time they shagged such-and-such a girl who was now going out with someone else. It seemed such a power to have, to know what it's like to shag someone else's girlfriend. And the girls, they were just so confident, so powerful, with their knowledge, their experience. They scared the shit out of us, but we were hypnotised by their aura, and that they had, and without shame, done it. And so what until then was just a pipe dream for all of us, something far away in time and space, had suddenly become frighteningly, excitingly real. Just out of reach, but still, very, very close. It could be us. It would be us. Had to be.

Most of the older girls were metallers, of course, and some of the younger ones were too. A few of the younger ones were indie-kids and we ignored them, but a lot of them were suburban and bland, ripe for conversion to the metaller cause. None of them were goths, thank Christ. There were a few indie-kid boys, but they weren't that much of a threat, except one, Damien, who the girls loved, with his floppy fringe and girly sensitive face. But then Thomas started a rumour that Damien had been caught bumming his dog and that put him in his place a bit. Thomas. He was in the centre of all of it, like a spider whose web we were all stuck in. He'd just reel everyone in, girls and boys, keeping the wrong people out and the right people in, with a single burst of nastiness

109

or sarcasm, and the withholding of the same. And the girls would all want him, and he'd just laugh at them and then they'd want him all the more. Then he'd get off with them in the alleyway, and he'd be laughing at them again the next week. And we'd all be speaking his language, with its silly words to describe things, mostly negatively – 'scrunty', 'wanger', 'flange', 'wankshaft'. You'd have conversations that went something like this:

'There's a bit of a flange on that dooferberry.'

'Yeah, fucking wankshaft.'

'Ah well, hang out with a girl with scrunty norks, you're going to get totally wangered, aren't you?'

If any of those words were aimed in your direction, even though their precise meaning was unclear, there was really no point in bothering to turn up the following week. The trick was always to use those words about other people, and never give cause to have them used against you.

It was a little slice of heaven, that youth club. If ever I've wanted to get back to simpler times, I think that's where I've wanted to go back to. It was our little paradise. And that's what, all those years ago, me and Ben were trying to protect, up in his bedroom, listening to AC/DC. Our place in the sun, right there in that church hall in Quireley. Such a little thing, but at the time it might as well have been the whole world. Within a few months we'd lose it, and find other worlds, but would any of them be as bright, or as wonderful? Sometimes I doubt it.

15

I think it was about November when everything began to change. We didn't see the signs at first. One thing that shook it all up was when Freddie Mercury died of AIDS. Now obviously we never listened to Queen because it was poofters' music. Even though it was meant to be rock and some of it sounded a bit like things we liked, like AC/DC, he was so obviously a bender that we just couldn't be doing with it. And you couldn't even forget it when you were just listening to it and not looking at him, because it was right there in the music, with all the opera and high voices and stuff. Only monger metallers listened to Queen. We all thought it was pretty funny when he died, Ben especially. 'Arse bandit got what he fucking deserved,' I remember him saying.

Only problem was, all the girls loved him, well a lot of them did. And they weren't having any of our talk of it being 'only right'. No, they demanded we respect his memory, and we had to listen to his bloody music all that Friday at the youth club, and keep quiet about it. This was a compromise for us, for some more than others. I could see Ben was on the verge of exploding all evening. But what some of the more enterprising of us realised was that the girls might need some comfort in their time of distress, so we held them as they rocked gently to the pre-recorded cassette of *Greatest Hits II* on a portable player, singing along to 'The Show Must Go On' with tears rolling down their faces, smudging their make-up. Then we got off with them in the alleyway. Well, Ben didn't. He ended up kicking the sponge football with the mongers that week.

Another thing that happened, and turned out to be more important really, was when 'Smells Like Teen Spirit' came out. You see, the thing was, we liked it. Now, we shouldn't have done, because it was an indie record in our eyes. It wasn't proper rock or metal. But even though it wasn't 'rock', it did 'rock', in that stupid Bill and Ted sense of the word that we never really used. Our attitude was always free of irony. Of course, not only did we like it, but so did the indie-kids, who liked it more than us. It was one of 'their' records. And perhaps more importantly, a load of the girls liked it as well. And the girls found themselves liking the boys who liked the record. Suddenly indie-kids other than Damien were getting attention. And Damien was getting so much attention it was ridiculous. Even though Thomas made up another story about someone walking in on Damien as he was getting his dog to lick his cock, it didn't make any difference.

Things really began to deteriorate when it became known that Nirvana were not a one-off, that there was a whole movement called 'grunge' built up around them, with its own style of music and fashion. Then the indie-kids started dressing up grunge. And the girls loved it. Then the girls started to dress grunge too: dreadlocks, checked lumberjack shirts and stripy jumpers with holes in and what have you. Doc Martens boots and fairy dresses. We were beginning to feel like yesterday's men. Soon the church hall had three poles. Us at one end with our fucking piano, the Horned Gods at the other, and indie-kid grungers in the middle. More specifically, they lined up along the right-hand wall while the mongers still shuffled about with their sponge football on the left.

We looked to Thomas to lead us. He did not let us down, but at the time it seemed almost like a betrayal.

Thomas bought a lumberjack shirt. Pale blue and black. When he walked in, on the last Friday before the Christmas break, we could not speak. We just stood at the piano, gawping. 'What's the fucking problem?' he snapped, only too aware all eyes were on him. He eyeballed us back through his jam jars. None of us could ever have told him what the problem was.

'All right, Tom,' said Jase. Jase, not being a metaller, had bought his own red and white lumberjack shirt some weeks previously.

'All right,' said Thomas. 'Someone dead?'

No one was, but we were all in shock and facing impending bereavement. As one, we knew that we were not true metallers any more. Things had changed with one shirt.

In fact, this was as much Neil's doing as it was Nirvana's. We'd been rehearsing round his house most Saturdays since October, and Neil had put his own distinctive stamp on all our material, both Jase's songs and the covers. For example, 'Sweet Child O' Mine' now went 'SWEET child! SWEET child! S-S-S-SWEET child o' mi-mi-mi-mi-HI-hine!' And 'Johnny B. Goode' went 'Go! Go! G-G-G-go-o-o-a-a-ah-johnny-ah-a-agh!' like water going down a plughole. They were pretty much unrecognisable from the originals. The only way you could identify them was from the guitar riffs. He'd throw in a bit of harmonica too, which he still hadn't learned how to play. Fortunately his excessive vocal style didn't leave too much room for this, although Ben didn't like it at all as it filled up the time meant for his guitar solos. One day Neil's harmonica went missing. We never found it.

Much to my surprise, the guys were warming to Neil as a person. Of course, they found a lot of the things he said and did pretty spazzy, but they didn't hold it against him that much. Even when he did do something really stupid, like drop a plate of sandwiches or something, sure, they'd take the piss out of him, but it wasn't followed by the unremitting abuse that you'd come to expect from Thomas, or even the more snide stuff you got from Ben. Somehow, Neil had charmed them. Maybe it was the way everything seemed to bounce off him. He didn't take it to heart and crawl away to die like your average monger. He just carried right on, singing the songs in his own strange way. I still hated it, and I don't know if Ben was ever too keen on it, but Thomas and Jase were really into it. Maybe it was because they were more rock than metal, they were more susceptible.

He'd even begun to widen their musical tastes a bit, making them compilation tapes of things he thought they should listen to. First, he went for really basic, obvious stuff, like the Rolling Stones, the Beatles, the Kinks and the Who, but before long he'd even got them listening to groups like the Velvet Underground, although they were a bit suspicious about that at first because some of it was so obviously gay. But crucially, that didn't stop them listening to it, and they even ended up liking it later on. That was a turning point, I think. Another was that REM broke big that year, and Neil had been listening to them for ages. Thomas and Jase decided that they were good and were quite excited to find that Neil had their entire back catalogue. Neil pushed them further and further from their original hard rock position, to the point that the lumberjack shirt shouldn't have come as a surprise.

So, as far as the band was concerned, things were going pretty well, it seemed, even though we still weren't anywhere near doing proper metal. Then something crazy happened. The day after the last Friday at the youth club before the Christmas break, just as we were packing up at our Saturday rehearsal, Jase was talking about the youth club, and what a bunch of wankers the Horned Gods were, and how Damien had bummed his dog and got it to lick his cock, when he said, out of the blue, 'You should come, Neil – you'd like it.'

Ben and I looked at him, silently saying 'No' with all the facial muscles we could work. Thomas looked out of the side of his glasses, his eyes slits, unreadable.

'Yeah, I'd like that,' said Neil. 'Do you have to dress up for it or anything?'

'What do you mean?' said Jase.

'I mean, do you have to wear a tie or a jacket? It's a club, isn't it?' said Neil.

'It's not that type of club, Neil,' I said through gritted teeth, marvelling at the series of associations that had led him from the simplicity and obviousness of a youth club to some gentlemen's drinking club from the 1930s or something. I really didn't know if he was being serious or not.

What I did know was that I wasn't happy about it, not one bit. I said as much to Ben afterwards, but it seemed that he'd gone as soft as Thomas and Jase, pretty much. 'Well, he can come if he wants to,' Ben said. 'It'll be a laugh, won't it?'

'He'll just make a tit out of himself and embarrass us!' I said. 'He'll hardly be a hit with the girls, will he?'

'S'pose,' said Ben. 'Don't really care, to be honest.'

'Well, if he bollocks it all up for us, don't say I didn't warn you.'

'I really don't know what you're talking about,' he said, and picked up the last copy of *2000 AD* he would ever buy from his bed.

115

And so, on the first Friday after the Christmas break, the other side of the New Year, Neil came to the youth club for the first time. Jase had been hassling about it on the phone for a few days previously. It seemed he really wanted him to come along. Of course, Neil was already there when we arrived. In fact, he was there before anybody. One of the God-botherers found him waiting patiently by the door of the hall and had to let him in.

'Hi there,' he said, as we walked in. He was standing at the wrong end, where the Horned Gods would soon pitch themselves. A few mongers were hanging around their allotted wall, and some of our girls were waiting for us by the grand piano.

'All right, Neil,' I muttered. I really didn't want this to be happening. Ben grunted. Thomas nodded.

'All right!' said Jase with enthusiasm. 'How's it going, Neil?'

He beckoned Neil to join us at the correct end of the hall.

'I'm fine,' said Neil. 'Are we allowed to play the piano?'

'Yeah, of course,' said Jase.

'Oh, great!' he said, lifting the lid and sitting down in a second, utterly unaware of the sexy teenage girls leaning up against it. They looked at him as if he were a new species, as yet unclassified.

Then he started to play. Well, I say play. More like he just picked out notes at random, without any relationship to each other at all. I mean, it was horrendous, just awful. But the thing was, like his singing, however horrible it was, there was some undeniable logic to it. It did make some sort of sense. Not an enjoyable sense, but there definitely was one.

The girls looked at each other, their mouths open and eyes rolling, that private form of communication that teenage girls always carry out in public. 'Sad,' one of them, Hannah, finally said to Jenny, another. But in a way it wasn't a statement, more a question. Because Thomas was not far away, and he was fascinated, his face frozen in concentration as he watched Neil's fingers.

16

'All right, Neil,' said Thomas. Neil was opening the door for him at that week's practice. 'I've got something for you.' Jase's dad was lugging something out of the boot of his car. It was a keyboard.

'Wow,' said Neil, as it was brought into the house and dumped on the floor.

'Yeah,' said Thomas. 'I thought you could have a go at playing this. It's pretty old. They bought it for my dad's social but no one could work out how to play it. Then they got a Casio with the drumbeats and they use that. But if you could do your spidery-widery playing on this, that would be splendid.'

Neil ran his hands over all the various knobs and switches on it. 'This is amazing,' he said to himself. 'Roland Juno-6, analogue but polyphonic. Best of both worlds. Absolutely amazing.'

'Yeah, we don't have a stand for it, though,' said Thomas. 'You'll have to play it on the floor, by the look of it.'

'That's OK.'

'And we'll have to put it through the bass amp. There's two inputs on that, but it'll probably distort.'

'Will it?' said Neil. 'Oh good.'

Thomas went to find a jack lead for Neil while Jase set up his drum kit. Me and Ben looked at Neil on the floor fiddling with his switches and levers. Then we looked at each other. I shook my head. Ben just shrugged his shoulders.

Thomas handed one end of the jack lead to Neil, who plugged it into the back of the keyboard. Thomas plugged the other end into the bass amp.

'OK, turn it on!' said Thomas.

Neil did so.

'Right, play something!' said Thomas.

Neil pressed down all his fingers on the keyboard. At first, nothing happened. And then, suddenly, a harsh crackling sound emerged from the bass amp. It grew louder. You could feel it in your teeth. The tourist trinkets on the wall began to vibrate and the windows and the drums started to shake. And then the crackling turned into a *zooooom!* that felt like a jet plane had just flown through your brain. With a tiny comedy *blip!* the sound ended. There was silence. Until a picture plate of the Alps fell from the wall and smashed against the fireplace.

'Shit!' said Neil, who swore very rarely. 'That was one of my mum's favourites!'

Me and Ben laughed, probably more than we really felt like. But Thomas and Jase weren't even thinking about the plate.

'That. Was. Fucking. Unbelievable,' said Jase.

Thomas just smiled a little smile. 'Yeah,' he said. 'We can use that.'

'Um, would it be possible to turn it down just a bit?' I said, wanting to say so much more.

'Yeah, s'pose,' said Thomas.

And so, from that moment on, Neil didn't just sing, he also made weird noises on the keyboard all over the songs. And not just rumbles and zooms, as he managed to work out a sound that you could play proper notes with as well. Like his singing, his keyboard playing kind of sat on top of everything else, fitting in some of the time, but not really that much. At first he almost had to lie down

119

to do it, and because he was still holding a microphone, he caused a whole load of wailing feedback every time he faced the wrong way. He didn't care, he liked it, said it was incorporating random elements or something, but even Thomas and Jase made him cut that out. So he saved up his meagre pocket money and bought a keyboard stand after a few weeks, which was the first financial investment Neil had made in the band. Pretty small, considering the amount of equipment the rest of us had bought, or at least got our parents to buy for us. But Neil wouldn't do a paper round because he wanted to concentrate on his schoolwork, and his mum was poor. She was still a dinner lady at the primary school and just did cleaning jobs on top of that. God knows how she ever ended up with that house. Divorce settlement maybe.

Anyway, the keyboard wasn't the only change that happened around then. It was just after the New Year that Thomas started going out with Jenny from the youth club. Christ, that was the love affair of the century, that was. She'd been going there since November, and for ages Thomas kept going on about how unattractive or 'scrunty' she was, then suddenly that first week after the Christmas holidays they were getting off with each other in the alleyway.

Jenny, now she was a funny girl. Well, when I say funny I don't mean she'd make you laugh or anything like that. Just that, well, she was a bit of a nightmare actually, not funny at all, in fact. Really, she was the devil. I think she might have been a psychopath. I've been trying hard to represent people fairly, to at least try to understand things from their perspective, but with Jenny I can't. I really don't have any memories of her that portray her in a good light. However hard I try, I can't find any motivation for the things she'd go on to do other than pure evil.

Still, she was attractive, sort of. Well, she acted like she thought she was attractive, anyway, and that's half the battle, I suppose. She had long straight dark hair, and glasses. But good designer frames, not NHS ones. Her family were quite well off, so she could afford them. And dark hair on her arms too. She didn't really go for the metal or grunge look, which made the fact that Thomas ended up with her quite surprising. But then, he was best mates with Jase. That tells you something. Jenny wore good clothes, I guess, quite expensive-looking. Not really your usual Quireley gear. Too upmarket, too chic, like what trendy people would wear in London. I particularly remember a pair of stripy trousers, for some reason. Almost a sixties retro look, like all that stuff that Neil obsessed over.

Christ, I hated Jenny. The way she used to swan about that youth club as if she owned it, practically from the first week she went there, taking massive strides in her stripy trousers as if she was marking out her territory. And the way she'd talk to you: being super-polite, with impeccable diction, and the odd clumsy attempt at a lower-class accent thrown in, but all the time making it perfectly clear that you were beneath her, like everyone was. She even talked down to Thomas. Occasionally he'd call her a stupid cow or something, then she'd stomp off very deliberately, and he'd have to go and apologise like a good boy. He'd make up for it a little bit, slagging her off behind her back. But mostly he just took it without question. Looking back, it's hard to fathom why he ever went out with her, but at the time we never questioned it, I guess because Thomas dictated our whole concept of what was normal. Still, they were the same in certain ways. They both managed to control large groups of kids, Thomas with his gang, and Jenny with her little twitty friends swarming around her all the time. Maybe she was all Thomas thought he deserved. A female, nastier version of himself.

It was heartbreaking really, to see him reduced to this. It wasn't as if he was doing it just to get a shag, because Thomas could have got one practically anywhere by now, including half the boys, I expect. No, he really seemed to care for her, for some reason. And not only that, after they'd been going out for a couple of months, word got out that she wasn't going to be letting him into her knickers any time soon. Not even a handjob. She was nowhere near ready, it was said she had said. But, and this was the deal, if their relationship matured and developed and blossomed, maybe, just maybe, she might be ready by the summer. Or possibly early autumn.

As for Neil, she really didn't like him. In fact, she was the first person at the youth club not to get on with him at all. Strange, because I think they were interested in some of the same things. But she looked down her nose at him, and encouraged all her girlfriends to do the same. She'd talk to him as if he was a child, patronising and cruel, and of course her twitty friends would copy her, and soon they were all doing it, every week. It got pretty fucking tiresome. I mean, she'd say things to him like, and this was in front of everybody, mind, 'Neil, you know that you can get brushes for clothes. You could get all that dog hair off your trousers. Then you'd look less scruffy, then maybe you could get a girlfriend. But aren't you gay? I heard that you were.' And Neil would just stand there like he didn't mind. But, Jesus, I wished he'd stand up to her and tell the stupid witch to fuck off. Mind you, no one else did either. If only we had, we'd have saved us a whole load of hassle over the years. But then I suppose at the time loads of other people were actually taking Neil deadly seriously, including Thomas. Maybe he just didn't think he needed to care what Jenny said or thought.

We all hated Jenny really. But the thing was, none of us had the mental discipline to work out why. It was just vague, unfocused bad feeling. And maybe that's why she had to put Neil down so much. She knew he was the one person clever enough to see through her, cut through her bullshit. What she didn't know was that even if he did, he'd never say anything to anyone about it. That's where Neil's troubles really started, I think, with Jenny. Perhaps, if she'd never entered the picture, maybe it would have all been different. Maybe he'd have ended up normal and happy, with a girlfriend and a job and money and stuff. Maybe he'd have been OK. Maybe.

17

Neil on work experience. That's a story in itself.

It began when we went back to school after the Christmas holidays and we all had to choose where we wanted to do our placement. Everybody was made to do it, something we had to go through before we took our exams and were thrown into the big bad real world. I suppose it was meant to prepare us for that. A lifetime of paid employment and drudgery. There was a list. On it were loads of local employers who would take kids on for two weeks. Sholeham wasn't exactly a manufacturing hotspot, so most of them were banks and building societies, or high-street shops or tea shops in Quireley, that sort of thing. I think my first choice was a bicycle-repair shop, for some reason, and my other one was the post office. It wasn't cool to put too much thought into it, especially in Thomas's gang, and even more especially in the band. Because, if we were really all just going to get proper jobs, what were we doing in the band? It was never said, but the band was going to be our life. Any daydreaming out loud was stamped on by Thomas, who was having none of it. I suppose he was thinking that if we failed, someone somewhere would remember us saying we were going to be successful, and laugh at us, or more specifically at him. But we were all doing it, in our heads, never quite able to share it with the others, but each of us knowing that we all felt the same way. Even Neil did, I think. You could never be totally sure what was going on with him, but I just know he was somehow. Meanwhile, outside Thomas's circle in the normal world of school, with its basketball and football and lessons and tutor groups, the kids who got too excited about their placements were still seen as being square. But some kids didn't even bother turning up for their placements at all, and nobody thought that was cool either. As usual, the middle ground was the safest place to be.

We all had to hand in the pieces of paper with our choices during our tutor group time. Neil was in the same one as me that year, and while we were waiting for the teacher to pick them off our desks, I mumbled to him, careful not to sound too interested, 'What did you put, then?'

'Oh, I put down Alliance and Leicester and Midland Bank,' he said.

Now, you don't need me to tell you these weren't right for Neil. Not only were there placements available in the art gallery and the local bookshops, but he'd all but declared war on what he called the dictatorship of commerce and finance several years previously. At the time I had just tuned it all out, like most of his usual bollocks.

'Why the hell d'you choose those for?' I scowled.

'Because I'm interested in those environments,' he said. 'I want to see how people act in them, and what they do to people psychologically. Also, they are prime targets for subversion.'

Naturally it didn't make any sense to me, and I thought it was obvious what working for an insurance company did to people, because that's what my dad did, so I just said he was making a mistake and left it at that. But it wasn't only me who thought it was strange. Even the tutor called him up on it. I remember him telling him to come to his desk, and murmuring something like,

125

'Do you really think this is what you're suited for? Wouldn't you get a bit bored?'

And Neil just said, 'No, I'm sure. This is what I want to do.' Then the teacher gave him a quizzical look, as if to say he knew that he was up to something weird, and if he knew what, he'd stop him, then let him sit down again.

Anyway, I didn't get my first choice of the bicycle-repair shop and had to spend a wretched fortnight in the tiny post office in Quireley High Street with some old biddy, hardly being allowed to do anything because if I screwed up the mail there'd be hell to pay. So I mostly monitored the stock of wrapping paper and worked the till if someone only wanted to buy a pencil. But Neil got his first choice, the regional office of the Alliance and Leicester building society.

To start with, everything seemed to be going well. In the first week of his two-week placement, Neil was apparently polite, well presented in a shirt and tie that his mum hadn't bought in Oxfam for once, and very eager to get on with any job they gave him. They started him out on the filing, but he made sense of their system so quickly that he was finishing it with hours to spare. Even the people paid to work there couldn't get it done as fast. And he was deadly accurate too. Not a file, letter or folder out of place. So after a few days, they moved him over to some basic data entry. Nothing important, just change of address and details stuff. Again, he got the hang of it nearly straight away, and it turned out he'd taught himself to touch-type and everything, something they were reluctant to teach us at our boys' school, presumably because it was such a feminine skill they were worried that it would turn us all gay. Anyway, by the end of the week, Neil was getting through whatever they threw at him in record

126

time, to the point that his supervisor, a middle-aged man who was like everybody's dad in Quireley, ended up telling him he could work slower if he wanted.

At the band practice that Saturday, we were discussing how things were going with our various placements. Jase was in a car dealers somewhere, making the tea while observing the salesmen's techniques. He was enjoying that, pretty much. Thomas was in a bakery, his fuzzy ginger hair kept under wraps by a dinky white hat. Ben was meant to be working with Ken on some building site, but he called in sick on his second day and hadn't been back since. We decided that this was fucking useless, especially seeing as it was his own brother who got him the placement, and we all called him a twat. Well, Neil didn't, obviously.

'How's yours going, Neil?' asked Jase.

'Oh, very well,' he replied. 'But it won't be for long.'

'Why's that then?' said Thomas.

'There's no room for creativity. It's dehumanising. It turns people into machines, essentially at one with the machines they use. At best, that makes them cyborgs. So the system must be exposed for the lie that it is through an act of play. I shall instigate a situation.'

It all went way over everybody's heads, naturally, but by this time everybody was used to that, and Neil was still in Thomas's good books back then. It went unchallenged.

Back at work on Monday, Neil began putting his strange little plan into action. This is how he did it. You see, he was entering onto the computer information regarding change of address, phone number or surname and things like that, either official forms picked up and filled in from Alliance and Leicester branches, or just handwritten or typed letters. Once he'd keyed in all the information from a batch of forms or letters, he'd take the originals and file them away. Now, remember, he was working faster than anybody else, and he'd proved himself so good at this stuff that no one was really watching him any more, even though they should have been under the terms of the agreement with the school. So, Neil had all this information to enter, and as far as anybody else was concerned, he was doing a fantastic job.

Then it was Neil's last day. He'd made a great impression. Everybody was pleased with him because not only had he done a good job, he hadn't been any trouble or really taken up anybody's time. In gratitude, his supervisor and a few of the office girls who thought he was cute had clubbed together to get him a book token. They all shook his hand, and some of the girls were giving him little hugs and pecks on the cheek. And he was five minutes from getting out of the door when some young oik with bog-brush hair piped up, 'Neil, can you explain this, please?'

The bog-brush guy had a bunch of letters. These had been printed off automatically by the computer, as they were at the end of every week, thanking people for informing Alliance and Leicester of the change of details. They were, of course, addressed to the new residence that the customers had supplied details of. Only, this time they weren't. In fact, where their address should have been, it read, simply, 'Underneath the paving stones . . .'

There were loads of them. Bags and bags of them, ready for the post room to send out. They looked on the computer. Every single address that Neil had entered that week said the same thing: 'Underneath the paving stones . . .'

'What have you done, Neil?' said his supervisor calmly.

'Oh no, oh no,' the girls said behind him, their fingers by their mouths.

128

Neil said nothing.

The supervisor shook his head. 'The only way we can sort this out is by looking in the files of all these customers for the hard copy,' he sighed. 'My, you're a bit of a one, aren't you, Neil?'

The bog-brush looked at Neil as if he was some shit he had to clean up. 'Better check 'em,' he said. 'Make sure he hasn't pulled any more funny business there.'

'Come along, Neil,' said the supervisor, and he, Neil and the bog-brush marched over to the filing cabinets that lined one wall of the open-plan office.

The supervisor found the file that matched one of the envelopes in his hand. There, on the top, exactly where it should be, was the original notification of change of address. But the new address wasn't there. It had been deftly blocked out in thick black felt pen. Written at the side of this black block, very neatly and elegantly, were the words, '. . . the beach.'

'Oh, Christ,' said the supervisor. 'Oh Christ almighty . . .'

18

Neil was in deep shit. This wasn't just him being a bit weird, which had been grumpily tolerated by the school up until now. Even that time he brought a knife into school, he got away with it because it turned out his mum had given it to him to sharpen his pencil with. No, this was wilful destruction of the property of a company that had kindly accommodated one of their pupils for a work-experience placement. Which made it a community-relations issue for the school. OK, the Alliance and Leicester staff had been negligent by not bothering to supervise him properly, but still . . . They now had completely lost contact with hundreds, if not thousands, of their customers. There was talk of expulsion.

It didn't come to that, or even suspension. Once again, Neil's saviour and number-one fan, Miss Millachip the lesbian art teacher, came to his rescue. She argued, loudly and deeply, with a slight smoker's rasp, that although as a member of staff she could not of course condone the destruction of private property, as an educator she could not help but point out that Neil was merely working in the tradition of Situationism, another of those art movements which she used to justify any crazy shit that Neil chose to pull.

At least that's what I thought at the time. But I've actually looked into it just to see what it meant, and I've found that in fact she was right. That's exactly what Neil was doing. Apparently, the Situationists were an art group back in the fifties and sixties who hardly made anything, because they didn't believe in work, and wanted to play instead. They had a thing about the capitalist, consumerist society which they tried to bring down by doing crazy things like stealing toys from department stores while dressed as Father Christmas and giving them to children, or lopping off the head of that statue of the Little Mermaid in Denmark. Mostly they stole and vandalised things, by the look of it. Obviously it didn't work, as the capitalist consumer society was still going strong the last time I looked, but the important thing is that they had something to do with the riots in Paris in the sixties. Now, during the riots they used to write graffiti on the walls, things like 'Be realistic, demand the impossible', and, this is important, 'Underneath the paving stones, the beach!' And what that means, I think, is that if you rip up the pavements of the streets, which are rubbish because of all the capitalism, then life will be better, like a nice beach.

So as usual, Miss Millachip saved Neil's arse with her incomprehensible arguments. By the time she'd worn down the head and the deputy head, Neil just had detention for a month, which was fine by him because it gave him a chance to get his homework done quicker. What's more, because it was an act of wanton destruction as opposed to plain weirdness, Neil became pretty cool in school after that, for about five minutes. Not that he seemed to care either way. I think he did a bit, though, and little did he know it, but that time, very early spring, that little window when people didn't all think that Neil was a total monger, was probably another golden age in itself. The golden age of Neil. It hardly lasted any time at all.

In fact, it was a great time for all of us. Why? Well, the first thing was, we nearly all had girlfriends. Neil didn't obviously, and

Ben didn't either, much to his frustration, but Thomas already had Jenny, and a load of the other boys in the gang had girls too. Including me and Jase. We all paired off pretty much simultaneously. I mean, not with each other, with girls. What happened was the youth club closed. That was pretty tragic, but also quite funny. Some of the older kids from sixth-form college were turning up pissed and stoned and just going crazy on church property, uprooting flowers from the garden and stuff, eating them, standing on the bench that was in memory of a dead old lady and jumping off, really crazy shit. Anyway, the church caretaker saw them and got in a right strop. Consequently the young Christians were told they had to close down their little youth club. When they rounded us all up and told us, with stony, defeated expressions on their faces, it felt like a kick in the gut, but at the same time, you really had to try hard not to laugh. They were just so wimpy. If they'd had any guts they would have come down on the troublemakers and stood up to the church people. They just needed some faith in what they were doing. Real faith, I mean. Not the airy-fairy kind where you believe in angels, but the type of faith that gets things done because you know that's how things have to be. But they didn't have it, so it all fell in a heap and they just had to tell us that they'd been bollocked and it was all over. So we were kind of laughing about it afterwards in the last hour of the very last night of the youth club, but on the other hand we were gutted because the youth club was the centre of everything. What were we going to do without it? We'd have nowhere to meet, and we'd actually have to phone each other up and organise stuff for ourselves now just to see girls, and that was going to be a fucking hassle.

And I think it was that realisation which caused the mass pairing that occurred that night. All of us had various crushes but without

132

the youth club, there was no way we could bide our time, knowing that there'd always be another week to make our move. Because now there wasn't. It was now or never. Some of us, like Ben, and no doubt all the mongers, realised this but didn't have the guts to do anything about it, so their desires went unfulfilled. As to some of the others, well, the Horned Gods had actually stopped going some weeks previously, as they had decided the youth club was 'lame', but more likely because they refused to stop being metallers and lost all their girls to us born-again grungers and indie-kids like Damien. Yes, I'm afraid I had a lumberjack shirt too by this time. And Neil, God knows what was going through Neil's mind about girls. All I know is he didn't make a move on anybody back then. Maybe he didn't know how to. Actually, he probably could have done at that point and no one would have found it weird, because despite Jenny's efforts, thanks to the work-experience incident he was pretty popular. I just don't think he knew that. As for the rest of us, in that hour, that last hour, well, we all moved in on our targets. Some girls even had to deal with more than one boy, and so needed to decide which one was closer to the mongers in the social hierarchy and then go out with the other one. But I got mine.

Her name was Hannah. She was pretty, nice doll features. Short, straight, nearly black hair. People used to think it was dyed but it wasn't. Big tits actually. I think I liked her. More than all the girls before, certainly. I definitely enjoyed her company, a little bit. But more than that, I knew I had to lose my virginity quite soon, and I thought it ought to be with her as she actually gave me the horn. I was looking forward to it, pretty much. But there wasn't too much of a hurry as I didn't turn sixteen until June. For Jase things were a bit more urgent. He'd been sixteen since

November. He definitely needed to be doing it in a hurry. And boy, did he pick a good bet. Kate was, well, horny, in a word. She was a sixth-form girl, which was very impressive in itself, but you just had to look at her and the way she moved and talked, and see the slightly crazy look in her eyes, to know that she loved to do it and she'd done it loads. Several of the sixth-form boys said they'd shagged her, either when they went out with her for a week or just when they popped round her house in the afternoon in a free period. Oh yeah, she'd relieve Jase of his burden, all right. Only problem was, everyone figured she'd break his heart in the process. He really liked her, I mean, really liked her, but she never seemed to go out with anyone for very long. But in the meantime, at the end of that hour, we all watched them skip down the street together hand in hand, her in her high-heeled boots and denims, red hair blowing behind her, him in his lumberjack shirt and townie trainers, and we figured she'd be doing him a favour soon enough.

We were right. Next day, at band practice Jase told us all that they'd gone down by the lock-up garages, where he'd fingered her and she'd sucked his dick. He said it was pretty bloody lovely, and kept on licking his fingers. This was momentous. One of us had done it, more or less. The first crack in the castle walls of our collective virginity had appeared. It was now much more exciting than it had ever been, what with the multiple pairings of the previous night. But for those without an outlet, it was all a lot more scary. That they'd be left behind. 'How long did it take – three seconds?' said Ben, very, very grumpily.

'No, half an hour, easy,' said Jase, blissfully not caring about taunts from such an obvious virgin.

Thomas said nothing. He just picked up my guitar and started strumming a chord sequence. 'Neil,' he said, finally, 'I've got these chords. Do you want to write some words for them?'

'Uh, yeah, sure,' said Neil. 'What did you have in mind?'

'Anything at all,' said Thomas. 'Just don't make them too gay like Morrissey or any of that homosexual stuff you listen to.'

'OK,' said Neil. 'I'll try and only use words known to be heterosexual in character.'

'That's my boy,' said Thomas, at a stroke neatly depriving Jase of his newly earned phallic power, at least within the band.

In life outside, there was little he could do about it. Jase had had his dick sucked; he hadn't. Simple as that. And he had always let Jase get away with stuff no one else could. But as for the rest of us in the gang, I don't know how he did it, but somehow, by some strange subliminal signal or maybe even mind control, it was made very clear that none of us would be getting even a handjob, let alone losing our virginity, until Thomas had. And seeing as Jenny was planning to hold out until at least August, that was a very depressing thought indeed. But, nevertheless, we all went along with it. We all had our hot new girlfriends, and our balls were the size of grapefruits, but we just wouldn't cross that line. We would honour Thomas's authority by staying pure. Not that we were saying that to each other out loud, but we all knew it was true. Somehow, he meant more to us than our girlfriends. We wanted to be true to him, we really did. But how long could anyone hold out?

Mind you, I was taking things slowly with Hannah. Way I liked it, to be honest. Just went round her house after school. Or she'd come round mine. We'd meet each other's parents. Watch *Robin Hood: Prince of Thieves* on video. All very sweet, all very innocent. Then afterwards I'd wank myself off like crazy.

The next week, at the practice session, after Jase had finally

135

finished telling us how much sex he'd been having with Kate, and all the mysterious acts and positions he was now intimately familiar with, Neil got out a neatly folded sheet of lined paper and handed it to Thomas. 'I've written some words for you,' said Neil. 'I hope they're sufficiently heterosexual. It's called "Town to Town".'

'Let's have a shufti,' said Thomas, scanning them with his beady eyes through his jam jars.

He mouthed the words as he read. Then he was silent. And looked up. He pinned Neil with his gaze. A smile broke out on his lips. 'These are absolutely fucking brilliant,' he said.

'Thank you,' said Neil.

'Can I see?' said Jase, reaching his hand out for the sheet. 'Oh my God, these are fucking amazing!' he said loudly, over and over, as he read them.

'Yeah, they're pretty good,' said Ben, grudgingly, once they were passed to him.

Finally, they made their way to me. This is what they said.

> It crossed the Atlantic in an aeroplane
> It's driven all of New York and Boston insane
> It's half a disease
> And half a dance craze
> It's been around for ever
> It's the latest phase
> And it's moving from
> Town to town
> Town
> To
> Town

136

And it takes you
On a magical trip
And it shakes you
When you're in its grip
Then it breaks you
And it gives you the slip
But it's taken you over

It's from the Earth's core but also from Mars
When it speaks to your soul you can speak to the stars
It's your own best enemy
Your very worst friend
And if it's yours to keep
Then it's yours to lend
And it's moving from
Town to town
Town
To
Town

I mean, they are pretty good, aren't they? For a fifteen-year-old, anyway. Actually, he would have been sixteen by then because Neil was one of those weird people who have their birthdays on Christmas Day. Anyway, those lyrics have stuck in my mind all these years, so they must have something to them. 'Yeah, these are good,' I said, finally saying that about something Neil had done and meaning it.

We were all happy, in that moment. I have to admit, it was a lot more fun with Neil in the band, even though we didn't have a clue what was going on most of the time. Sometimes I wonder:

even now, in their quieter moments, do the rest of them look back on that time and realise how good it was? I like to think so. And as I unravel the threads, I can see now that was when all our golden ages met. Ours, the band's, Neil's, mine. And by the same time the following week – although it would take Neil a painfully long time to realise it, and maybe even longer for the rest of us, far, far too long – it would be over. The golden ages would begin to die, and no others would take their place.

19

'Oi! Hurry,' Thomas shouted to me from the grass verge. Morning break, Wednesday.

'All right, Thomas,' I said. 'What's up?'

'We've got a gig.'

'Fuck me!'

'Well, thanks for the offer, but no. I'm not that way inclined, unlike you.'

'Where?'

'Just in the social club my dad goes to. Said we could play twenty minutes if we brought loads of our friends.'

'Well, we can do that. When is it, anyway?'

'Uh, August the first.'

'Cool.'

'Only thing is, they need a name to put on the entertainment list. Our band doesn't have a name.'

He was right. We didn't. And up until that point it had never occurred to us to think of one. At least not to admit to thinking of one out loud.

'Right,' said Thomas. 'So we're going to have a band meeting in the bike shed to decide a name. We need one by tonight, my dad said. If you see Neil, tell him, yeah?'

'Yeah, sure.'

'OK, twelve forty in the bike shed, then. And don't try and feel me up!'

I found Neil in the art room, talking about Andy Warhol to some swot who'd just done an overly intricate drawing of a church for his GCSE coursework. Neil was going on about democratic art and photocopying or something, while the swot, smug expression on his face, started making a dickhead motion from his forehead, copyright Jasper Carrott. I took that as the moment to get Neil's attention.

'Neil,' I said, 'two things, both of them quite exciting. Firstly, we've got a gig.'

'Excellent,' he said, his eyes lighting up.

'I'll tell you about that in a minute, but also we've got to think up a band name. We need to do it quickly, so there's going to be a band meeting in the bike shed this lunchtime. You're going to be there, yeah?'

'Of course,' said Neil. 'Do you want me to bring some suggestions?'

'It would be an idea,' I said.

'I've got quite a few,' he said, 'but I'm particularly fond of just one. It's—'

'Right. Well, save it for the band meeting, yeah? Then we can hear everybody's ideas and decide on the best one.'

Of course, I knew that the best one would be Neil's.

I gave Neil the details and left him to it. Naturally, he was already waiting in the bike sheds when we all got there about five minutes late.

'I've made a list,' he said, before any greetings could be exchanged. He had in his hand another of his neatly folded pieces of lined paper.

140

'Yeah, well, I've got some ideas too,' said Ben. 'One, anyway.'

'What's that, then?' said Thomas.

'I'm not going to tell you if you're going to take the piss.'

'We won't take the piss. Actually, we might do if it's crap,' said Thomas. 'But spit it out anyway. Or don't. I don't care really.'

'All right then, I'll tell you. Well, it's . . . Motörhead II.'

'What?' said Thomas.

'Like Motörhead, but we're a new version of them, like a sequel. So, we're Motörhead II.'

'That's so fucking shit, it's unbelievable,' said Thomas.

'It's not shit, you know,' said Ben. 'It's fucking good.'

'No, Ben, it really isn't,' I had to say.

'Fucking well is,' he said, under his breath.

'What about you, Hurry, you got any ideas?' said Thomas.

'No, sorry,' I said.

'Jason?'

'Yes I do, actually.'

'What's that, then?'

'Guns N' Roses II.'

'You've got to be fucking kidding.'

'Yeah, I am.'

'Thank fuck for that.'

'Fucking hilarious,' grumbled Ben.

'Right, what have you got then, Neil?'

'I've got a list.'

'Yes, we know that, but what's on it?'

'Well, first one I've got is . . . the Garden Party.'

'Sounds fucking queer. No.'

'OK, how about . . . Unlimited Dream Company.'

'No.'

141

'The Corridor People.'

'That sounds queer too.'

'Why?'

'Just does. Next.'

'All That's Solid Melts into Air.'

'You what?'

'It's a quote from Karl Marx.'

'Fuck off. What's next?'

'Piss Christ.'

'I like it,' said Ben.

'I don't,' said Thomas. 'Next.'

'Well,' said Neil, 'I've only got one more. I just put it down as an afterthought, really. It's not very good.'

'What is it?'

'It's . . . well, it's really not very good.'

'We'll be the judge of that,' said Thomas, 'or I will, anyway. What is it?'

'It's . . .' said Neil in a low, nearly mumbled voice, 'Animal Magnets.'

'Say again?'

'It's, ah, Animal Magnets. You know, like animal magnetism. If you can have animal magnetism, then you should be able to have . . . animal magnets. I said it wasn't very good.'

'I like it!' said Thomas.

'Me too!' said Jase.

'Yeah, it's . . . good,' I piped up, having no idea whether it was good or not, truth be told.

'It's all right, I s'pose,' muttered Ben.

'Yeah, well, it's better than fucking Motörhead II, eh, Ben?' said Thomas.

'Fuck off,' said Ben.

'Ah, fuck yourself, you moany old fucker. Right, Animal Magnets it is, then!'

As usual, we agreed to meet at Neil's for our weekly practice on Saturday. How or why his neighbours put up with it, I'll never know. I mean, we were fucking loud, especially Neil with his synthesiser distorting through that bass amp.

And sure enough, that Saturday, there we were, playing away at our first practice as a band with a name. Not only that, as a band with a gig. We were working on 'Town to Town', Neil and Thomas's song. It was coming on pretty well. I'd just about got the hang of the chords, and Ben had written the beginnings of a lead part. Jase was being suspiciously slow coming up with a decent drum pattern, but even so, one was emerging. We'd been through it about seven times, including a couple of false starts, when, during the inescapable and painfully long clatter that marked the end of every song we ever played, the result of Jase making his way round his kit umpteen times, Thomas's raised voice could be heard.

'Shut! Up!' he shouted at Jase, which he finally did once Thomas started to make his way over to the drum kit, punching his palm.

'Listen,' Thomas said.

We tried, but our ears were still ringing from our own noise pollution.

'I think the door bell's ringing.'

It was. Neil clambered over furniture and amps to get to the hall to answer it.

'It's for you!' he cried from the front door.

'Which one?' Thomas shouted back.

'All of you, I think. It's some . . . uh, girls – I mean women.'

We all made our way to the front door, Ben lagging at the back. Sure enough, there at the door were, I think, five or six girls. One of them was Jenny. One of them was Hannah, the others . . . I forget. Probably all called Louise, because nearly all of Jenny's friends were, but it doesn't matter. More girls than had ever been on Neil's doorstep before, I'll wager.

'Hello,' said Jenny. 'Sorry to interrupt, but we were wondering if you'd let us hear you play? We promise we won't be a nuisance.'

Neil just stood there looking perplexed, his brain trying to process the unique event of girls wanting to enter his house, and probably some obscure issue of artistic integrity thrown in. It looked pretty clear he wasn't going to make a decision any time soon.

Thomas turned to the rest of us. 'What do you reckon?' he said. 'Is that all right by you lot?' Strange for him to be asking us. Maybe he was hoping one of us would say no. We didn't, although I doubt any of us thought it was a good idea. But six teenage girls on a doorstep, you always say yes to that, don't you? It's something you can't argue with. So in they came.

It was cramped enough in that front room already, but somehow they managed to make a little circle for themselves on the floor, between the amps and coats and leads. Their collective perfume mingled with and temporarily smothered the usual rehearsal stench of boy smell and dog. 'Just carry on as if we weren't here,' said Jenny. Fat chance of that. Her and Thomas immediately launched into a mumbled conversation that lasted minutes while the rest of us fiddled about. You could tell he was uncomfortable from the way he shuffled about from foot to foot, as if he really wanted to leave. But Jenny had some power over him, which always made him stay in her presence until he was dismissed. Hannah just looked at me and smiled. All the other girls looked at Jase, pretty much, after glancing briefly at the crazy decor and deciding not to look at it any more because it was doing their heads in. Ben and Neil were probably invisible to them.

Even by our standards, the rehearsal had drawn to a complete standstill. Ben lost patience. 'Are we going to play something or what?' he snapped.

'Yeah,' sighed Thomas. 'OK, "Town to Town", again.'

He nodded at me to strike the opening chords. I did so, and he joined in with the bass on the third bar, Jase on the drums on the fifth. We had hit a groove, I suppose you'd call it, and the girls started nodding their heads, following the lead of Jenny. So far so good. Ben's lead part came in, smooth, pretty much professional standard. They nodded their heads even more, which meant they were into it. And then Neil started singing. And they stopped. At least they stopped when they noticed that Jenny had stopped. She frowned. We were halfway through the song now. Neil's keyboard solo, if you could call it that, was cutting through everything, a sonic tear through the sound. We were used to it by then. It was just what happened. Jenny shook her head. The other girls watched her. Hannah was alternating between smiling at me and watching Jenny.

The song ended. Amid the usual jamming and drum fills, even more frantic this time because we were so nervous, Jenny beckoned Thomas over and talked into his ear over the din. There was something the matter. An issue that needed to be addressed. An action that needed to be taken. Thomas said nothing, but had the look of someone who was only too aware he had sold his soul to the devil. And now I realise it was then, at that moment, when music lost its hold on me. I would still hear it, I would still enjoy it, I would enjoy making it, but never again would it transport me to that state of elation. Here is the moment I have been looking for. When the spell was broken. When I had to make my first grown-up decision and I chose to remain a child, the very choice ensuring that a child was something I could never be again. My innocence was lost. I knew that something bad was going to happen to someone I loved, and I did nothing to prevent it. Right then and there, when I betrayed Neil, somehow I betrayed music too. I no longer deserved to hear it. So it went away, leaving me to chase after it in vain, destroying all I touched as I went.

And with that little word in the ear came the end of not just mine but all our simultaneous, interconnected golden ages, though they would only reveal themselves as such much later. But there are still threads to be untangled, so I must continue, picking them apart, one by one.

20

And from that point on, nothing was quite the same. Jenny's sniping at Neil entered a new phase, not just influencing her twitty friends, but trying to turn the otherwise iron will of Thomas Depper. She, and only she, had the power to do that, but the field of music was the one area in which he would take a stand against her. He said to her face that she had rubbish taste in music, and at first her impassioned opinion that the noise Neil made was, in fact, horrible seemed to fall on deaf ears. But, nevertheless, little by little, the trickle of bile that left her mouth could not help but make some impression. But I don't want to talk about that yet. Because there's something, one little thing actually, that happened after that practice which was beautiful, and which I'll cherish for ever. Probably the last thing involving Neil that didn't get corrupted and shit.

It was the May Day bank holiday. Same as every year, there was a funfair on the Fields. Jenny was going with all her little friends, including Hannah, of course. Boyfriends were obviously to be dragged along for multiple purposes – winning soft toys, holding on to on the scary rides, buying things with their hard-earned paper-round money, keeping at bay the seedy fairground workers, with their shirtless and tattooed bodies. The thing was, neither me nor Thomas were into the fair. I'd never liked it as a kid, and I certainly didn't like it now. Townie scum in shell suits everywhere. Metallers, or metallers in grunge disguise, didn't go to the fair. But there we were, me and Thomas, press-ganged into going. We'd stick out a mile, and probably get the shit beaten out of us behind the dodgems by some gang of thugs from Raneleigh Park.

Both of us were thinking along the same lines. Safety in numbers. We'd take as many of our friends as possible, so we weren't too much of a target, and also in the hope that Jenny's friends might sponge off someone other than us. We sent out a message along the grapevine that this was happening, and people should join us. Only problem was, our GCSEs were nearly upon us, and practically everybody we knew was revising like crazy, memorising packs of cards with science facts on them and whatnot. I mean, we were too, of course, but we had girlfriends, we had responsibilities, we couldn't revise too much. It wouldn't have been tolerated. But for the boys not blessed with a serious, heavy, committed relationship, an evening at a townie funfair wasn't an option. Even if they wanted to, their parents had barricaded them in their bedrooms with a pile of textbooks. Ben wanted to come, because there would be girls he could fail to get off with, but he didn't because his dad couldn't drop him off and pick him up in the taxi that night, and he was too fucking lazy to walk. Jase said he would probably be too busy 69ing to make it, but he'd be there if he could. He'd fit right in anyway, seeing as he looked like a townie half the time. But other than that, there were no takers, or so we thought.

We didn't ask Neil, but he found out about it anyway. And as soon as he got the opportunity, there he was, on the phone to me, wanting to know the details. Only thing was, I knew how big a problem Jenny had with him, and I didn't want the evening to turn ugly, partly for Neil's sake, but mostly for my own. 'Tell you what, yeah,' I found myself saying, 'I'll phone up Thomas and get him to ask Jenny if it's all right for you to come, because it's kind of her thing.'

'Ah. Oh right, OK,' said Neil. Even he must have seen how wrong it was. Why would you need to ask permission to go with a group of friends to a funfair? It's a public place, for Christ's sake! But like a total fucking arse, I didn't just say, 'Fuck it, Neil, come.' No, I went ahead and phoned Thomas, who phoned Jenny and phoned back half an hour later to say it was OK. A bit of a surprise; maybe I'd got her wrong. Or maybe Jenny just knew the old saying about keeping your friends close and your enemies closer. Fuck knows what excuse I'd have come up with if she'd said no.

So I phoned Neil back and told him where to meet us. And then I thought it was obvious that Neil would want to come because I remembered that Neil absolutely fucking loved funfairs and amusement parks and fairground rides and stuff. He obsessed over it all, the same way he did about loads of things. How he found room in his head for it all, I don't know. For instance, he could tell you the complete history of rollercoasters: how and why and where they were invented; how they evolved from sleds dropped down a slope; when they started going round corners; who made the first one that went upside down, all of that. He'd even collected pictures of old ones from the nineteenth century and put them in a folder, along with photos he'd taken of ones on tatty seafronts when he went on holiday. And not only that, he had a separate folder for dodgems and waltzers and what have you, with all the pictures in historical order to show things like how one ride would always have a musical theme in the decoration, and there'd be pictures of someone who looked like Elvis painted on it one year, the Beatles the next and John Travolta ten years later. The last one in the sequence had the ride renamed the Thriller, and a giant Michael Jackson painted on the front. Christ, I hope that's not still doing the rounds.

So I suppose I shouldn't have been surprised Neil wanted to come. I wasn't that comfortable with the idea of walking around with a bunch of girls and him being weird, but at that point no one else seemed to mind, so I thought what the fuck. And I also shouldn't have been surprised when we got to the entrance to the Fields and found Neil waiting for us. Neil never really got the hang of the teenage thing of not being quite on time. He was visibly excited. I mean, not in that way; it was just that he couldn't wait to get in, you could tell. He was pacing up and down, banging his hands on the gate, straining his neck left and right, not knowing which direction we would be coming from. We saw him before he saw us, as we'd used a side path he hadn't taken into account, so we got a full view of his angsty spaz dance.

'Oh dear,' said Jenny in her stripy trousers. 'Look at him. How sad.'

'Oh, he's sweet,' said Hannah.

'But sad, too,' Jenny corrected.

'Oh yeah,' said Hannah, remembering her place, 'very sad.'

'What do you think, Thomas?' Jenny said. 'Do you think Neil's sad?'

Thomas said nothing.

'I said, what do you think, Thomas?' she said again. 'Is Neil sad?'

Thomas shrugged.

'He is sad, isn't he?' said Jenny.

'S'pose,' he said finally.

150

'Oh, he is, he's very sad, very sad indeed,' Jenny said to nobody and everybody. 'I bet he'll jump when he sees us,' she said, as we got nearer to him. 'Watch!'

She crept up behind Neil, who'd finally stopped pacing and had sat down on the gate, as he stretched his neck as far as it would go to the left, while rubbing his back for some reason, then to the right, switching arms to rub his back with. She waited until his neck was stretched completely to the right, and the tendons were sticking out of his neck. Then she edged herself closer and closer, until she was just a few centimetres away from his ear.

'Boo!' she shouted.

Neil nearly wet himself. He jumped right off the gate and yelped.

'Hello, Neil,' said Jenny. 'Didn't mean to surprise you.' Then she laughed, a horrible, undignified laugh. Neil laughed too, out of politeness. Jenny's friends also laughed dutifully. Even I managed a smirk. Thomas was stone-faced.

It was a beautiful evening. I mean truly beautiful. Spring, with the promise of summer in the air. Smell of blossom, excitement in the breeze. You had to feel good on an evening like this. The future was rushing towards you and you just had to let it carry you away. You had to ride it. Ride it like a fairground ride. Ah, the fairground.

Now, as I said, I've never liked funfairs. Not the rides, anyway. I think it's the loss of control; I don't like it. You just sit back and whatever happens, happens. And because of the rides, which are everywhere, and someone's always hassling you to go on one, I don't like the funfair. But here we were, on this beautiful evening, in the pink and the blue with the pale moon and the first stars overhead, going into the funfair, and for the first time it felt like a good place to be.

The funfair's odd when you're just that bit older. Nobody wants to make a fuss about going on a ride in case they appear childish. So everybody just saunters along being casual, almost like they're bored. That's unless you've got Neil with you, of course. In which case he'll be running up to the first ride that he sees, nearly jumping up and down trying to find someone to go on it with him, which in this case was one of those things where everybody stands in a cage that ends up getting flipped upside down. Of course, everybody was too cool to agree to go on, even if they actually wanted to. 'Nah, no, not really,' they all said. Me, you wouldn't get me going on one of those things if you put a gun to my head. Neil looked despondent.

'Never mind, Neil,' said Jenny, 'I'm sure someone will go with you on one of the rides.' She made out like Neil was retarded for wanting to go on anything, even though the whole funfair thing had been her idea. Christ, she was evil.

After effectively stamping dead the ride idea, she made us go into an arcade, where she bullied Thomas into pouring half his money into one of those machines with a claw you control to pick up a cuddly toy. Of course, it's a con and it's completely impossible, so he was just pissing his money up a wall. Thomas danced about impatiently – he hated arcade games, never even had a computer or a games console – while all the girls waited patiently, too cool or too gormless to actually do anything. Me, I stuck my tongue down Hannah's throat, just to pass the time.

After wasting several quid out of Thomas's paper-round money, Jenny then threw some more away by demanding candyfloss. She ate about a tenth of it, and then decided she didn't want any more. She offered it to her friends, who turned their noses up as if it was dog shit – after all, if Jenny didn't want it, why would they? Then she gave it to Neil. 'Here you are, Neil,' she said. 'You can have this. Nobody else wants it. Yuck!'

Neil tried not to look self-conscious as he ate the evidently diseased candyfloss, as we passed ride after ride that he desperately wanted to go on. Then we came to the dodgems. 'Let's all go on them!' shrieked Jenny, clapping her hands together as if she was five. Suddenly it was all right to be a child, and soon all her friends regressed as one too, clapping and cheering, 'Yaaay! Dodgems! Dodgems!'

It was two to a car. Me and Hannah. Thomas and Jenny. Two twitty friends. Another two. As usual, Neil was the odd man out.

'Oh no,' said Jenny, with mock concern, 'what are we going to do?'

'It's OK,' said Neil, 'I don't really like dodgems anyway. They're not like any other fairground ride.'

'Why's that then, Neil?' said Jenny. 'Please tell us, do!'

'Well,' he said, 'on any other ride, once you're sat down and strapped in, you have no control over what happens to you. The ride begins, and it will not stop, however much you scream. You have no choice but to go through it to the very end, or try to throw yourself from it and almost certainly die. But with dodgems, it's different. You're faced with countless decisions. Where to go, which way to turn, when to stop, to stick to the sides or aim for the centre. And most importantly, whether to go by the official definition of the ride, which is dodgems, i.e., you are aiming to avoid the other drivers, or to go by its popular name, bumper cars, which suggests that the point is to deliberately drive into everybody else. Now this in itself lays down the grounds on which you establish a relationship with authority, which in this case is represented by the fairground workers. By treating them as bumper

153

cars, you risk antagonising them. At the same time, you could also be potentially recognising the outsider status that fairground workers have within society, and validating it by the very breaching of their own rules, of which they make a token gesture of enforcing by the use of the term "dodgem", but in reality have very little interest in. So, for me, the bumper car ride does not embody the suspension of existential responsibility that other rides do. It's what Foucault would call a heterotopia, a site of alternate ordering, existing within the larger heterotopia of the funfair itself—'

'OK, Neil, that's enough now, lecture over,' said Jenny. 'Why don't you wait for us like a sweetie?'

She made that gesture that means something's gone over your head to her friends, then grabbed Thomas by the arm and led him to the booth to spend his money. We all followed her, except Neil. He just waited at the barrier, looking forlorn. I don't care what he said, he wanted to be with us on those dodgems. Then I looked at Jenny. At that moment, I was so filled with loathing for her, and her stripy trousers, that I made one of those radical existential decisions that Neil was always going on about. And this is the beautiful part, more beautiful than the sky or the evening or Hannah's sixteen-year-old smile. Something that the memory of Jenny and her trousers and everything that happened afterwards can't corrupt.

I found myself turning round, no, I chose to turn round, and I pulled Neil round the barrier. 'Come on,' I said. 'I know you want to go on.'

'No, really, it's all right,' he protested, not very hard.

'What's going on?' asked Hannah.

'I'm going on with Neil.'

'What about me, then?'

154

'Go on with one of your mates.'

'There's an odd number.'

'One of you could go on your own.'

Of course, teenage girls don't do anything on their own, so between them they decided that none of them were going on. Thomas had already sat down with Jenny in a car and paid for both of them, and had no choice but to see it through, even though Jenny's wonderful idea for fun was now effectively ruined. By me.

I paid for Neil myself, so he couldn't get out of it by kicking up a fuss about money, seeing as he never had any, and we sat in a car, waiting for the swarthy fairground man to take our money and lock us in the car. Naturally, I took the driver's seat.

Neil looked nervous, but excited. Then he was calm. 'What's it going to be, then?' he said, once we'd been clamped to the seat. 'Are we in a bumper car, or is this just dodgems?'

I looked at Jenny, bad-mouthing me in Thomas's ear, while he stared sullenly forward in the driver's seat. 'Oh, bumper cars, definitely.'

The power came on. We were live. And I spent the next five minutes just ramming the fuck out of Thomas and Jenny's car, hitting Jenny's side as often as I could. I've never been happier. Thomas was holding on for dear life, but he was loving it too, I could tell. We were both laughing our tits off at the wildness of it all. And in that moment, I was really getting the whole thing about choice and freedom that Neil was always banging on about. Right then, I did not give a fuck about keeping Thomas and Jenny happy to maintain some stupid position in a teenage social struc- ture; I just wanted to smash the fuck out of them because that's what I wanted, and had chosen, to do. In that moment, just that one little moment, and not for nearly long enough, I was looking through the door inside me that Neil had shown me all that time ago at the talent show. Beautiful. Absolutely beautiful.

I wasn't really concentrating very hard on how Jenny and Thomas were taking it, but I doubt they were enjoying it that much, especially since Thomas never managed to recover sufficiently to bash me back. Team sports, you see. Improve reflexes and coordination. Teach him to spend every break for the past four years on the grass verge. And none of the funfair folk were stopping me. Turns out they really didn't give a fuck, like Neil said.

Then, when the power was switched off, and I was stopped with my bumper five centimetres away from another successful ram of Jenny, everything collapsed. Jenny looked straight at me with a furious gaze, and I was back, trapped in that silly prison I'd built for myself where it actually mattered what a stupid cow like Jenny thought. But the memory of looking through that door stayed with me the rest of the evening, and that was what made it so magical.

Jenny sat there glaring at me while we waited for the cars to unlock, for what seemed like for ever, and when the collective click of the release was heard, it was no release at all, because now I had to face Hannah. Me and Neil got up out of the car, our knees weak, while Jenny and Thomas strode ahead the best they could to where her friends were waiting for her to verbally destroy me. Neil was still laughing to himself. 'Have fun?' I asked him, putting off the shit I was inevitably going to walk into for another few seconds.

'Yes,' he said, between chuckles.

'I thought you didn't like dodgems.'

156

'Well, I've never had anybody to drive me before.'

Obviously. His dad. Not there.

We took the walk of death off the dodgem track. Except the execution never came. Because Jase and Kate had turned up, and Kate's bouncy, horny excitability was now the light bulb that the girls were flittering around, entranced by her one extra year of life and evident knowledge of what spunk tasted like. Even Jenny had to take a back seat to that.

'Hi, Chris! Hi, Neil,' she called, waving.

'Nice of you to make it,' I said. Jenny gave me a sideways glance.

'Yeah,' said Thomas, 'thought you'd be too busy taking it up the arse or something.'

'Thomas!' cried Jenny, slapping him in the chest. 'Don't be disgusting!'

Kate just laughed. She wasn't a girl who minded people talking about her getting it up the arse. 'No, no,' she said, 'not today. I didn't have any jelly. No, just the front way today. With this big lovely cock!' She grabbed Jase in a very inappropriate manner. He looked quite embarrassed, but somehow, quite smug too. The girls sniggered. Neil looked shocked, as if he hadn't heard a girl talk that way before. Truth is, neither had I, none of us had. I mean, we'd been saying far worse things in the playground for years, but here was a real girl talking about a real dick she was really touching, through denim and boxer shorts. It was all getting more and more real. Yet I knew the best thing was to appear nonchalant about these things. I just hoped that Jenny didn't pick up on Neil's reaction. It's the sort of thing her evil mind could use against him.

'Look! Look!' Kate cried out suddenly, still rubbing Jase's

157

manhood absent-mindedly through his jeans. 'I want to go on that!'

It was a Cyclone. Now, a Cyclone is kind of like a waltzer, only it's in the open air and the tattooed fairground man can't spin you round to make you go faster. What essentially happens is that the whole thing goes round and round while your car is thrust forward as if you're about to hit the barrier and die, until it pulls back at the last minute, and then you think you're safe for about half a second until it shoves you forward again, and you think you're going to die again, and it happens about a million times before they let you off. I didn't want to go on the Cyclone.

But everybody else did because Kate did. Like a shoal of fish, everyone moved towards it. Somehow making a fuss about how I didn't want to go on didn't seem like a very cool thing to do right then. So, like everyone else, I stood at the barrier, waiting for the ride to stop and the previous victims to unload.

Just watching it made me shit-scared. The whole thing was held together by big iron bolts that seemed destined to ping out, sending the cars straight at us at a thousand miles an hour and decapitating everybody. But I couldn't show my fear. No, I had to hold Hannah close, because she was pretending to be scared to show off. At least it stopped her making a fuss over the dodgems, I guess.

The ride slowed, and stopped. There was the click of the lock on the bar that pinned your legs in, and the dazed evacuation of whooping teenagers with wobbly legs. It was time.

I've never had a panic attack, but I think that was the nearest I've ever come. I was so close to just legging it, it wasn't funny. But then, and this will sound soft, when I saw that there were three people to a car, and that Neil, who'd been excitedly leaning

158

over the barrier like a dog sticking its head out of a car window, would have to go on with me and Hannah, it seemed all right. Right then, I trusted Neil to make it OK.

And you know what, it was. Hannah was screaming, all the girls were screaming, Neil was screaming, Thomas was looking bored and I was screaming inside, but it was OK. However violently we were thrown towards the barrier, at whatever speed, and despite the fact that we were hemmed in with no means of escape, I actually didn't mind. I'm not saying I enjoyed it or anything, but I just felt that, having Neil there, I could see things through his eyes a bit. The idea of letting go, letting things happen, having an adventure, it was like him and the music. He wasn't in control, but he let things happen, and occasionally it would sound . . . OK. Just for that brief few minutes – which seemed to last a very long time, by the way – I understood, I really understood it all. Choices, control, responsibility. Sometimes the choice you make is to jump off a cliff and see what happens. And maybe the fall isn't always so bad as it looks. Maybe that's why Neil could stand in front of the entire school screaming and not worry about what happened next. The fall doesn't kill you. At least it shouldn't do.

Eventually the ride was over, thank God, and we got off. Kate wanted Jase to win her something by shooting, so it suddenly wasn't cool to want to go on any more rides, although Neil would have given his arm to. Not that he had any money left. No paper round, you see. And so the evening gradually wound down, and we all went our separate ways.

Once I'd walked Hannah home and got a bit of an ear-bashing about the dodgems, it was time to go home. I was on my way back, down the so very suburban streets of Quireley – Cresston Avenue, I think – when I saw ahead of me someone standing still, looking up at a street lamp. It was as if they were in deep concentration, no, more than that, rapture even. As I got closer I could see that it was Neil. In fact, apart from looking at the light, and the surrounding semi-detached houses, and up at the clear deep blue starry sky, the moon half-full, I could not for the life of me work out what he was doing.

'All right,' I said. 'Not gone home yet?'

'No,' said Neil, still staring at the light.

'What are you up to then?'

'It's beautiful,' he said, softly.

'What is?'

'All of this,' he said, a big happy smile on his face as if he'd just seen Jesus. 'These houses, what's inside them, the street, the light, the sky. It's just so beautiful. Suburban beauty.'

'Ah, I guess. Well, I'll see you in school tomorrow, yeah?'

'Yes, indeed,' said Neil, not taking his eye off the light.

I walked off, but before I turned a corner I looked back at him and his light and his street and his sky. He was right. It was very, very beautiful.

21

It was the last day of school, ever. Well, not exactly, as half of us would be shipped off to the sixth-form college on the other side of the Fields after the summer holidays, and we still had to sit our exams, but you just came in specially for those, you didn't have to stay all day or anything. And besides, we were all doing different options, so some of us finished about a week before others. Which was tough shit for the kids who were doing German, who had to wait ages for their very last exam, but pretty fucking funny for the rest of us.

But this was the last day of school proper, with lessons and stuff, and the last thing in the day was one final assembly for all the fifth-years. They had us all sat in the hall on stackable chairs, like they did at the talent show. There were chair monitors who laid them out and stacked them back up again at the end. All the chair monitors were mongers. Fuck knows what they got out of it. A badge or a different-patterned tie, I think.

So there we all were, in rows. Ben next to me, Thomas and Jase not far behind. Neil somewhere over the other side. Teachers standing like guards along the wall. We were all being as rowdy as we liked because it was the last day and we just didn't care any more. Just a few exams and all those cunts would have their power over us taken away for ever. And this is what the assembly was about, of course. It was almost like we'd won.

The deputy head called for quiet as the headmaster looked on, too senior to have to ask for it himself. Five minutes later, once the repeated requests had turned into bad-tempered demands, he just about got it. The headmaster stepped up onto the stage to speak, the closed curtains behind him.

Can't remember what he said. Probably some speech that was meant to prepare us for the world outside and our life ahead, our freedoms and opportunities, and naturally and far more importantly, our responsibilities. Some words of advice that we should always remember. But they can't have been much use because I can't remember any of them. What I do remember is this. After he'd made his silly speech, the headmaster paused. Then he said, 'And now, gentlemen, we have a surprise for you.'

We all raised our heads like meerkats, trying to see what it might be.

'Mr Evans has very kindly agreed for the brass band to play a few numbers for you. So without further ado, take it away, Mr Evans and the Quireley Boys' Brass!'

There was a mass groan mixed in with the perfunctory applause as the curtain opened to reveal the mongers who made up the band already launching into the first piece, the theme to *Van der Valk*. Mr Evans stood in front of them, his back to us, the tails of his velvet jacket flailing behind and his silver hair exploding as he gesticulated wildly. Actually, not all the boys were mongers, some of them were OK, but they were the sons of hard-working blue-collar real-ale drinkers. We didn't really mix in the same circles. Brass bands probably made more sense to them.

The sheer volume of the band pretty much blocked out the sound of any criticism. Even so, I could hear Thomas muttering behind me about the 'queer' and how he was 'fucking them all up the arse'. Jase said something but I didn't hear it. 'I don't care, he's a fucking queer and they're fucking shit,' Thomas said in reply.

The music finished. We all applauded, not really thinking about it.

'That was fucking rubbish,' muttered Ben next to me. 'Why can't they play something decent, like "Overkill" by Motörhead?'

I didn't say anything, but something clicked in my head when Ben said that. There, in his velvet jacket, with his crazy hair, bent as a thrupenny bit and not giving a fuck, Mr Evans was rock 'n' roll. He was the real deal. He didn't play rock 'n' roll, but he was rock 'n' roll. Different thing, and I didn't get it before, but I got it then, for a few minutes. He knew we all hated it. He knew we all took the piss and called him a queer who bummed the band, but he didn't care, he really didn't care. He had what Lemmy had, and what Axl Rose and everyone else we liked had. He went out of his way to entertain, but if you didn't like it, that was your tough shit. Because he knew he was doing things the way he felt they should be done. He had what we needed.

Like the dodgems, this was a lesson I forgot immediately afterwards for years, but now after everything, it's crystal clear in my mind. If only I had held on to it, maybe it would have worked out for us. If only, if only, if only.

They played a few more things from the nineteenth century, and stuff from the twenties with Mr Evans turning round and doing the Charleston. He just did not give a fuck. Then it was over. The curtains closed to a bit of applause, the deputy head pushing his hands up in an attempt to raise the volume.

'Right, clear off, you lot,' he said, as the chair monitors stacked their chairs for the very last time.

163

'That was a load of total fucking wank,' said Thomas as we left.

'Yeah, fucking cock,' said Ben.

Jase shrugged. 'Well, it's not really my thing, but at least they're doing something, know what I mean?'

'Fucking wish they weren't,' grumbled Ben.

'Listen,' said Jase, knowing a lost cause when he saw one, 'there's something going on down the Fields tonight. Do you lot fancy coming?'

'What is it?' I asked.

'Well, do you know about the bonfire?'

'No.'

'There's a thing on the Fields, and basically it's a clearing where the council sometimes have a bonfire to burn up all the dead wood. Now, all the dead wood's kept there until they have enough for a big fuck-off bonfire. Some of the lads from college have been going down there the past couple of weekends and lighting it up, getting drunk, stoned, just hanging out really.'

Drunk. Stoned. Mystical words of power.

'Yeah, I'll be down there,' said Ben.

'Yeah, sounds good,' I said.

'Thomas?'

'Yeah, s'pose.'

'What about Neil? Do you think he'd be interested.'

'Nah,' I said, 'he'll just say he's revising.'

Neil was taking his exams very seriously, despite being so ideologically opposed to the system that made him do them. I think he just liked proving to people he was clever. As we spoke we could see him walking across the playground with a load of textbooks heading for the school library. Someone had said they'd seen Miss Millachip giving him a goodbye hug earlier.

'Right, I'll see you down there, then,' said Jase after we'd agreed to meet at the entrance to the Fields with our bikes and girlfriends. Well, not that Ben had a girlfriend, but the rest of us. Jase with Kate, me with Hannah, Thomas with Jenny. Ben on his own.

And so there we were, half seven, that evening. We hung around at the entrance for a bit, talking crap, as if we weren't that bothered about it, but really we were probably all a bit scared. Going to the bonfire was like going to meet our adolescence full on. It just seemed decadent, sitting round a bonfire like that. Dangerous. Anything could happen round a fire. In my mind I pictured everyone getting off with each other while wild crazy sixth-formers jumped through the flames. And besides all that, we weren't entirely sure where it was. Then some guy called Jeff, one of the sixth-form metallers, rode up. He was cool, and everybody liked him, even though his name was Jeffrey.

'Wotcha,' he said. 'You lot going down the bonnie?'

'Yeah,' said Thomas.

'Yeah, so am I,' said Jeff. 'Do you mind if I ride down with you?'

'No, s'pose not,' said Thomas, his usual accommodating self.

And so Jeff led us like the Pied Piper to the bonfire. Only I suppose we weren't going to drown like the rats in the story, because it was a fucking bonfire, obviously. Maybe we'd disappear like the children, though. And maybe we did disappear as children that night. Maybe our adult lives started there, purified of the last vestiges of our immature selves by the fire. Or maybe we never stopped being children at all.

You could smell the smoke and feel the heat as you made your way down the dirt track through the trees. But you had to clamber up a ridge before you could see it. And there it was. A huge fucking bonfire right in the middle of the Fields that none of us even knew existed until that day. To get to it, you went down the other side of the slope and over a pile of logs and branches at the bottom waiting to be burnt, but the view from that ridge was really what you needed to see. It was almost what I imagined it to be. Metallers and grungers and half-and-halfs, some gathering wood or stoking the fire, some running about like lunatics, including some nutter who actually was jumping right through the flames, and the rest who were just kind of hanging out, sitting on logs, smoking roll-ups. It wasn't quite the mass orgy I'd pictured in my head, but there were a few couples snogging or holding hands. How many were there? In my mind now I see about a hundred, but I expect it was only twenty or thereabouts in reality. But this was it, our Promised Land. We'd been waiting for this all our lives, we just didn't know until we saw it. We slid down the bank.

We were the first kids our age to go there, but as the first weeks of the summer passed, and more and more exams were sat, it was inevitable we'd be joined by others. Still, we felt being first gave us a kind of superiority. Greeted by the sixth-formers we knew from the youth club, it seemed like we were being made honorary members of their society. The society of adulthood. Adult in the cool sense of drink, drugs and sex, not the boring sense of having to go to work all the time and growing old and going bald and having kids and stuff.

There was no spliff that night, although we were told that other nights there had been and they'd try and get some next week.

There was beer, though, and cider. We all took a swig, well, other than Jenny, who was teetotal and tedious about it. We were all practically teetotal anyway because we were all underage, but we were allowed to drink a little bit at Christmas and family occasions, and every now and then our dads would let us have a beer and the girls had wine. But Jenny didn't even do that. She didn't think people should drink or do drugs. But she fucking smoked, so she was full of shit.

We didn't take more than a swig from the communal cider, because we knew that wouldn't be cool. But some of the older guys said they'd buy stuff for us from the garage if we gave them the money, and so we said next week we'd bring some. And we did, and we got drunk on cider, at least us boys did, and it was the most fantastic, blissfully happy thing we'd ever done and Ben wandered into the road on the way home and nearly got run over. Then he was sick in a bush and Jenny sighed and made a fuss about how embarrassing it was while smoke from her menthol went in my eyes. I told her to put her minty cigarette up her arse and shut the fuck up, then I burst out laughing and Thomas punched me. And I lay on the ground and the stars were spinning and I was spinning and I was laughing so much as I moaned, 'You fucking punched me, you wanker!' Then I was sick too in the middle of the pavement and everybody just ran off, even Hannah. And no one wanted to walk with me and Ben when we caught up with them because we stank of sick, but Hannah let me walk her home. She wouldn't let me kiss her because of the sick on my breath, although I kept on trying, but she pecked me on the cheek and sent me home, saying, 'Are you sure you're going to be all right?' And I said I was fine and I wasn't even drunk. Then I went home and I managed to get upstairs without anyone catching me because my parents were already in bed and Nicki was out. Then I went to bed and fell asleep and was sick in my sleep and I could have choked on my vomit and when I woke up the dog was eating it.

22

> I live in a red house
> With bricks the colour of blood!
> And if I leave the red house
> The bricks they turn to mud!
>
> I'm going to detach my situation
> I'm going to try for a revelation
> Ro-oh-oad! Ro-oh-oad!

That was another one of Neil and Thomas's songs. It was called 'Road'. How did the rest of it go? Oh I remember . . .

> Build me a house by the river
> Build it out of dreams!
> But if you fall in the river
> It's deeper than it seems!

Then it's back to . . .

> I'm going to detach my situation
> I'm going to try for a revelation
> Ro-oh-oad! Ro-oh-oad!

I don't think there were any more verses. It just went back to the beginning again after Ben's guitar solo. What other songs were there? Let's see, there was 'Sound of Sound', and I think that just went 'Nothing sounds better than the sound of sound!' over and over again, sort of alternating with a guitar riff. And what else? There was 'Fly'. Don't really remember that one, except the bit that goes 'I look at the sky! I look at the ground! I look at the world! All around!' Can't remember if the song was about someone who could fly, or someone who was a fly, or whatever. Maybe he could see the sky and the ground and everything all around because he had giant fly eyes with 360-degree vision or something. There were other songs later, but they were different. After what happened had happened.

The rehearsals continued, even during our exams. Not even Neil was so much of a swot that he'd pull the plug on them. But although the material was coming out as if it was on a conveyor belt, with Thomas just presenting Neil with some chord changes, and some lyrics magically appearing out of his notebook that would hang on top of them, in a more or less neat fit, it wasn't quite the same. There was something going on with Thomas. You used to be able to rely on him. He was a cunt, everybody knew that, and he didn't disappoint. But with Neil, at least at first, here was somebody he'd normally be ignoring, swearing at or beating up, who he actually, sort of, got on with. Somehow they managed to tap into each other's wavelength and work together, and come up with some stuff that, Neil's presentation style aside, was pretty decent. And Thomas obviously knew this and didn't want to mess it up. So he wasn't overly rude to Neil, and he didn't talk about him behind his back and turn everyone against him, like he did to pretty much anybody else he hadn't known since he was five. And the reason, I think, was that Neil had given him something to actually believe in. The songs. If the songs were good, then

170

that meant that Thomas wasn't all bad. And if he wasn't all bad, then he wasn't the total cunt he'd been persuading himself and others he was all this time. And you could tell, he was lightening up a bit, slightly.

But then there was Jenny. Jenny bollocked all that up completely. Because Jenny didn't like the way Neil sang or played his keyboard. And she'd told Thomas that. And she wasn't bothering to say the songs were good, either. The way she was putting it, Neil in general was an embarrassment. And hard as he made himself out to be, when it came to Jenny, Thomas was, well, I don't like the phrase, but it's true, pussy-whipped. What Jenny said went. And if Jenny said that something wasn't good, then in Thomas's mind, at some level, it had to be true. Because Thomas was a piece of shit, in his head. And Jenny was the embodiment of the voice that had been telling him that all his life. The only thing that made Thomas see himself as something good, Jenny was going out of her way to destroy.

And once she'd started on that, Thomas started behaving a bit weirdly towards Neil. The better Neil's lyrics got, and the more they fitted in seamlessly with what he was coming up with on the guitar, the more the old-style Thomas came back. For instance, the first time Neil came up with 'Sound of Sound', and it was just the same line over and over again – which, looking back, was genius and was exactly what the song needed – Thomas said some-thing like, 'Yeah, well, it's probably less painful listening to you sing one line than lots of different ones.' Which didn't even mean anything when you think about it, but it was still nasty.

Or another time, we were getting ready to play a song, and Ben was working out his solo, and he said, 'What key's it in, Thomas?'

And he said, 'It's in A but Neil's going to be playing in G, D and F Sharp Doofucker,' another of his made-up words that everybody copied. But by then Neil had actually grasped the concept of keys and why it was a good idea to play in the same one as everyone else, so that was unnecessary as well.

But then, Neil sometimes did try people's patience a bit too much, and he should have known better. I think the thing that really wound everybody up was 'Flying Saucer Rock 'n' Roll'. It was a song Neil had taped off the radio that he thought was amazing, and he wanted us to play it. Fine, we were up for that. Only problem was, he wouldn't let us hear it.

'How the fuck are we supposed to know how it goes, then?' said Jase. Even he was pushed too far with this one.

'You don't. I'll just sing the melody and you can all work out your own parts.'

'Why the fuck would we want to do that?' I said.

'Because then we wouldn't just be copying. We'd be doing a truly new version of the song. It's the only way we'd be able to come up with something as essential as the original.'

'Bollocks,' said Ben.

'Well, Otis Redding had never heard the Rolling Stones' version of "Satisfaction" when he did his. The guitarist had just sung it to him before they recorded it.'

'Never heard it,' said Thomas. 'Bloody nig-nog.' He was coming out with even worse stuff a lot of the time, but I don't see the point of documenting it.

'OK,' said Jase, wearily, 'let's hear it.'

'Yeah, all right,' said Thomas. 'Let's hear you sing this fucking song and get it over with.'

Neil began to sing.

172

'Well, the news of the saucer been a-flyin' around
I'm the only one that seen it on the ground
First thing I seen when I saw it land
Cats jumped out and they formed a band . . .'

We tried not to laugh. For about two seconds. Then we all started sniggering. Not just because the song was ridiculous, or seemed so at the time, but because Neil really couldn't carry a tune in a bucket. There was no way we could work out what was meant to be going on in this song.

'. . . Flyin' saucer rock and roll,
Flyin' saucer rock and roll
I couldn't understand the things they said
But that crazy beat just a-stopped me dead'

By the time he got to the chorus we were in hysterics. He tried to start the second verse but we were all laughing too much.

'OK, Neil, we'll give it a go,' said Jase between laughing fits. Everyone else was laughing too hard even to protest.

'I can't believe we are doing a fucking song about aliens,' moaned Ben.

'He's from another planet, what do you expect?' said Thomas.

'Yeah, Planet Monger,' said Ben. Even Jase laughed.

We started jamming underneath Neil as he sang it again, still laughing. Pretty soon we worked out that it was essentially a blues chord sequence, and just played that. It probably turned out a lot more ordinary than Neil was hoping, maybe even like the original record, although to this day I've never heard it so I can't be sure, so occasionally I'd play a little weird chord that didn't fit just for his sake. But in the end, though, we'd done what we'd been asked.

Then, after we'd been fiddling around with it for half an hour, Thomas started making a horrible piercing sound by taking his jack lead in and out of his bass. This wasn't good for his amp at all, and Thomas was usually very fastidious in taking care of his equipment. The rest of us stopped to see what the problem was.

'No, don't stop!' cried Neil. 'That's what I want!'

'We're not going to be fucking playing that again!' said Thomas, making the horrible scraping noise one more time. His face was pale, his eyes small. He didn't look like someone who'd been laughing helplessly not long before.

And that was what was happening with the band. We had that gig coming up soon as well at Thomas's dad's social, and we had to drum up an audience for that. It would have to be the gang from the bonnie. Naturally, we planned to go down there the first Friday after the last exams. We were going to celebrate in style, because we'd heard that the old guy at the garage would sell you booze, and he didn't care how old you were. This was incredible news, and we just had to test it out. So, half seven that Friday evening, me, Ben, Jase and Thomas met outside the garage. Ben was shitting it, you could tell. Thomas didn't care. I was shitting it too a bit, but I wasn't such a wuss as Ben. Jase wasn't that bothered, and waited outside for us on his bike. He never did drink that much, even later.

We walked in. The right guy was behind the counter. The old guy. Looked a bit damaged. Should have been doing something more dignified at his age. Like being retired. Thomas went straight over to the drinks section. Ben hovered around the crisps for ages. I considered studying the crisps too, but thought, no, we're here for one thing, may as well get on with it. Not that we had that much money between us, though. It had all gone on buying stupid gifts for our girlfriends. Well, Ben didn't have a girlfriend, but he didn't have a paper round or anything either. So he only had what his dad gave him, which, mind you, was more than any of the rest of us got. But for the amount we each had, which was just a few quid, there was only one thing that was guaranteed to get us as blind drunk as we were aiming for. We'd seen the college kids drink it and get absolutely wrecked. It was some eastern European beer that had come over when the Berlin Wall came down or something, and was about 9.5% alcohol and tasted like paint stripper. I can't remember what its real name was but I can remember its industrial-looking silver can, devoid of anything other than the required legal information. The sixth-formers called it Napalm.

Thomas took two cans. I took two. Ben, although he was shaking with fear, took four. I looked at him. 'Yeah, well, it takes a lot to get me pissed, dunnit?' he grunted.

Of course it didn't, he was a lightweight, but that's what he liked to believe.

Thomas got to the counter first. The guy didn't even as much as look at him before asking for £1.98, or however much that stuff cost back then. I was more baby-faced than Thomas, so I thought he might still pick on me. But no, not a glance, just money handed over, in the till, cans in a little blue bag. Ben, still shaking even then, and virtually white, placed his four cans on the counter. 'Jesus,' said the old guy. 'Four Napalms. You'll be sorry tomorrow!'

'Yeah, well,' muttered Ben, looking down at the chewing-gum rack.

We walked out and over to our bikes where Jase was waiting. By the time Hannah and Jenny met up with us on a bench by the path that led to the bonnie, we'd already cracked open our cans and taken our first swigs. It was without doubt the foulest thing any of us had ever drunk. But somehow we kept it down, and swallowed some more, even though our bodies were begging us to throw it back up. After just a quarter of a can, we were all feeling quite funny.

Naturally, Jenny was disgusted. 'Do you have to drink that stuff?' she said to Thomas, as she blew out minty nicotine.

Thomas just belched.

'Thomas!'

'What?' he said.

'Don't do that, it's disgusting!'

'Yeah, so what?'

Jenny didn't have an answer to that watertight argument.

Time speeded up because of the Napalm and next thing we knew we were by the bonfire. The sixth-formers had already lit it and there was quite a crowd. Soon, pretty much everybody would be there. Andrew, Will, John, Alex, Jon without the H, James, the other James, Ewan, Karen, who was now going out with James, the other James, that is, the girl with the big tits from the sports centre the year before, Kate, of course, loads of Jenny's little friends, all called Louise. And Damien was there too, hitting on all the girls. Normally we'd have tried to get him to piss off, but by the time we got there the Napalm had made us all deliriously happy, so we were running about hugging people and telling them we loved them, even Damien. Well, Thomas wasn't, but he wasn't telling them to fuck off either, which was more or less the same thing in his world. Ben got through all four of his Napalms and

176

ended up shouting at girls to get off with him before some sixth-former punched him in the stomach and everyone cheered. He ended up asleep in a bush. No idea how he got home.

Anyway, I was feeling really drunk, and everything was dancing in my head, and everybody was there, literally everybody I'd ever known, it seemed, at least thirty of them, like it was some amazing party, and it was, although still nobody had managed to get hold of any weed, when Hannah tugged at my sleeve. 'Honey,' she said, because she always called me that, 'there's someone I'd like you to meet. Louise, this is Chris, my boyfriend. Chris, this is Louise. She's my friend.' She lisped self-consciously when she said it. Looking back on it, Hannah did talk like she was six a lot of the time. It could never have lasted.

'Christ,' I said, 'not another Louise! There are too many already. You must change your name to Graham!'

'That's the sort of thing Neil would say,' sighed Hannah. She'd been down on him too recently, no doubt because Jenny had told her to. 'Have you spoken to him yet?'

'Yes,' I said, 'I've known him since I was five!'

'No, I mean tonight, silly.'

'What on God's earth are you going on about, woman!'

'Chris, don't be cheeky. He's over there.'

I couldn't coordinate my head to turn in the direction she was pointing, so Hannah turned me round herself. Sure enough, there Neil was, talking to some sixth-formers who appeared to find him quite amusing.

'He's come over already to talk to us. Just going on about Spam and lard or something silly like that. You took quite a shine to him, didn't you, Lu-Lu?'

'Oh, he's sweet,' Louise said. She was quite sweet herself.

She had an elfin pixie face and was dressed in dark goth clothes, with her hair dyed black, close to Hannah's natural shade, but you could tell she didn't walk about thinking about death all the time. A petite little thing with just too big an arse for her body, and her eyes didn't exactly line up. She was a weird cross between a normal person and someone a bit freaky. She was a borderline case. It could go either way for her. She needed to be careful.

'Neil! Neil!' I screamed as I ran over to him. 'What the blazes and fuck are you doing here?'

'Oh, Jase said I should come down, so I did. My last exam was yesterday.'

'Well, good to see you, my old chum,' I said, hitting him on the back very hard. 'I must go now, as I've got to hug a tree.'

And I did, and from that point on the evening's a mess of colours and dizziness, except for one thing. I remember looking across and seeing Neil talking to Louise, and he was talking his usual surrealist nonsense and she was laughing and laughing like she was going to wet herself. Well I never, I thought, Neil's going to get in there. And then I looked to the left, or the right, or somewhere. And there was Jenny. And there was Thomas with her. He was looking very sober now, despite having downed his two cans of Napalm. They were both looking at Neil and Louise too. And the look in their eyes – I can't describe it. Whether they were both thinking the same thing, or for the same reasons, I can't say, but that look. It was chilling. Jenny was saying something again in Thomas's ear. Thomas just nodded. He looked at Neil some more. Then he turned and stared into the fire.

23

That whole month of July was one of the happiest times of my life, I think, maybe the happiest. But I can't remember it that way. It's certainly not one of the little golden ages, like the summer before, or the youth club, or the time in the band when we hadn't played a gig and we were still rehearsing and Jenny hadn't started turning it all sour. It can't be, because every time I think about it, I can't help but remember what was being planned. At the time I was blissfully happy, and now I'm sick with guilt, because on some level I knew that something was up. If it was a golden age, it was a dishonest one. A fool's golden age.

It wasn't even perfect at the time. Nothing ever is, of course. I remember being quite annoyed that my parents made me look for a part-time job. I found one in a newsagents in Quireley High Street, which I pretty much hated from the start. Still, it brought in a bit of money, though not that much. It was just on Saturdays and a bit on Sundays, because shops weren't open long on Sundays back then. And though I was pissed off at having to do it so soon after finishing school, I really needed it, seeing as there was no way I was going to carry on doing my paper round now I'd left. Thomas actually carried on doing his, which would have been hilarious if we weren't all too . . . well, whatever it was we felt about him to make a joke about it. Jase immediately walked into a bit of work through his dad's car-repair firm, just odd jobs and stuff, but it was obvious they'd train him up. Ben and Neil didn't get jobs. Neil because he was too weird, and Ben because he was too lazy. Looking back on it, there was really no hurry, and they probably had the right idea, just enjoy our freedom and the summer for a bit, but I had a girlfriend, and girlfriends swallow money, or at least they seem to when you're sixteen. Besides, I wanted to be drinking something other than Napalm, because I couldn't help being sick every time I did.

The whole Fields thing just got bigger and bigger. There were so many kids round that bonfire, and it wasn't just on Fridays any more, it was most nights of the week. I remember it being beautiful every night, clear skies and sunsets, then stars in the night sky on the way home. I think I remember one rainstorm, and us all sheltering under the trees, except for the crazy kid who jumped through the fire, and he just ran about in it getting soaked. It was a whole month of blue and green and pollen in the air, long before I started suffering from hay fever. And girls, and friends, and laughing, and music on a portable tape player, that last summer of hard rock and metal. Funny how it didn't sound as good as it had just a month or so ago.

So, it wasn't all so perfect. There were a few things we could really have done with but didn't have. The promised weed, for example, never showed up. Either the person who said they knew someone couldn't get any after all, or they got it and smoked it all with their college mates in the afternoon, then turned up that evening at the bonnie totally mashed, but with none to share. They say that anybody who wants to do drugs knows where to get them, but we fucking didn't.

Another thing we weren't getting was sex. Jenny was still holding out on Thomas, and that insane thing he had over us meant that none of us could or would cross that line, even though some of the girls were obviously up for it. Instead, we just stuck our tongues in their mouths and occasionally felt their tits. Tit feeling was OK, because Thomas had let it be known that Jenny had shown him her little lumps and allowed him to run his hands over them and tweak her nipples in her bedroom one time, but anything below the waist or above the neck was out of bounds. Thanks to Thomas, we were all getting up to a lot less trouble than our parents feared, at least in that respect. Not that we were angels. Some of the college boys vandalised a plastic frog on a spring or something in the kiddies' play area, which I didn't think was cool, although Ben did. But I wasn't going to stop them; how could I? And we were pissed out of our minds on cider and Napalm, of course.

Obviously, one of us had been getting laid and that was Jase. But July didn't turn out to be such a good month for him because Kate dumped him all of a sudden, giving one of those weird reasons that girls come up with, something about needing time, or needing space, or needing some particular combination of time and space that Jase couldn't give her. In reality she just wanted to go out with a crusty from college with disgusting dreadlocks and camouflage trousers who never washed and always smelt like a wet dog. They ended up together for ages. In fact, I don't remember them breaking up. Maybe they're still together. Perhaps Kate's cock hunger could only be satisfied by someone as dirty as she was. Anyway, Jase was pretty depressed about that for a week or two and didn't come down to the bonnie for a bit, but then he did and he was back to normal.

And then there was Neil and Louise. It wasn't as if they were going out, they weren't, but they always talked together the nights they were both at the bonfire, although neither of them came as often as the rest of us. She lived quite a way out, and Neil, well, Neil was Neil. God knows what he was up to some of the time. I know he stayed in on Mondays because there was a radio programme that played all this weird music that he used to like to tape and then walk around listening to all week on his Walkman. I think that's where he found 'Flying Saucer Rock 'n' Roll'. He tried to get the rest of us into it, but we never quite remembered to listen. Besides, I heard one of his tapes and it wasn't my sort of thing. Other than that, he might not have come out much because he didn't have any money, but then he didn't drink so he didn't really need any. Neil was into abstinence from mind-altering substances, which is odd because all his heroes from the sixties were off their tits on drugs. But in the world of Neil I suppose it all made sense. Anyway, Jenny didn't like the idea of him and Louise getting on so well one bit. She was always having a go at Louise about what an embarrassment Neil was, and Hannah did too, seeing as she just did what Jenny did and everything, but Louise was having none of it – she liked Neil and always talked to him. Maybe they met up during the day somewhere, I don't really know. So that was July. Everything felt . . . ready. Ripe. We enjoyed that ripeness so much, we forgot that unless fruit is plucked and eaten, then it falls off the tree. And rots.

It was intoxicating, that blend of sunset, grass pollen, fire and friendship. The gig almost sneaked up on us. Not that we weren't rehearsed, we'd been meeting as normal every Saturday. But it was only in the last week that we really began to talk about it and persuade people to come. And sure, loads of people said they would. Jenny did her usual sniping about Neil's abilities, but that didn't stop people from wanting to go. We were happy, that last week in July, in that summer, by the bonnie, on the Fields. And

182

then one day it was the first of August. And our dads were shifting all our gear over to that dingy little social club on the other side of town. And we were there setting up at seven o'clock, doors at eight, ready to go on at half eight. This was it, our big moment, the one we'd been dreaming about for so long we'd forgotten we were even dreaming it. If only it had stayed a dream.

24

For the first time that summer, it wasn't just warm, it was humid. As we took all that gear out of the cars, Neil hitching a ride with Thomas, seeing as he didn't have a dad to get him up there with the keyboard, big black clouds hung above. And the air was heavy. We could feel it pressing down on our shoulders as we lifted the amps out of the various car boots. Suddenly everything had turned. The summer had passed that invisible moment and was no longer ripe on the tree. Now it was pulling the branch down.

'All right, Neil,' said Thomas, 'you grab the other end of your dooferberry.' What he meant was for him to pick up his end of the long, heavy, outdated keyboard. 'Tell me when I'm by the door, if you can see that far ahead.'

Neil had recently started wearing glasses, something that Thomas had been making various snide references to, ironic considering his own four-eyed status. But then consistency was never Thomas's strong point. As they carried it across the car park towards the concrete bunker of a social club, Thomas walking backwards and Neil obviously struggling with his coordination – but then, no change there – one giant raindrop, and then another, then a third, splattered on the plastic keys and dials and levers.

'Hurry-it-up-a-fucker,' said Thomas. 'We're going to get fucking electrocuted at this rate. Well, you will anyway. I'm not touching this once we're inside. So go as slow as you like.' Strangely for Thomas, instead of letting the insult hang in the air to do its work, as was his usual style, he followed it up with a strange high-pitched giggle, almost like an old woman laughing. What it meant I was not sure.

The rest of us, along with the various dads, quickly carried in any remaining electrical equipment, draping some of it with car-seat covers or dad jumpers or whatever was handy, leaving the drums, our only acoustic instrument, until last. That grim feeling that had bothered us all afternoon grew once we got inside. The social club was a dark, alien space. Nothing like what any of us were used to. Maybe Thomas had been there before, I don't know. But to me, and at least Ben and Neil, this was something new. It wasn't just dark, it was stained, a strange, sickly yellow. The carpet looked like it had been new about ten years ago, with its flecks of pastel, but now it had holes in it, and tears that had been nailed down to stop people catching their feet on them. And the furniture looked coated in fag ash, while on the bar were towels soaking up lager, a token effort at cleaning up after lunchtime opening. I'd been to the bowls club with my grandad, and that had a bar, but that was different: even though everyone was drinking, it felt jovial, but proper, respectable. This wasn't quaint decay, this building was ill. It reeked of defeat.

We were all on edge. Our dads could feel it too and arranged a time to pick us up, then left, with the usual dad-like whistle and jangling of car keys. 'I don't want to find you've been drinking,' my dad warned me, as he disappeared out into the car park. Obviously, none of our families were invited to the gig.

185

Not even Thomas's dad, who'd got us the gig in the first place. This was for our friends. Was meant to be, anyway. But something about that place, the desperation, the despair, got to us, and we were beginning to wish none of this was happening. There was some old guy from the social doing the sound desk. He looked like an overgrown Teddy boy, with big bushy sideburns. His job was really just getting the volume right for Neil's vocal and his keyboards, because they were the only things going through their PA. It was just him and some barman there at the time, and the barman kept on popping out back to rustle crisps. Both of them had the red-faced look of men who had spent far too much time in places like this. They were ill like the building.

'Are you Animal Magnets?' said the Teddy boy.

'Yeah,' Thomas said, suddenly embarrassed by the name. We did 'Sound of Sound' as a soundcheck. At first you couldn't really hear Neil at all, so the old Teddy boy put both the vocals and the keyboard up loud. He listened for a bit, and frowned, his haystack eyebrows pointing down. Then he slid the fader down with them and made Neil quieter. A lot quieter. Now you couldn't hear him at all. We finished the song. None of us were quite sure what to say. There was silence as we all just stood there, which Jase broke with some nervous drum banging. The barman exchanged weary glances with the sound guy. Finally, I thought I should say something. 'Um, could we have the vocals and keyboards a bit louder, if that's possible?'

The sound guy squinted me a puzzled look. 'Are you sure?' he said.

'Well, yeah,' I replied.

'OK,' he said. The 'your funeral' was silent.

He told us to go again, and he pushed Neil's parts up. Not as much as they should have been, but up. 'Is that what you want?' he said.

'Yeah,' I said, sensing that was as much grace as we were going to get.

I looked around at the others. Ben and Thomas looked back, their eyes a mix of worry and bubbling anger. Jase just stared up at the ceiling while he broke into a violent drum roll, and Neil didn't even seem to be in the room. What he was thinking I don't know, I still don't, but I knew what was going through the minds of the rest of us. This isn't going to work.

We knew then that we had been deluding ourselves. We'd been sucked in by the spell we'd cast on each other, compounded by the dreamland that had been the summer, but the utter, irrefutable reality of this dingy, depressed and depressing little social club woke us up with the sickening feeling of having over-slept and being made to look foolish. Idiots who had hung on to their dreams far too long because they couldn't even tell they weren't real. But the beer-soaked towels were the things that were really real. And the ashtrays. And the dartboard and the snooker table with the beer spills on it. And the sound man and the barman who thought Neil couldn't sing or play the keyboard properly. And they were right. Which meant we were going to be humiliated. We were going to be humiliated by Neil.

Next thing we knew, the girls were there. Jenny and Hannah, of course, Louise, a couple of other Louises, and some more of Jenny's twitty entourage. Neil, seeing Louise, finally remembered what building he was in and bounded over to her, smiling like a Jehovah's Witness on a doorstep. Jenny rolled her eyes. 'I suppose you'll always have one fan, Neil,' she said. 'Well, depends. Louise hasn't heard you sing yet, have you, Louise?'

'No,' she said softly, looking at Neil. 'I'm sure he's very good, though.'

Jenny placed her hands on Louise's shoulders. 'Louise, Lou, Lu-Lu, darling,' she said, 'just don't be surprised if it's a bit . . . strange. It's different, anyway.' All of this while Neil was standing there, mind you. Maybe a week ago Thomas would have told her to shut up, but now he was silent, just like the rest of us, the social club's absolute reality clogging up our heads like the concrete blocks it was made out of. Jenny, having finished trying to brainwash Louise, took Thomas's hand. 'Shall I get you a drink?' she asked him, as if he was five. 'I bet you'd like a Coke.'

'S'pose,' he grunted.

I couldn't bear to look at Jenny any more, so I turned the other way. Already, Neil and Louise had disappeared.

More people started to arrive. Every one of them soaked from the rain that had bucketed down on the way. James, Will, Jon, other James, loads of the college kids, some of whom were even old enough to buy drinks from the bar, and Damien, and the crazy kid who jumped through the fire, Kate with her new crusty boyfriend, there apparently to prove some point to Jase that they could still be friends, but succeeding only in depressing him further by turning up, and some others, plus the old alcoholics and manual labourers who went there anyway. Because it was a club, Thomas had to keep a list of them, which he had to give to his dad afterwards in case anybody started any trouble. It didn't sound that legal, but the people who ran the place didn't care really, they didn't even ask the college kids for ID. I don't know why Thomas's dad went there. He had quite a good job. Mind you, it was in a warehouse. He did mostly paperwork and stuff, but he was still really dealing with moving boxes about.

'Is this going to be good?'

'Are you looking forward to it?'

'Are you nervous?'

They were all asking me questions, and I was doing my best to answer, supping on my pint of lemonade, but I was miles away. No, not miles away, minutes away, ahead in time to the moment when we had to start playing and everybody was going to laugh. Laugh at Neil because he can't sing, and us for being stupid enough to go onstage with him. Christ, why did we have to hook up with a monger, no, worse, a spazzer? Spent all this time, all these years, getting popular, keeping my position, making sure I had a girl-friend, and now this. It was all going to come tumbling down now.

The minutes dragged, the minutes flew. Then, as the sick feeling in my stomach somehow managed to slip up my throat and into my head, and my hands, and my legs, it was time. Time to go on. Ben and I looked at each other, defeated. 'Better get on with it, I suppose,' muttered Ben. Jase, who had been sitting behind his drums, tapping along to the jukebox so as to avoid Kate and crusty, nodded sadly. Thomas, seeing us move towards the stage that was not a stage, just a seating area with a table moved, stopped snogging Jenny up against the bar and came to join us.

'Right, where's Neil, the little twerp?' he said.

Good point. Where was he?

'He must be outside,' I said. 'I'll go get him.'

'I'll come with you,' said Thomas.

We went outside. The rain had stopped, and the sky was lighter, although black clouds still sailed above, threatening another down-pour. Neil wasn't there amongst the various wall-sitters, drinking their cans of Napalm and bottles of cider and Newkie Brown they'd got from the garage on the way over and the old guy who'd sell anybody anything before they got on their bikes. We went out into the car park. We couldn't see him there either.

'Where in fuckery duckery has he gone?' hissed Thomas.

Then I saw him. He was there, with Louise. They were holding each other, no, holding on to each other, their faces about a centimetre apart, their noses occasionally rubbing, as the sun went down and the rays broke through the spent rain clouds behind them, by some railings beyond the car park that overlooked an old piece of railway that very little, if anything, ever travelled down now. Old terraced houses, their bricks glowing in the sunset, were on the other side of the track. It was almost as if Neil had arranged it. I just knew he was getting off on the romantic industrial bleakness of it all, the same way he had got off on that suburban thing the night of the fair, because that was Neil.

Thomas's eyes burned like the sunset behind his jam jars. 'Right, let's get him,' he said.

We walked towards them. 'Oi! Wank-wrangler!' shouted Thomas. 'You doing this or what?'

'Yeah, sorry,' said Neil, walking towards us. 'Just lost track of time.'

'I bet you did, you dirty little fucker. Stick your finger in her hole, did you?' Although a few paces behind, Louise could probably hear.

'Ah, no, no I didn't,' said Neil.

'Good,' said Thomas, a little too quickly, and a little too much like he cared. 'Right, let's get this fucking thing over with.'

'I think we should play "Flying Saucer Rock 'n' Roll",' said Neil.

'No. It's shit.'

Louise caught up with Neil and squeezed his hand. 'Good luck,' she said.

We walked back into the social club. I'd leave a couple of hours later, tamed, damaged, changed.

25

I never normally have lie-ins, but the next morning I stayed in bed for hours. It made my dad think I had been drinking, but really I hadn't, not that time. Truth was, I didn't want the day to begin, and if I stayed in bed I thought I might be able to stop it. Didn't work that way, of course. Ben phoned and asked if I wanted to meet up at the Fields at lunchtime. Apparently, quite a few people were going to be there. Thomas was going to be there, anyway. I didn't want to, but if I stayed in it would probably look worse, so I said yes.

Every minute of that morning, I tried not to think about the night before, and of course spent every minute of that morning thinking about it. The gig itself was terrible. Neil's singing was even worse than usual, his keyboard playing all over the place. I don't know what he was thinking. And because we were all so embarrassed, we didn't play well either. I'd miss a chord change, or Ben would play a wrong note in a solo, or Jase wouldn't know the song had ended and would just carry on playing. Thomas played all right, pretty much, but he just stood and stared out into nothingness, as if he wasn't really anything to do with what was going on. After the first song, people clapped, and there were a few cheers from our girlfriends, and the Louises and Kate, but by the third song in, I could definitely hear people laughing, and soon they weren't even doing that, they weren't listening, they were bored. Neil's hiccuppy, stuttering vocals just didn't hold their interest. They probably didn't even count it as music. Not their sort of music, anyway, which was metal and grunge. We managed to get a bit of applause for every song, but by the end it was just Louise, Neil's Louise, I mean, all on her own. Everyone else was talking, or wandering outside, or simply not paying attention. Kate, who had cheered the loudest at the beginning, was busy snogging her crusty and didn't even notice we'd finished.

Once it was finally over, the four sane members of the band started packing up our instruments as if we were racing against time. Truth was, there was no hurry at all. There weren't even any cars to load them into. Ben used the payphone to ask his dad if he could come and pick him up early. Naturally, Ben's own personal taxi service was soon on its way.

When we finally ventured out to our friends, no one acted as if we'd done anything. None of them wanted to mention what had just happened. Well, that's not quite true. Unlike the rest of us, Neil wasn't in a hurry to get packed up. As soon as he'd finished singing he made a beeline for Louise, with a big goofy grin that suggested he was unaware of the fact that he'd just made a total tit of himself in public. She started talking animatedly, far too animated to fit in with the rest of the girls we knew. I couldn't hear what they were saying, but she seemed to be telling him how great he was. I could see Jenny about two feet away, glowering at them like there was no tomorrow. Thomas also had them in his sights as he wound his jack lead. It was as if they were psyching themselves up for a pincer movement, and looking back on it, I'm not sure they weren't.

Jenny rested her hand on Louise's shoulder and said something in her ear. It looked like she was persuading her it was time to go. It wasn't at all, but Jenny suddenly had something she had to be back for and if Louise wanted to get home with her and all the other Louises then she'd have to go now. Hannah, her trusted lieutenant, began to rally the twitty troops into formation, and within two minutes they had their coats on and handbags clutched. It was definitely time to go.

When Hannah snuggled up to me and whispered a sweet goodbye I wasn't remotely listening to, I saw Neil and Louise do the same, as all the while Jenny hovered at Louise's shoulder, haranguing her that they had to leave now. They didn't kiss, I don't know if they ever did, but they held hands as their faces nuzzled, and only broke apart when Jenny manoeuvred Louise away, her arm round her as if she was really her friend.

Neil just stood there, looking a bit lost, but happy. I wonder if he had any idea. He couldn't have. Meanwhile, I went to phone my dad to see if he could pick me up earlier, but he wasn't in, so I had no choice but to stay and wait. Fortunately Jase didn't seem that bothered about getting home in a hurry because some college kid had bought him a drink, so at least I had him for company, not that I really wanted any. Thomas had got hold of his dad, though, and so he needed Neil to pack up his keyboard and sharpish. 'Right, get a move on,' he snapped, as he knocked Neil in the ribs with a loose fist. Neil did as he was told, and pretty soon Thomas was grimly helping him lift the keyboard back into the car. It had started raining again, not as heavy as before, but a miserable, spitting drizzle. If the keyboard hadn't been his family's property, I wonder if Thomas would have given him a lift at all. Neil got in the back seat. The boot door slammed. Thomas waved goodbye with an efficient dart of an arm, and they were away, out of the car park and into the black and neon-yellow night. To this day I cannot imagine what it must have felt like to have been inside that car.

I joined Jase at the bar with his college kid mates. He offered me some of his beer casually. I said no and he shrugged.

'So how do you think it went?' I asked, finally. I just had to talk to someone about it.

'Fine,' he said.

'Do you think anybody liked it?'

'Dunno, maybe.'

That was as much as I could get out of him, and he went back to talking to his college mates. I sat there, pretty much in silence for the next hour, waiting for my dad.

Now, after Ben's phone call, I wanted to crawl back into bed where it was safe, but I needed to get washed and dressed if I was going to get to the Fields in time. I wasn't hungry.

After the rain the night before, the air was fresh and a strong wind buffeted me from side to side as I rode my bike up Cresston Avenue. The suburban houses did not seem beautiful like they did on the night of the fair. Now their beauty seemed an awful one. They seemed to be screaming. Clouds as big as spaceships zoomed across the sky, blocking out the sun and quickly releasing it again. The light flickered through the trees as I sped under them, and made my head hurt.

From a distance, I could see Jenny, and Thomas, and Ben, and Hannah, and an army of twitty Jenny-friends, and Louise, some way from the entrance on a grassy area half hidden by bushes. I had the awful feeling I was about to witness a lynching. What happened was almost as bad, in its own way. As I rode up, a circle was forming. Jenny was hovering around Louise, moving from side to side, sometimes at one shoulder, sometimes at another, sometimes in front, mostly behind. The twits stood behind Louise in a crescent, Hannah directing them in a smirking chorus line. Thomas was in front of her, rolling backwards and forwards on his bike. Ben was to his side. The only place for me was the other side of Thomas. I guess I must have looked as if I was part of it all too.

'Neil wasn't very good last night, was he, Thomas?' said Jenny as she paced.

'No, he was fucking shit,' said Thomas.

'Made himself look stupid, didn't he?'

'Yeah, fucking useless twerp.'

I wondered where Jase was.

'Do you fancy him then?' said Thomas, rocking ever closer on his bicycle.

Louise looked down and bit her lip.

'Do you? Do you?' giggled Thomas.

'Well, he's sweet,' mumbled Louise to her shoes.

'Sad! Sad! Sad! Sad! Sad!'

Thomas emphasised this with a peculiar pointing dance aimed at Louise's head. It was weirder than anything I'd seen Neil do, but Neil wasn't Thomas.

'Neil is a mongoloid! Neil is a spastic! You can't fancy him!'

Hannah giggled and all the twits giggled too. Normally they didn't laugh at those words, they didn't approve of them, but they laughed at them now. Ben also laughed, which didn't happen often. It was a low, moronic sound, like a distant road drill. Jenny just looked sadly at Louise, then smiled.

'There, there,' she said, hugging her, 'we'll find you a new boyfriend, one who's not such a weirdo.'

Louise began to cry. Jenny clutched her face and looked into her watery eyes.

196

'What's the matter, babe, what's the matter?'

Louise just kept on crying.

'Tell me what the matter is, Lu-Lu honey. I can't help you if you don't tell me what's the matter.'

I looked at Ben. He glanced back, his face hard, then looked away. Thomas just stared into the distance. Those stupid little girls would not stop smirking.

'Look, I can't help you if you don't tell me what the matter is. Now, stop being silly and tell me what's wrong. Come on, stop messing me about.'

Finally, Louise tried to speak. 'I want Neil,' she sobbed. 'I like Neil. I don't care . . .'

'What did you say? What did you just say?'

'Does – doesn't matter.'

'No, what did you just say?'

'I like Neil and I want to go out with him and I don't care what you think, you stupid townie!' cried Louise in a sudden burst of red-faced fury.

Jenny slapped her. Louise cried out. Jenny put her hands to her mouth.

'Oh, honey, I'm sorry, I'm so sorry.'

She wrapped her arms tightly round Louise, in an embrace that ensured she could not get away. Louise sobbed quietly into Jenny's pink T-shirt.

'There, there. I'm sorry, I'm really sorry. Do you forgive me? Yes, I'm sure you do.'

This was horrific. I felt sick. I wanted to tell her to leave her alone, I wanted to tell them all to go fuck themselves. But my mouth wouldn't open. I couldn't make a sound. I realised then that this was all much bigger than I was. This was evil, pure and simple, manifesting itself through the medium of teenage girls. I knew that if I went up against it, I would be crushed.

'Now, why don't we take you back to my place and we'll have a good chat, a nice cup of tea, and you'll feel a lot better. You'd like that, wouldn't you?'

Louise said nothing, her face a red and black mess, her body trembling.

'Look, guys, we're going to go back to mine for a bit,' said Jenny. 'Think it's going to be girls only, I'm afraid.'

'S'pose,' said Thomas.

Jenny wrapped her arms around him and kissed him on the lips. Hannah did the same to me, but I didn't even feel it.

'What's the matter?' she said.

I shrugged my shoulders.

'There's something the matter, I know there is.'

I said nothing.

'Oh well, be like that then,' she said, and went to take her place by Jenny's side as they led their prisoner away.

It was known by twelve o'clock the next day that Louise no longer wished to see Neil.

I never laughed. I didn't stop it, I couldn't have done anyway, but I never laughed. Surely that must count for something? Doesn't it?

26

The summer was on the ground, a fruit you wouldn't want to be eating. We still went to the bonnie as always, but it was turning shit. There were more and more kids there, but most of them weren't our type of people. The Horned Gods came along a few times, and stood by themselves sneering. Fortunately they hated it so much they stopped coming. Some of the others were virtually townies. Every so often you'd see a tracksuit top or something and you'd just know it wasn't what it used to be. We should have told them to fuck off, but the college kids wouldn't have put up with it. Some of them were old enough to have been to raves and had this thing about everyone being together and chilled. Mind you, a lot of the college kids gave up on the whole thing, and just went to the pub instead. The weather wasn't so good anyway, it was pretty muggy a lot of the time. Many of the old faces disappeared, like James, the other James, John, Jon without the H. Some of them were simply bored, I think, a few probably went on holiday or something. But there was another reason some kids dropped out, and that was to do with the whole sex thing, the doing it, or the not doing it.

I mean it was just ridiculous, a bunch of sixteen-year-old boys, most of them with girlfriends, and none of us were up to anything because we were all waiting for Thomas to get some. And one by one, a lot of guys got tired of waiting. So they'd finally give in and let their girlfriends wank them off or even give them a blowjob or something, and of course the plan was not to let anybody know, but being sixteen-year-old kids it naturally stayed a secret for about five minutes. Within a day, the information would have got back to Thomas. Just one cold stare from Thomas from behind those jam jars the next evening would be enough to inform these old comrades of his, some of whom had known him since primary school, that their presence was no longer welcome, and something very bad would happen to them should they turn up again. You see, they remembered. They knew what he could do. Some of the new kids didn't get it, because it had been a while since anyone had seen Thomas in action, but if you'd been around a few years, you knew, all right.

One of the guys tried his luck. Will, it was. He'd known Thomas for quite a few years, and he'd been on the grass verge for as long as I could remember, but maybe he'd never seen Thomas in full swing at first hand. That's the only way I can explain why he was still hanging around, even after he got his dick sucked at a party on the other side of Quireley that the rest of us weren't told about. He'd have been OK if he'd just kept his trap shut, but of course he blabbed. And there he was at the bonnie the night after. Thomas gave him the look. Maybe he thought Thomas had gone soft. Maybe that's why he came back again two nights later. He really shouldn't have done.

He was standing on the ridge above the bonnie talking to his friends from school when Thomas came up.

'Oi! Did you call Jenny a bitch?' said Thomas.

He got the fear right then. He tried to save himself but he knew it was no use.

'No. Who's been saying I did? I swear I didn't.'

200

'You fucking liar!'

With that Thomas pushed him over, and he rolled down the slope, landing by the bonfire. He got a few scratches from the branches piled against the slope, waiting to be burnt. When he stood up, it looked like there was something wrong with his ankle, although he was trying to hide it.

'Hey, are you OK?' asked a sixth-former. 'What was that about? Do you want me to talk to him?'

'No,' said Will, 'it's fine. Don't worry about it.'

Will kept his distance from Thomas for the rest of the evening, went home early on his own and didn't come again.

The girls didn't really want to come out that much either. You'd see them now and again, Jenny and Hannah and all the Louises and the one who used to be Neil's Louise who just turned up with them like she was hypnotised or on drugs or something, but mostly they just started going round Jenny's and did whatever girls do together, fiddle with their hair, put on make-up, slag us off, watch *Pretty Woman* on video. That's what we imagined, anyway. If we wanted to see them, we'd have to go round theirs in the afternoon, or take them to town and spend money.

So that was what was happening at the bonnie. But the really weird stuff was what was happening with the band. Yes, the band. The band kept going. It's hard to believe, I know, but it did. And not only that, Neil still turned up at the bonnie. God knows what he was thinking. For a start, the first anybody heard from Neil was the evening after that incident on the Fields, with Jenny and Louise. After Jenny had Louise holed up at hers all afternoon doing God knows what to her head, she and her twitty friends took her home. Apparently when they got in the front door, Louise's mum said that Neil had been phoning nearly every hour all afternoon. Sure enough they'd been in about ten minutes when Neil phoned again. Louise's mum handed the cordless phone to Louise. With Jenny and Hannah perched on either shoulder, they had a conversation that went something like this:

'Hi, Louise, it's Neil.'

'Oh, hi, Neil.'

'How are you?'

'Fine.'

'Great. Um, are you free tonight?'

'Not really, no, sorry.'

'Oh, OK. What about tomorrow?'

'Uh . . . no. I'm busy tomorrow, sorry.'

'Oh right, OK. How about some other time next week?'

A pause.

Then, 'No, I don't think so, sorry.'

Another pause. A very long awkward one.

'Ever?' said Neil.

'Ah, I gotta go. Listen, you take care, OK. Bye.'

And that was that.

That was Sunday. We didn't often go down the bonnie on Sunday, so it wasn't until the next day that we got to hear about it. Jenny gave Thomas the story in luxurious detail on the phone that morning, and when we met up to go down the bonnie as usual, Thomas told us all about it and we had a good laugh. Well, Jase didn't see the funny side, but Ben thought it was hilarious, and I pretended to, even though it actually made me feel a bit sick. Still, appearing to find it funny was probably necessary for my social survival, so I laughed nearly as much as Ben.

Then, when we got there, all the other guys found it fucking hilarious too. Well, some of the college kids didn't seem that impressed, but overall it got a huge laugh from pretty much every-body. Now that it was obvious we'd disassociated ourselves from Neil's performance, everyone felt free to discuss how terrible it was. Neil was the joke of the moment that evening. Even when he turned up.

None of us could believe it as he made his way over the mound towards us. 'Oh no, it's Neil,' said one of the Louises, loudly. There was a general murmur of ridicule and disapproval. Thomas's face was a mask.

'All right, Neil,' said Jase, as if Neil was actually a human being.

'Hiya,' said Neil, jovially, like a total fucking idiot.

The rest of us said nothing. Neil circulated. He got the cold shoulder everywhere he went, except for a few of the college kids. Some people just mocked him to his face. Then, unexpectedly, he found himself in front of Louise. It was the first time she'd been out in her new zombified state, with an invisible leash tethering her to Jenny, who hovered not too far away. Neil mumbled a hello, but Louise said nothing, as if he wasn't even there. Although they would come across each other several more times that summer, they would never speak again.

(I wasn't there, but apparently around this time, Jenny got Louise to burn a photo of Neil taken at the gig. People said she was laughing and crying more or less simultaneously as she did it.)

Later that evening, Neil sidled up to Thomas. 'Hi, Thomas,' he said.

'Yeah, what do you want?' he snapped back.

'Just wondering if we're still on for the practice on Saturday.'

It was unbelievable. How could he think we were still in a band with him? We all waited to see how Thomas would deal with this. It was bound not to be pretty, we all thought.

But we were wrong. 'Yeah, why not?' said Thomas.

And so the band continued. And Neil kept on turning up at the bonnie. He still got the brush-off from most people, including us – except Jase, of course – but we were still in a band with him, and we were still going round his house on Saturday for our practice.

At first, you could be forgiven for thinking that it was just like old times. The practice was civil, if a little tense. There was the odd dig at Neil's performance, but nothing major. We mostly just got on with it. We turned up at the usual time, plugged in and got ready to play. Thomas had some more chords and, as ever, Neil had some new lyrics. This time, though, they were a bit different from his usual surrealist wordplay. They seemed a bit personal, although I didn't see exactly what the point of them was. They went,

> You live in a secret room
> But you ain't got the key to your secret room
> And we'll be friends to the end of time
> And it's getting very near the end of time

I couldn't work out who was in the secret room. I was thinking about it all week, though. Louise, perhaps. That sort of made sense. Or maybe it was about us. Me, even. But surely if anybody lived in a secret room round here it was Neil, with his weird ideas about what music was and how you went about making it. We lived in the real world, where lead singers had to sing in time and in tune.

Over the next week, Neil kept on coming to the bonnie, and still he got ignored. There was a fair bit of abuse now too. Some of it was coming from Thomas, it has to be said. Some from Ben too. I just pretended I couldn't see him, like most people. It was round about now that we began to see less of the girls; I think they only came once or twice that week. And also that was when people started getting sent to Coventry left, right and centre by Thomas. The new kids too, who the week before had only been a little group, were beginning to move in en masse, smiling too much and their hair too short. On Thursday, Neil asked again, after he'd just been called a mongoloid twerp by Thomas, whether we would be practising that Saturday. 'Yeah, may as well,' said Thomas.

So that Saturday we were round again, although only Jase made it on time, and as ever, more chords and more lyrics were unveiled. Both were slightly depressing. Thomas's chords were mostly minors or minor sevenths strung together, unlike his usual power chord riffs, while Neil's words were pretty maudlin. He called the new song 'The Haunting', the only bit of which I remember went, 'A record plays but I don't hear its tune, just footsteps' echo in a nearby empty room.' They weren't his best by any means. Nowhere as good as the other stuff. The atmosphere was worse that week. Ben was bored, and Thomas was in a pretty foul mood. There was an incident. After we'd been through 'The Haunting' five or six times, he slammed his bass down. 'This is fucking dreadful,' he said. 'Let's chuck it.'

'I like it,' said Neil.

'Yeah, well, so fucking what,' said Thomas. 'You like your own fucking singing.'

'I'm just trying to do something different,' Neil said quietly.

Finally, Ben came to life. The first time in months, it seemed. 'Neil,' he said, 'no one, absolutely no one, liked your singing at the gig. No one at all.'

Neil said nothing. Maybe he had no way of defending himself, or maybe he didn't feel he needed to.

'That's not true, actually,' said Jase, from behind his drum kit.

'What the fuck are you talking about?' sneered Thomas.

'Damien said he really likes what Neil does, and actually I happen to like what Neil does as well, and I'm not going to stop liking it just because someone tells me to. Now let's play "Sound of Sound".'

There was obviously a coded message for Thomas in there about Jenny, and only Jase would ever have got away with giving it. But there was another clue in there as well, if only we hadn't been too stupid to see it. Not just about the music, but about the strange cloud that was August. If only we'd realised what a small world the bonfire was, and exactly what was going on outside it.

In the third week of August, things really started to get bad. Those kids who we suspected of being townies brought their mates, who most definitely were townies. Naf Naf jackets, baseball caps, rave music blasting out of their boom boxes, the works. They were all called things like Wayne, Shane, Darren and Dean, like the flash kids from school. In fact, we had been to school with a few of them. But that meant nothing now they'd turned townie. It wasn't like they were hostile, in fact they seemed pretty friendly, on the surface. But you could feel the latent violence. They wanted us out.

The townies were all over the bonnie. It was like an ant infestation. Practically all our girls had gone now. The townies had their own girls, horrible shrieking ginger things, who, we suspected, might not be as innocent and pure as our own. Also gone were so many of our mates, ostracised but no doubt in their bedrooms with a smile on their face while they sampled their first tastes of carnal pleasure, their innocent suburban girlfriends turning less innocent underneath them. But there at the bonnie, it was just us, a few of the hardcore from Thomas's old circle, and some college kids. Not many left now.

Something needed to be done. Fortunately for us, the crazy kid who jumped through the bonfire was there to do it. And on the third night of the townie infestation he saved us all. We saw him coming over the ridge with several cans of Napalm, wearing an old Army and Navy shop coat, which was actually fashionable at the time, whistling the theme from *The Dam Busters*. Nobody drank Napalm any more, so we thought it was quite odd that he had some. We weren't that bothered, though, because he was a mad bastard. Good mad, not Neil mad.

The townies were everywhere. I mean, there were loads of them, absolutely fucking loads of them. It was like that Alfred Hitchcock film *The Birds*, if the birds had worn shell suits. In what used to be our special place, we were now outnumbered nearly five to one. There was no way we could have taken them on. But that didn't matter now, because the crazy kid was here to save the day.

He stood up on the ridge. Then he put up the hood of his Army and Navy shop coat and zipped it right up. He opened the first can of Napalm and poured it on his head. All of it. There was froth rolling right down him. A few of the townies saw it and laughed. The crazy kid's doing something crazy, ha, ha, ha. Then he opened the second one and did the same. Then the third, then the fourth. Everyone was watching now and laughing. What a mental. If only they knew. He walked back a few paces. And started to run. And yell. He built up momentum as he went over the ridge, and much more as he skidded down the steep bank. He nearly tripped and fell at the bottom, but he recovered and kept right on going, very, very fast. Right into the fire.

He came out the other side a fireball, the absurdly high alcohol percentage of the Napalm transformed into flame. And he just kept on going. Straight at some townies. He was screaming his head off, the loudest scream I'd heard since Neil at the talent show all that time ago. They ran for their lives. He kept on going, lapping round the bonfire, flames leaping out from him, townies scattering like mice. He must have been round three times before he slowed down and started to pull off the Army and Navy shop coat. The alcohol had burnt out now, and he really was just on fire. He frantically tried to get it over his head, but the red-hot zip burned his hand when he tried to tug at it. Finally, just when we thought he was going to die, he managed to pull the coat off and flung it in the fire, which leapt up as it absorbed the last of the Napalm.

The crazy kid laughed hysterically. He didn't seem to mind that his hair was singed and his skin was black and blistering. But it had done the trick. The townies had gone.

And in their place was Neil. 'Hi,' he said.

We were too excited to ignore him or tell him to fuck off.

'Did you see that?' I asked him, laughing.

'Yeah, that was like a Chris Burden thing or something. It was great.' No one knew what the fuck he was talking about, obviously.

'What can we do you for, Neil?' said Thomas.

'Just wondering if we're going to practise on Saturday,' he said.

'You and your practices,' said Thomas. 'Always hassling me for one. OK, yeah.'

'Great,' said Neil. He turned to go.

'You not staying?' said Jase.

'Nah,' said Neil, and he disappeared into the woods.

That last rehearsal was not good. Ben was not in a cooperative mood at all, me and Thomas had just had a conversation about how hacked off we were that we could never get to see our girlfriends any more, and even Jase wasn't exactly chipper. Don't know why, maybe he just didn't feel like it that week.

Neil had a new set of lyrics for Thomas's chords which he hoped he would like better, but they were even more depressing. They went:

> Everyone is born without form
> Until with time the edges are worn
> I've lost my faith in cause and effect
> What's wrong with me
> I can't connect

None of us were really enjoying it, and the new song was as much of a dirge as ever. Then there was another incident. As Neil started trying to play his keyboard over the miserable chords, and somehow ended up playing in a major rather than a minor scale, Ben just got up, went over and turned the volume down. I mean right down, to silence. OK, Neil's playing was pretty bad, but even I could see that was a bit rude. Neil didn't say anything. Nobody said anything. Instead we just carried on, and Neil didn't try to play the keyboard any more. The hours dragged on until it was mercifully time to go. Then, without any of us really saying much, we packed up, and for the last time left that weird house, with its smell of dog and all the strange souvenirs from the seventies on the wall.

We had the bonfire to ourselves that night, just us, a few of the college kids and the crazy kid. No townies, thank God. But no girls either. Then on the Monday, I was cycling through the Fields to the bonnie, when I saw Jeffrey on his bike.

'Hi, Chris,' he said.

'All right, Jeff.'

He got off his bike and motioned me to do the same.

'Listen, mate,' he said. 'It's not easy for me to tell you this, but I think I'm going to have to. You know your girl's been spending a lot of the time round Jenny's recently?'

'Yeah,' I said. I could already feel something gnawing in my gut. Things were about to get very bad.

'Well, ah, how can I say this? Look, fuck it, I'll say it. There's been stuff between her and Damien.'

I tried to say something but the words wouldn't come out. It hit me that I hadn't seen Damien at the bonnie since the girls stopped coming.

'Yeah, apparently Jenny's parents went away on holiday for the month, and basically Damien's been over there a lot, and stuff's happened.'

I felt as if the path was sinking and the trees were falling on me. It's funny, I thought, Thomas never mentioned Jenny's parents being away. Did he know?

'I mean, he's just been a total sleaze, apparently. Just, ah, doing stuff with a lot of the girls there, really taking the piss.'

I felt stomach fluid in my mouth and I had to stop myself from dribbling.

210

'Look, I think you should go and talk to her, but whatever you find out, be careful what you say to Thomas.'

I was in so much shock it took hours for it to register how odd it was for him to say that. What had it got to do with Thomas? I thanked Jeff for telling me and he hugged me in a manly way. I gave up on the idea of the bonnie and went home, where I stared catatonically at the TV for hours and then failed to sleep all night.

The next morning, I surprised Hannah on her doorstep. I told her I knew about her and Damien, and I could see she was about to deny it, but then she thought better of it. Instead she said, 'Oh,' and took me up to her bedroom to explain. Turned out that Damien had felt it was his duty to introduce her and a few of the other girls to the joys of oral pleasure one night, and he was such a gentleman about it that afterwards he didn't even ask for anything in return, and just wanked himself off in the toilet.

I was crushed. Half of me wanted to punch her face in, the other half wanted to get her to pull me off just so I could get something out of this whole sorry relationship. 'I'm going to go now,' is all I ended up saying. And I let myself out. I can't remember if she said she was sorry.

On the last Friday of August, three things happened. Firstly, on the day before Jenny's parents flew back from their holiday, she finally let Thomas where some other man, or indie-kid, had most probably gone before. All the way, right in there. The drought was over. We were free at last to have our way with all the girls Damien had deflowered behind our backs while we weren't paying attention. Secondly, me and Ben went down the bonnie. We were the only two people there. None of us ever went there again. Thirdly, Jase got a call from Neil. He was just phoning, he said,

211

to say he didn't want to do the band any more. Jase couldn't believe it, and begged him to reconsider, but Neil said no, they'd won. He'd had enough.

The last ripple of all our golden ages disappeared from sight. There would be no more. Finally, it was all over. Now real life could begin.

II

The Aftermath

1

And with real life, real time began. Before then, in the golden age, and all the little golden ages contained within it, time hovered, like a bubble we floated in. Now it began to move, like the current of a river. Very slowly at first, barely noticeable, but definitely there, a build-up of days lived began to grow, and that build-up would come to be known as a life. It was constantly being added to, with the days stacking up more and more, and at a faster and faster rate, until a long time was no time at all, and years would take what once was a month to pass. Birthday would follow birthday, and after a while, we would have to think twice before we could remember how old we were. And before we knew it, we were no longer at the very start of our stories. We were many chapters in.

But it was not like that at first. At first, it was almost as if the golden age had never ended. It was mid-September, summer was dead and buried, and we were all about to start sixth-form college. Well, they called it the sixth form, but it was actually a different place altogether from school. It was in a flash new building on the other side of the Fields. There were probably about half the kids from our school going there. Most of the boys from the lower sets just went out into the world and got jobs. I could never get over how one minute they couldn't be bothered to turn up on time, or at all, never did their homework and were abusive to all the teachers, and the next they had become good little workers, doing exactly what they were told by their boss and bringing home the bacon for their pregnant girlfriends. The school sociopath ended up manager of the local Spar.

College was totally different from school. For a start, there was no uniform, you could wear what you liked. Amazing. Also, you called the teachers by their first name. This was a hard habit to get into, and it was pretty embarrassing for the first few weeks because I just couldn't remember to do it. And not only that, it was so informal you could pretty much swear in front of the teachers and they wouldn't care. Most of them wouldn't, anyway. But obviously the biggest difference was that there were girls. Oh yes, girls. The college took on the pupils from not just our school, but the local girls' school as well. I'm glad to say, though, that Jenny and Hannah didn't end up there. They went to some special Catholic place run by nuns that they had to go to church for ages pretending to be religious just to get into. Anyway, as you can imagine, having girls about changed absolutely everything. The way we talked, for one. Spastic, mongoloid, spazzer, spacker were all gone for good, except for the odd furtive, sniggering use when there were no girls about. And the way we behaved, how cruel we could be seen to be in public, that all changed for us. You couldn't just swear at a monger in the corridor for no reason, for example. Nevertheless, it was funny watching all the monger kids who hadn't been around girls that much struggling to deal with them suddenly being there. They made right twats of themselves trying to be cool and impress them, and ended up looking desperate.

Still, it wasn't just the mongers who had problems with change. I think we all did. For a start, there was the whole clothes thing.

216

For instance, the first day there, me and Ben turned up in our metaller gear – and really that was when we realised we'd outgrown it. I mean mentally, not physically. We hadn't gone lardy or anything. We'd been mixing the metal with the grunge look all year, but for some reason we both thought that on our first day we should show our colours and go in hardcore metaller gear. But when we were surrounded by all the other kids, who looked pretty normal except for the odd crusty, I think we both felt a bit stupid. It wasn't as if it meant anything to us any more. We'd been listening to the music less and less, but there we still were in our leather jackets, black denim and studs. Neither of us ever wore that stuff again. It was the grunge look all the time from then on. You were safe with the grunge look. We'd grown our hair way over the collar during the summer anyway, so we could pull off the look quite well.

Actually, round about that time we were at a loss as to what music to listen to. We couldn't be bothered with the old stuff any more, but we didn't really get any of the things that Neil had got Thomas and Jase into. So there was grunge, and I experimented with the Wonder Stuff and the Senseless Things and bands like that. I went to my first gig sometime around then. FMB. Stood for 'Fuck Me Backwards' or something. They were a band off a TV show that followed them round as they tried to make it big in the music world. They never did, but they did play a gig in Sholeham in its only proper music venue. We weren't really old enough to get in, but none of the audience was. I remember somebody's mum came in and pulled her fourteen-year-old daughter out from the mosh pit. Funny to think I'd played a gig before even going to one. None of that music was really me, but it filled a gap.

But I suppose I was just at a loss generally. I hadn't really thought hard when I chose what A-levels to do, because I was in that weird dream state at the time when we believed it didn't really matter because all we were going to do was the band anyway. But now the band didn't exist, and I was stuck doing subjects that meant nothing to me. French, because it's always good to have a language, so my dad said; something called Communication Studies, the point of which I never quite understood, so a bit of a breakdown in communication there, I suppose; and English Literature, which was a laugh really, just reading books for two years. I wish I'd kept it up, to be honest. I guess it was a shock to the system for all of us in some way. We'd lost the band, and Thomas had lost his gang, so we were all pretty aimless for a bit. But the one who really couldn't handle it was Neil. Neil changed.

I found that out that beautiful first day in early autumn. The trees were beginning to turn golden on the Fields, the sunlight was incredible and the air felt fresh as I cycled through. I passed loads of other kids, and if they were walking and I knew them I said hello, and if they were on their bikes then I rode with them. Everyone was really excited. When we got there we found this crazily modern-looking building, with loads of unusual round windows, and light fittings that looked like flaming torches and stuff. We all waited outside for the big welcome speech and, OK, I was feeling a bit stupid about the metal gear, but other than that, I was hyped up like everybody else, when, out of the corner of my eye, I saw a figure I vaguely recognised, standing on his own. He was wearing a black polo neck, his hair shaved to a number two, with thick-rimmed glasses that wouldn't stay on his face properly, through which he was looking about as if everything around

218

him was vomit. Then I realised. It couldn't have been, but it was. It was Neil. And then he was gone.

We were all ushered into the main hall for the speech. All very liberal. You're adults, we will treat you as adults, we respect you, we won't discriminate, please don't bring a knife in, blah, blah, blah. Then we were given a map and a welcome pack of various bits of crap, and sent off to our first tutorials. After wandering round the maze of a spaceship that was the college, I finally found the right room. I waited outside for about five minutes, until some townie oik barged past me and walked straight in.

'You can just go in,' he said.

There were a load of chairs in a circle. Quite comfy ones with padding, not like the old stacking chairs that really hurt your arse in school. The oik was already slouched down in one. I sat on the other side, careful not to face him directly. Neither of us said anything. He exhaled long and loudly, turning it into a tune at the end. More townie oiks, girls and boys, fresh from schools the other side of the city, came in, wearing their Naf Naf jackets that made them all look like the Michelin Man. The sitting oik knew most of them already, and he called the boys 'mate' and the girls 'babe'. Outnumbered, I thought I was going to be the social outcast of the tutor group. Until Neil turned up.

He poked his head round the door. He sighed when he saw all the townies. Then he saw me and sighed some more. He realised that the only way he was going to get a seat was if he sat near me, and sighed yet again. He sat down.

'Hi, Neil,' I said.

'All right,' he mumbled, almost inaudibly.

'What do you think of this place, then?' I said. 'Pretty crazy building, huh?'

219

'Postmodern crap,' he sneered.

'Really?'

'Yes, really,' he replied, as if I was retarded.

Fortunately at that moment I was saved because Will, still hobbling slightly from being pushed down the slope at the bonnie by Thomas, and one of the Jameses came in. Neil saw them and sighed.

They sat either side of me and we chatted for a bit, until our tutor arrived with a register. Middle-aged woman in casual clothes. Jeans and a woolly jumper. Bad, scraggly hair. She sat down in a spare seat, one exactly the same as ours, not a proper teacher's chair or anything, and let us talk loudly and eff and blind to our heart's content until she was ready to start.

She asked for our attention in a little meek voice, and by the third time of asking, she had just about got it, the townies shushing each other as loudly as they talked. She introduced herself by her first name and then went through some clarification of what the tutor group was for, and how often we were meant to turn up and stuff like that. And then she said, 'Right, what I'd like us to do now is a little exercise to help us get to know each other better. What I want you to do is to pair up, and I want each of you to tell your partner who you are and a few things about yourself, such as your hobbies, what music you like, or films, things like that. And what I also want you to do is to say something about what you want to do in the future. Where you would like your life to be headed. Then I want each of you to report back to the group what it was your partner told you. OK, let's go!'

I paired with Will because it was easy. I already knew him. James didn't want to work with Neil because he'd always thought he was a bit weird, even before the whole gig thing, so he ended up with some townie girl, which I don't think he minded because she had big tits and a low-cut top, and Neil was with some poor Asian lad. We had about five minutes to do it. The room was a pit of townie noise as they discussed their love of banging techno and street corners.

'All right! All right!' shrilled the tutor. 'Let's stop now!' Another round of loud shushing followed, and eventually the last townie was silenced. 'Now what I want us to do is to go round the room and each of us tell the group what they found out about their partner. We'll start from my left.'

The townies all pretty much told the same story about how their partner liked rave and/or hip-hop and just liked 'hanging out with their mates', which of course meant taking drugs and vandalising bus shelters. I told them about Will's swimming trophies, and Will told them about . . . what could he tell them? About the band? Or about the bonnie and drinking Napalm? No, I just told him to say that I was about to start Venture Scouts, which was like Scouts but for older kids and loads harder, with mountaineering and stuff, and girls were allowed to do it and everything, and that I liked to 'hang out'. I didn't even try to claim I 'hung out' with anyone I could call a 'mate'. The big-titted townie, meanwhile, liked ten-pin bowling and 'hanging out'. James liked watching *The Mary Whitehouse Experience* and doing tae kwon do. I knew full well he hadn't been for two years.

Then it was the Asian lad's turn to describe Neil. He didn't look as if he wanted to do it. 'He said his name was Neil,' he began. 'That he likes being in a band but his band doesn't want to play with him any more. His favourite music is someone called, uh, Throbbing Gristle? And I think . . .' There was a long pause. 'I think he wants to . . . blow things up.'

221

The tutor's mouth fell open, revealing a good few fillings in her bottom teeth. 'Blow. Things. Up?' she said.

'Yeah, is that what you meant?' asked the Asian kid of Neil.

Neil said nothing.

'What . . . kind of things does he want to blow up?' asked the tutor, looking very, very concerned.

'Ummm. I think . . .' Another long pause from the Asian kid. 'Everything, really. I think he wants to blow up everything.'

'You mean, buildings, property, even people?'

'Uhhhh . . . yeah. Yeah, that's pretty much what he said.'

'I see,' said the tutor, quietly. 'Neil, what did your partner tell you about himself?'

'He told me his name was Sanjit and that he was a sheep.'

'I didn't!' protested the Asian kid. 'Miss, I didn't say that.'

'Not "Miss",' said the tutor. 'Please, call me Hilary. Neil, Sanjit says that he didn't say that.'

'He didn't say it,' said Neil.

'But you said that he did. Are you not taking this seriously?'

'He didn't say he was one. But you asked me what he told me, and what he said about his silly, boring life and his silly, boring way of looking at things told me that he was a sheep. A total, stupid idiot who was going to do exactly what he was told to by his parents, by the government, the media and by the multinational company he'll no doubt end up working for. A perfect son, a model employee and a happy consumer. A sheep. Not even that. A robot. A robot sheep! Look in his head and there's nothing there! Nothing—'

'Neil, that's enough.'

'Nothing to indicate he even has a brain to think for himself and question what he's—'

222

'Neil, that's enough!'

Neil stopped and sighed. 'What's the point?' he muttered. 'You don't want real answers, you just want sugary crap.'

Sanjit was crying. 'OK, I think we'd better stop there,' said the tutor. No one moved. 'You can go!' The townies shuffled out, their Naf Naf jackets rustling as they giggled. Neil had just earned himself a whole new set of enemies.

The tutor went to sit by Sanjit and offered him a tissue.

'Neil,' she said as he got up, 'could I see you in five minutes, please?'

He shrugged and left the room.

2

It was tough adapting to the new Neil, not just for me, but for everybody. Kids from school would go up to him, expecting him to go on about fish and lard and all that surrealist crap, and he'd just tell them to get a lobotomy because it would make them more intelligent. And if you ever reminded him of something he said or did not so long ago, like the screaming at the talent show, he'd just shake his head and turn his face away as if it was too painful to deal with.

He was in my English class. He'd sit there, looking bored, as if he knew it all already, and fair enough, he had read more books than the rest of the class combined, but if anybody said anything, like the book made them sad, or they didn't understand it, he'd tut loudly and roll his eyes behind his new glasses. Sometimes he'd just lay into some poor soul, usually a sweet bookish girl, and accuse them of being 'naive', or 'sentimental', or 'brainwashed'. The English teacher tried to put a lid on it, but she didn't want to restrain him too much as he was the only person in the class who ever said anything intelligent. Often he'd be the only person in the class who'd read the book.

I didn't go out of my way to speak to him any more, but just the mildest greeting would result in a torrent of interrogation and accusations. I remember once I was talking about getting the new Senseless Things album, and he just had a go at me about it. Well, about rock music in general. He said something like, 'Rock music is the result of the appropriation by white people of musical forms developed by blacks whilst enslaved and socially degraded. Without slavery and segregation, rock music would not exist. What would you rather, a world in which slavery never existed, but as a consequence also no rock music, or one with both?'

'Well, I suppose it would have to be the one without the slave trade,' I said, finding it a bit of a chore to think about it, truth be told.

'So then you wouldn't have your wonderful new Senseless Things album. Would you be happy about that?'

'Uh, I guess . . .'

'What, no rock music at all? No Hendrix, no Metallica, no Motörhead, no Napalm Death, nothing?' It was quite hurtful that he'd mentally been keeping a list of all the music I'd been into over the past year or two seemingly just to throw it back in my face now. But what was my answer?

'It's a stupid question,' I said, 'because you can't turn back time. It's all already happened.'

'Yes, it's what's called a hy-po-thet-ic-al question,' he said, breaking down each syllable of the word for me to digest with my feeble mind. He shook his head and sighed. 'Never mind. You don't get it, do you?'

'No, I guess I don't.'

Another time I got one over on him, though. He was having a go at some lad who was doing Business Studies as one of his subjects. 'Why do you want to sully your soul like that?' he was saying. 'An A-level in Oppression Studies!'

I couldn't take any more of this crap. 'Neil,' I said, 'if it wasn't for people setting up businesses and employing people, you

225

wouldn't be able to listen to any of the music you like, not the Velvet Underground, not Iggy and the Stooges, not your precious Throbbing Gristle, or read any of your clever books. You wouldn't have your sodding polo neck or your lovely glasses. They were all made and sold to you by businesses and business people. So fucking lay off.'

'I'm not asking people not to use businesses,' he replied. 'You can't escape them. But what I do think is that people should stop being so fucking dense and unquestioning about it all and think about what's going on!'

'Of course, because nobody else thinks but you. It's just you who's worked it all out. And everybody else is a stupid sheep who never questions anything. Has it ever occurred to you that maybe sometimes other people do think about it all, and maybe they don't like it, but they have to get by, and live their lives, and provide for their family? So they compromise, because unlike you, they're not just locked up in their own little worlds, and have responsibilities and some desire to actually connect with people?'

I had no idea I had that inside me. Neil said nothing. For a second I thought he was going to cry. It nearly made me cry too. Because this was all beneath him. It was as if he'd become less intelligent now that he was bitter. What had happened to him in those two weeks between that final phone call to Jase and the first day of term? The horrible wake-up to reality he must have experienced in order to pick up that telephone in the first place must have been over-whelming. All the things that he'd been denying for all that time would have hit him at once. The fact that all his friends, his band, had shafted him. That someone wanted to see him hurt so much they broke a poor girl's spirit just to do it. The fact that I didn't stop it. The grim reality that regardless of whatever conceptual spin

226

he tried to put on it, what he did at the gig hadn't really worked. The way he really felt about his mum being such a weirdo. And where had his dad been all those years anyway? And most importantly, the realisation that even though he'd pretended on a day-to-day basis, year in, year out, for as long as I'd known him, that he didn't give a shit what people thought of him, he really did. Christ. It must have been devastating.

What he never understood, though, was that at college it was different. Nobody was thinking about the summer any more. He could have made a new start and it would have been fine. New friends. New opportunities. Parties. Beer. Girls. He could have had it all, if he'd reached out for it. It was there for the taking. No one would have stopped him. And he nearly did have it, a taste of happiness, not long before. But we'd stomped all over it, gleefully, maliciously. No wonder he had no faith left.

But one thing I will say for Neil during that time. He was the only one who saw through Spencer Macleavy for the poser he was from the off. Spencer Macleavy was the college punk. He had a very mild Mohican dyed green, a safety pin through a gangrenous hole in his left ear, a rucksack with an anarchy symbol painted in Tipp-Ex, a leather jacket and Tartan bondage trousers. He used to wander round, shouting 'Pogue mahone!' at random people. They'd just look at him funny and carry on doing what they were doing. Then one day he did it to Neil while he was in the dinner queue. Neil just gave him a withering look and said, 'Yes, I know it's Gaelic for "kiss my arse". Every Pogue fan knows that, because that's where they got their name from. The entire population of Ireland also knows that, because they speak Gaelic there. You're about as subversive as Tesco's. Try harder.'

227

Spencer ran off with his bondage strap between his legs and you never heard him say 'Pogue mahone!' again.

Unfortunately I heard him say a whole load of other stuff, and sing it. I was in the smoking sheds one day, not smoking, when Ben came up to me. 'We've found a new singer for the band!' he said. The band. I didn't even know the band was meant to continue. I hadn't wanted to think about it at all, although having Neil's glaring presence around me practically every day made that difficult.

'Really?' I said, as if waking from a dream. 'Who?'

'Spencer Macleavy!' said Ben. 'Thomas tried him out and he said he's really great!'

'Oh, right,' I said. That meant nothing to me any more.

'We're going to have a practice this Thursday night.'

'Where?' We couldn't really go round Neil's.

'Oh, Spencer knows a place.'

The place in question was a warehouse on the outskirts of town. It was pretty close to the one where Thomas's dad worked, and not that far away from the social club. It was an even more depressing sight than that fucking place from the outside, as our dads dropped us off for that first rehearsal. Spencer had cadged a ride down with Thomas. He got out first to unlock the enormous doors of the warehouse. He stepped inside, and one after another a series of lights could be seen coming on through the reinforced windows. Just like in the old days, we began hulking the gear into the building, players and dads alike. Spencer just stood by the door as we hauled in the heavy amps and drums. Inside it was a symphony in brown and grey, boxes stacked everywhere, and not a shred of joy in the place. You could lose your soul working somewhere like this, I thought; it's worse than the newsagents. We brought in the final piece of equipment, the big heavy bass amp. Spencer still hadn't lifted a finger. He was now slouched in a corner, chuckling to himself. 'That's the good thing about being the singer,' he said, 'you don't have to carry anything.'

We should have taken that as a warning sign and told him to fuck off. But we didn't. Instead, we went ahead with the practice. In fact, we set up the mike for him and everything. Just that day, we'd managed to get our old mike off Neil, who had been looking after it during his tenure in the band. It wasn't easy, as he'd goaded Ben into an argument over Jimi Hendrix being gay just before he eventually agreed to go home and fetch it for the next period, but we did it.

After the usual twenty minutes of faffing about from Jase on the drum kit, Spencer finally got up from his crouching position and in a brief moment of calm asked, 'All right, what are we gonna do, then?'

What were we going to do? The old stuff? Neil's songs? That felt very, very wrong to me, like desecrating a grave.

'We haven't written anything yet,' said Thomas.

'We just jam,' said Ben.

'What about my stuff?' said Jase. '"Soul in Torment" anybody?'

We all pretended we hadn't heard him.

'Do you know any Pistols?' said Spencer.

'Nah, not really,' said Thomas.

'Well, do you know "Johnny B. Goode"?'

'Yeah.'

'We can do that, but we'll do it the Pistols way.'

And we did. Well, we just played it the way we always played it, but Spencer sang it in a Johnny Rotten whine, complete with a word-perfect recreation of the can't-be-arsed ad-libs that Rotten had come up with sixteen years earlier.

We did that for what seemed like for ever. Then we just played some awful sludge that we made up on the spot, with Spencer whining vaguely anarchic things over the top, like 'Never trust a hippy!' or 'Ever get the feeling you've been cheated!' or, most weirdly, 'Love is two minutes and fifty-two seconds of squelching noises!' It was awful really.

But for some reason we kept coming back for more. Every week we wouldn't know what to play. We'd suggest stuff to Spencer, but he'd shoot it down because whatever it was, he'd always say it was a love song, and there wasn't room for love in Spencer's musical world, just hate. Then Spencer would suggest something which fitted into his rather bleak world view, and he'd do it like he was Johnny Rotten. Invariably it would turn out there was a Sex Pistols version of that song already. Then we'd jam for a bit and more old punk slogans would have the cobwebs blown off them and turned into some excuse for lyrics, until it was time to go home, which got earlier and earlier every week.

I hated every minute. I think we all did. It was as if we were putting ourselves through it as some sort of purgatory. Maybe if we did this, we thought, or at least I did, a little bit, we'd feel less bad about what had happened before. It didn't work.

By the fourth or fifth week, we'd accepted the inevitable and were working out the chords of Sex Pistols songs at home. Don't get me wrong, I quite like the Sex Pistols, did even then, but I didn't like them that much. I didn't like them so much I wanted to play in what had become in effect a Sex Pistols tribute band. But still, that's what we did, and come December, we had most of *Never Mind the Bollocks, Here's the Sex Pistols* pretty much down, along with some non-album B-sides and the out-takes found on *The Great Rock 'n' Roll Swindle* soundtrack.

We'd look forward to each rehearsal with less and less enthusiasm, knowing that we were demeaning ourselves, and knowing that we had once been part of something a lot more special. 'I wish we were still playing with Neil,' said Jase finally in the smoking shed one lunchtime.

None of us could stand Spencer. Not only was he lazy, unimaginative and a total parasite, constantly cadging fags, lifts and lager off people, without ever providing anything in return, but he wasn't even good company. One week, he pissed nearly all of us off when we were having a five-minute break between recreating side one and side two of *Never Mind the Bollocks*. 'Right,' he said, 'what do your dads do?'

He looked at me first. 'Uh, he works for an insurance company,' I said.

'Yeah, thought so,' he said, 'middle class. Bourgeois. You'll be first up against the wall when the revolution comes.'

'Cheers,' I said.

'What about you, Ben?'

'He's a taxi driver,' said Ben.

'Good man,' said Spencer. 'Good working-class occupation. Real proper job.'

'Hang about!' I said. 'His dad earns far more than mine does! Ben doesn't even have to go out to work! I do!'

'Bloody right, he shouldn't go to work,' said Spencer. 'Working's for tossers.'

'But you just said that it was great that his dad was a taxi driver. You can't have it both ways!'

'I fucking well can,' he said. 'Taxi drivers are fantastic, but compared to people who don't work, they're tossers. The underclass, mate, that's where it's all going to happen.'

By the end of the conversation it was established that Jase and I didn't deserve to live, but that after the revolution Ben and Thomas would be treated like royalty because their dads were manual labourers. Not that Thomas's dad was really, but he worked in the vicinity of some heavy boxes, so that made him OK. Compared to Spencer's, Neil's arguments actually seemed to make sense.

I think the final straw came when Spencer wanted us to learn 'Friggin' in the Riggin'', some dirty comedy song the Sex Pistols did after Johnny Rotten had left. Me and Ben listened to the tape Spencer had done us round Ben's house one afternoon. It had to end.

Not long after that, in the final week before the Christmas holidays, me, Thomas and Jase walked down Birch Tree Avenue, the distinctly suburban-looking street where Spencer lived with his mum and dad and sister, in a large four-bedroom house with garage and sizeable front and back gardens. We made our way up the long, winding path through the front lawn and between the gnomes, into the porch and to the front door. I pressed the doorbell, and it played 'Greensleeves'. A balding man in a red V-neck jumper, shirt and tie opened the door.

'Can I help you?' he said, as if he was a butler or something.

'Could we speak to Spencer, please?'

'Just a moment.'

He trudged upstairs. 'Spencer? Spencer?' he called, the plum in his mouth almost getting in the way of his words. 'There are some young men to see you.'

The sound of bondage trousers clinking made its way down the stairs, closely followed by Spencer himself.

'Hi, guys,' he said, 'what's happening?'

For some reason, I was the spokesman. Pissed me off a bit. Especially as Ben didn't even bother showing.

'Spencer,' I said, 'well, there's no easy way for me to say this, so I'm just going to say it. We don't want to be in a band with you any more. Sorry.'

Suddenly Spencer was a five-year-old boy looking back at us. His eyes went watery. 'Merry fucking Christmas,' he blubbed, and slammed the door.

3

By the following September, we had played our first gig, as just the four of us. A lot had happened in that year, mostly involving our cocks. Thomas had broken up with Jenny, then got back together again, then broken up, and got back together, and so on, several times. Usually the pattern would be that one of them would declare the relationship finished because they were pissed off with the other one, then Jenny would immediately be seen out with another guy, usually someone several years older, which is quite creepy looking back on it now, then go out of her way to stick her tongue down his throat in public, and let him shag her senseless for a fortnight, even up the arse on a couple of occasions, rumour has it. Then she'd get back together with Thomas, until the next crisis, and they'd have loud make-up sex for a week. People said you could hear her in the street, but I don't know if that's true. Her dad's liberal policy on letting her have boyfriends stay over must have been stretched to the limit, though. Poor guy. That must mess with your head, listening to that.

Jase always had loads of girls. Some he went out with, some he just shagged on the floor of the bathroom at parties. And I'd finally done it. For ages, I'd almost lost interest. I'd already seen sixteen come and go while still a virgin. But it didn't bother me that much because there were loads of kids who still hadn't lost it by the time they were seventeen and they were OK, they weren't mongers. They were just a little more comfortable in themselves and had less to prove. Eighteen, though, that was just sad. But merely the thought of it brought back the bitter, sick taste of the summer, and, I don't know, I think it was having to see Neil all the time, it was as if he was haunting me. I just couldn't put my mind to it. Then sometime after my seventeenth birthday, I must have thought, fuck Neil. I mean, not fuck Neil, obviously, but forget about Neil. And fuck someone else.

It was on a Venture Scouts camping weekend. Those things are meant to be about orienteering and stuff, but really they're just an excuse for teenagers to shag in tents. They're affiliated with churches and everything. Someone needs to tell the vicar, I think. It was with a girl called Kelly. I could have done better, I suppose, but I knew she was dirty. There was a story going round about how she had refereed a speed-wanking competition in a tent one night with three of the boys, not even cool boys, three mongers really. They were nearly at the finish line when she just started sucking one of them off and swallowed it! Then she did another one, but the poor last guy got too excited and just sprayed the tent wall with a big jet of his cum. That's the story, anyway.

So one night, after we'd downed cider round the campfire, I started getting off with Kelly and we went into her tent and we did it. It wasn't that nice, partly because I was too desensitised from the alcohol to really feel anything, and the only noise she made was a single low grunt, but I definitely did it, it was definitely inside, pumping away, shrink-wrapped in a borrowed condom. Then I could feel the warm sensation of coming, and I just thought, 'Thank fucking Christ for that.' The next morning, when I came out of the tent, everybody was waiting, and gave me a big round of applause. I'd even had witnesses to verify this momentous occasion.

The ironic thing was, a few weeks later I met Caroline, so I could easily have lost it to someone I actually cared about. Ah well, you can't get too sad about that sort of thing. Meanwhile Ben wasn't shagging anybody, even though he'd say he'd done it loads of times. He just couldn't name names. He got a snog, though, I remember that.

And it was probably our collective sexual adventures that finally got us over our phobia of singing, and our bizarre idea that it was in some way an inherently homosexual thing to be doing. Thomas and Jase had been writing songs together, and when they called me and Ben round one afternoon to hear them, it was quite a surprise to hear them not just play them, but sing them. And not just that, their singing wasn't bad. Soon we were all in on the act, first me, and then Ben, who due to his lack of experience was probably the most worried that singing might reveal his latent homosexuality. But he needn't have worried, because Ben was the best singer of the lot of us, and his voice was very manly.

We'd found a new place to practise, some garage somewhere, and we had to pay for it, but we all had jobs except for Ben, who got wads of pocket money anyway. And we'd go there once a week, and we'd play. We only had the one mike and no PA, so we couldn't do harmonies or anything, but we'd share the vocals between us, putting them through a guitar amp like we did with Neil. Even Jase sang while he played the drums. Ben was definitely the best singer, though. We'd have given him all the songs to sing if he didn't grumble so much about having to do it. But he liked it secretly, I'm sure.

Anyway, we'd been playing together steadily for a good few

236

months throughout the spring, when Jase got talking to some guy behind the bar at the Falcon. The Falcon was the main student pub in Sholeham. We used to go there every Friday. We didn't always get served, but sometimes we did, depending on who was behind the bar. If it was this guy Gerald, some university student, I think, then we always would, unless the landlord was lurking about. So Jase was talking to Gerald, and telling him about the band, and Gerald said we should play at the Falcon as they'd just got a live music licence. And suddenly we had a gig.

We needed to get a set together. We were meant to play for an hour and a half because there was no support or anything, and there was no way we could fill that, so we just planned to play the same forty-five minutes of music twice. A lot of the songs we prepared were covers, which was right for a pub because you don't want too much unfamiliar material. Did a few REM songs, a bit of Crowded House, I think, some Jimi Hendrix, which sounded great with Ben singing in his gruff voice and playing lead at the same time, just like Jimi did. Our own stuff was quite fast, so we didn't think people would have that much of a problem with it. One song we were particularly hopeful for was called 'The Age of Teenage Hysteria'. 'We turn the page, enter the stage, feeling the rage, into the age of teenage hysteria,' was the hook line. I think it might have been about the youth club, or the bonnie. Probably the best song we ever did, after Neil left. It sounded quite like the Undertones, looking back on it.

So we played the gig. And it was fine. We called ourselves the Honey Trap. We'd have that name for the next four years. None of us knew what it meant. Jase had heard the phrase on TV and liked the sound of it. We weren't nearly as nervous as before, I think because we really believed that our stuff was good. I mean, we all liked it. And it was easy to like. It was well played, and the singing was good. And people did like it. OK, we packed it out with our friends and our girlfriends and everything, but the locals in the pub liked it too, people who didn't know who we were. Even Jenny approved. She made some snide remarks about Neil, pretty much along the lines of how much better we were without him. I think she'd got things the way she'd always wanted them.

Yeah, the gig went very well, a lot better than you would imagine for a first gig – well, first gig proper, anyway. There was one weird thing, though. During the second half of the set, or the second time we played the one set we had, whichever way you want to look at it, I was looking out, and you couldn't really see much except the bar, and there were quite a few people in the room, but I could have sworn I saw Neil at the back, standing by the stairs. He was just looking at us. He wasn't with anyone or anything. And then when I looked again, I couldn't see him. Once we'd finished I did a quick scout around the pub, but he wasn't anywhere. I asked a few people if they'd seen him, they all said no, except for Damien. I could talk to him now, I didn't give a shit about Hannah. Nobody saw her any more anyway. But Damien said he thought he'd seen Neil, but hadn't had a chance to speak to him, and that was all. It was as if he'd appeared and disappeared like a ghost. I never thought to mention it to Neil when I saw him next, but it really did look like he was there.

4

And then, nothing happened. Or if anything happened, it was just the same things happening over and over again, which is only slightly better. But in the long run, it all adds up to a big load of nothing, pretty much. At least that's how it feels looking back on it. I mean, obviously stuff happened, stuff always happens. But as we waded through all that little everyday stuff – the exams, the jobs, the relationships, the living – slowly, step by step, we screwed up.

It started out all right at first. It seemed to, anyway. We got asked back to play the Falcon a lot, and by the time we were finishing our A-levels, coming to see us play there was a bit of a social event for the college kids. We had quite a few songs now, some of them pretty good. We always went down well, and Ben even finally got to do it. With a girl, I mean. He was going on about it for days afterwards, which was funny because he was meant to have done it loads of times already, so it shouldn't have been that much of an event.

And I'd met Caroline. Friend of a friend, not even at college. Worked in a shop, selling pens, nice ones, not biros. She was about a year older than me, and I wouldn't say she was what I consider my type. Thin, not that stylish, not very well stacked. Not like the little doll girls with tits I'd gone for before. But I think that was why she made me feel good. I knew that she'd never take me to the dark place that going out with Hannah had led me to. She was a grown-up. Strong emotionally. Comforting. Comfortable.

I don't know, maybe I loved her back then. I probably did. But as time went on, she was always just there, and nothing seemed to happen to us. Things would never develop. Every day was pretty much the same. I'd go round hers week nights. She'd come round to see me at my parents' at the weekend. Of course, we'd do things like go on holiday to Cornwall and stuff. And we'd hang out with friends down the pub and we'd go to a rock club every fortnight or so. But it didn't take us long to get settled into our routine, and we were doing it for nearly four years. Only the band, and the vague notion that I was meant to be trying to get somewhere with it, stopped us from discussing seriously in those four years whether we should be having kids.

But in the band we never really talked about stuff much, what we were doing with our lives. I think we saw that as a sign of weakness. Not even back when we'd nearly finished our A-levels, and we were all thinking about what we were going to do next. The thing was, Thomas and me were actually doing OK with our coursework and it looked likely we could both easily get into university. Not Oxford or Cambridge or anything, but some jumped-up poly was well within our reach. Jase and Ben would be lucky to pass. Jase was never that academic, and Ben couldn't be arsed. But me and Thomas, we had a chance. We also knew, though, that if we went away, that would be the end of the band. We'd heard about other local bands that tried to stay together even when members went to uni and only played in the summer and Christmas, but it never worked. They'd always start playing with other people at uni and that would be that. Long-distance bands are harder to maintain than long-distance relationships, I reckon.

We might have stayed at home to study, but the local uni didn't do any courses we wanted to do. So we decided, individually, without really discussing it, that we were all going to get full-time jobs. Nothing too demanding, because that would interfere with the band, and we'd all live at home with our parents to keep our lives simple, but enough to support us while we worked towards our goal. My parents didn't mind really, as long as I was capable of making a living. Sometimes I wish they'd pushed me a bit harder. Looking back, if we'd only defined a bit more clearly what our goal was, then maybe we would have stood a chance of getting there.

Jase was already working nearly full-time at his dad's garage anyway, which is half the reason why his grades were so shit. Thomas finally gave up his beloved paper round. Me and him both signed up with an agency. They got me various admin jobs in offices. Dull stuff mostly, filing, data entry. Photocopying. But still, I got a bit of money coming in, and I started saving up for a new guitar. Took me a while, but I finally had enough for a pretty decent one. As good as Ben's, at least. They got Thomas a job mending snack and drinks machines. It was only meant to be temporary. Little did he know he'd still be doing it four years later.

Ben went on the dole, of course. Made no effort to find any work at all. Just sat on his arse for years while his parents waited on him hand and foot and picked up his shit after him. I mean, he literally did nothing, not a single household chore, and just sponged. In the end, the dole office told him he had to actually get a job or they'd take his benefit away. He'd been filling up that little book they give you with lies for absolutely bloody ages, about all these jobs he'd supposedly applied for, even made up interviews he'd gone on, but he hadn't really done anything at all. Then when they were one week from taking his money away, he finally got a job on the bins. Pretty ironic that he'd end up picking up other people's shit.

In time, I proved myself to the agency and they found me a permanent position in a bank, just fiddling behind a computer with stacks of application forms, trying to convert people's illegible scrawl into usable information. And, Christ, it was dull. But it was all dull, really. Not just work, but the band, Caroline eventually, everything. It took Neil to make things come alive again.

The band. Four years in a nutshell. Once we'd finished at college, we decided we should play gigs somewhere other than the Falcon. We weren't that great at persuading anyone to book us, so my sister Nicki, who I now had realised was actually a person and not just my older sister, said she'd be, well, our manager, I guess. She wanted to go into events management, so it was good practice for her. Something for the CV, anyway. And pretty soon we had a lot of gigs lined up. The problem was, without college, it was difficult to get people to come to them. Our friends would be there, and our girlfriends, and their friends, but we could never really fill a room, and sometimes landlords would get grumpy about that. Still, we always played well, and people enjoyed it, so usually we were all right. But we never built a following. The people who enjoyed one gig would never come to the next, even when they said they would and we gave them the details and everything. No matter how much and how well we played, we just could not get the people to come back again. And you need a following if anybody in the music industry's

242

going to pay attention to you, which they never did, however many demo tapes we sent out.

Another thing that went wrong, in retrospect, is that we got into the Eagles. Well, not just the Eagles, but that whole laid-back West Coast sound, Fleetwood Mac and that. Don't know why really, just felt safe, comforting, like metal used to be. And by this point we could afford our own PA so we could do harmony vocals. Our songs got slower, we used acoustic guitars more, and we even started playing on stools. We actually bought some stools specially for the purpose.

The problem was that our friends weren't into that West Coast stuff the way we were, and it was harder to win over the regulars of wherever we were playing. And looking back on it, the songs we came up with weren't that great. They didn't really go anywhere, and they didn't have any proper hooks, so they just didn't stick in the mind. I remember one was called 'Epitome'. The problem was that Jase had only ever seen the word written down, so he wrote this chorus that went 'You're the epitome', and had it rhyming with 'And I never want to roam'. I think it was Jenny who pointed out that the 'e' wasn't silent. It made me miss Neil right then. Neil would have known that, I thought, and he wouldn't have been an arse about pointing it out like Jenny was, at least the Neil I used to know anyway.

Ah Jenny. We freed ourselves of Jenny in, I think, '97. After breaking up with Thomas umpteen times, she finally ran off with a skiing instructor she'd met taking lessons on a slope at the sports centre in preparation for a holiday with her mum. Her parents had divorced a couple of years earlier and, Christ, did she go on about it. Hours and hours of Thomas's time wasted listening to her whingeing about how it made her feel. But he needn't have bothered because she ended up shagging the ski instructor and moving to be with him in a village about ten miles away. I'm pretty sure they had kids, and I think someone saw her once and she'd put on loads of weight. I'd like to see her get into her stupid stripy trousers now.

So Jenny was out of the picture, thank Christ. Unfortunately, she took half our audience with her. On the plus side, Jase finally stopped shagging everything in sight and got a proper girlfriend called Charlotte, or Charlie, for short. She brought along a few of her friends to every gig, but nowhere near the gang that Jenny could command. By this point Jase was making good money, probably a bit too much money, I was later to discover, and moved out of his parents' house and got a flat with Charlie.

But generally things were just winding down. Slowly, so slowly, over four years, our audience got smaller. But we'd never stop and ask each other why. None of us could ever find the guts to stand up and say what we were doing was shit and we had to ditch it all and start again. None of us believed, quite enough, that we could do it. We never went out of our way to really make it happen. We didn't have the courage to stop either, so we'd just carry on. It was as if we were in a trap. Or a nightmare from which we couldn't wake up. And you know what, to be honest, if I had been in a car crash at that point, and lost a limb so that I couldn't play any more, I think I'd have been secretly fucking delighted. I'm pretty sure the same was true of the rest of them.

Mind you, we weren't the only band that was changing. When Britpop hit, or about six months after it hit, come to think of it, the Horned Gods finally ditched the leather jackets their dads had bought them, had their slightly long hair cut, all started wearing Fred Perry and mod target T-shirts, and changed their name to

Union Jack, which was exactly what they hung as their backdrop when they played the Falcon. Made it look like a National Front rally. They were really terrible. That was the last we heard of them, thank fuck. As for us, we never went all the way with Britpop. We liked Oasis and Cast and Dodgy, the blokier side of it, but bands like Suede or Gene or Chessington's World of Dementia weren't our thing at all. Way too ambiguous. Much too Neil.

It's easy to understand why it felt as if I'd been saved when I got the phone call from Neil. Nicki took it. She'd come round on Sunday afternoon to do some washing. She had a flat now too, with her boyfriend, Mark. I liked Mark. At least he wasn't smashing up Metallica records with a sledgehammer. Nicki burst into my room without knocking, something she'd always done, causing no end of anxiety during my earlier masturbation years. 'You'll never guess who's on the phone for you,' she said.

'No, who?' For a terrible moment I thought it might be Hannah.

'That weird friend you used to have – Neil.'

'You're fucking kidding me.'

'No, I'm not, and mind your fucking language.'

I went down the stairs into the hall where the phone waited for me. I hadn't seen Neil in nearly four years, not since we'd finished our A-levels. In fact, our English Literature exam must have been the last time I saw him. It's funny, he actually calmed down a lot towards the end of that year. He became less argumentative, more sullen, practically silent. People said they'd seen him hanging about St Edmond's, the posh bit of town that Louise lived in. He'd just be standing in the street looking at houses. Once or twice I saw him down the Falcon, but he always came on his own, and one time he turned up really drunk, as if he'd downed cans of Napalm or something, which wasn't like him at all. It was just embarrassing; he was shouting incoherently and really bothering people. I think he fell backwards over a table more than once.

I don't think he did that well in his A-levels. Apparently a lot of his coursework turned out weird, with rambling arguments that went nowhere, about loneliness being the only valid and authentic human experience. It wouldn't have been so bad, but that was for a Geography assignment. I remember in the last year of English Lit his essays became odd and he was no longer the teacher's darling. And he said practically nothing all year in lessons. The one thing he did say, which was really strange, was when the teacher asked if anybody had any questions at the end. Neil raised his hand and said, 'What effect does isolation have on the individual?'

Everybody just went, 'What?'

The teacher quickly moved on to something else.

I remember just before that last exam. We were all sitting waiting for the tutors to start the big clock, and tell us to turn our papers over to start. Neil was in the row to my left.

'Good luck,' I said.

'Thanks,' he mumbled.

'What are you going to do after this?'

'Art school,' said Neil.

'Really? Where?'

'Anywhere that will take me,' he replied.

'Is that what you want to do then, be an artist?'

'Everybody's an artist, Chris.'

'Yeah, but I mean, get paid for it and stuff.'

'I guess. I don't really think in those terms.'

'You haven't thought about making any more music?'

'We're making music now. We're talking, breathing, moving. It's all music. Silence is music too.'

'If you say so. Anyway, good luck.'

'Yeah,' he said. Then added, 'You too.' It was the first nice thing I'd heard Neil say in nearly two years.

I was told by someone later that because his grades were so bad, the only offer he got was from this little place in the middle of the Welsh countryside. And as far as I knew, that was where he'd ended up.

I picked up the phone.

'Hello?' I said.

'Hi, Chris, it's Neil.' He sounded chipper.

'Wow. Long time, no hear. How are you?'

'Ah, I'm OK. Listen, it's my degree show in a couple of weeks, and I was wondering if you'd like to come and have a look at it. I know you'd have to travel down a long way to Wales and everything . . .'

'Ah, well, I'm glad you thought of me, but—'

'You see, the thing is my mum died a couple of years ago, and there's no one else who could come. And I want someone to see it. So I was wondering if you'd like to.' He spoke fast. With nerves probably. Excitement too, though, I sensed. 'The opening's on a Friday, but you can come down on the Saturday if you like. You can still get in to see it then. That's if you don't work at weekends.'

'No, it's OK, I'll take some time off work. Yeah, sure, I'll be there.'

I said yes partly because his mad mum had died, obviously, but it certainly wasn't convenient, seeing as I'd be spending bloody hours on a train just to walk around looking at student paintings and stuff. I don't even look at proper paintings. But I knew I had to say yes, regardless of all that. Maybe I knew I'd lost something important, about four years ago, maybe five, and Neil was the only person who could find it for me. Or at least remind me of how to find it for myself.

'Great,' said Neil. 'I'll phone nearer the time with train times and stuff. I'll meet you at the station, if the System allows it.'

What the hell did that mean? Little did I know it, but I'd just been thrown into the heart of the latest manifestation of Neil's craziness. This would be like the screaming of the talent show, amplified a hundred times over.

5

I went by train because my car was in too bad nick to be trusted with such a long journey. We all had cars now, except Ben, of course – I had to pick him up every week to take him to band practice. The journey to Wales lasted fucking ages. I set off at half past eight in the morning or something, and I was still on it at four o'clock in the afternoon. I had to change twice, once at Bristol, then again, until finally I was on this slow stopping service working its way through all these tiny Welsh villages with their crazy names. Can't remember what they were called now, of course. Can't even remember the name of the place where Neil was studying. It wasn't much bigger than all the other places we stopped at. All those small towns. They could go on for ever. An eternity of them.

Finally, just as the blood was refusing to circulate round my body any more and I thought my left leg had fallen off, we pulled into the station. I got off the train, as did a bunch of other people. I presumed they were all going to the degree show too. Everybody dithered on the piss-smelling platform for a few seconds until somebody worked out where the exit was and we all followed like cattle. It was a bright sunny day. I was too hot in my jacket, but I had nowhere else to put it. I just had a small travelling bag where it would barely have fitted. We passed through the gate – there was no ticket hall – down some steps and into the car park. Neil was waiting for me.

'Hi, Chris,' he said, smiling. I nodded. I wasn't sure what to do at first. I walked over and shook his hand. He looked more or less the same. Not angry, not depressed, but, I don't know, strained, I guess. His eyes looked tired. He had an old leather satchel hanging from his shoulder. He was still wearing a black polo neck. It looked as tired as he was. I guessed it was the same one.

'Hi, Neil,' I said. 'How's it going?'

'Very well at the moment,' he said. 'Of course, that could all change.'

The fact that pretty much the first thing he said to me was weird suggested that nothing had changed. I had a horrible sinking feeling and suddenly regretted coming.

'Do you want to see the town?' said Neil. 'There's nothing really here, though, other than the art school.'

'Actually,' I said, 'is there somewhere we could get a drink? I'm pretty dehydrated.'

'I don't know,' said Neil. 'There used to be a drinks machine on the station, but they took it away because kids kept on pissing in it.'

'To be honest, I was thinking of a pub.'

'Oh, OK. Actually, what's the time?'

I looked at my watch.

'It's just gone seventeen minutes past four.'

'Right, we can go to a pub, but I can't guarantee I can stay in it after four thirty.'

'Ah, OK. Do you have to be somewhere?'

'I'll show you in a minute. It's a bit hard to explain.'

Neil clearly didn't know where to find a pub. He just looked into the distance awkwardly trying to spot one. Fortunately I could see one myself. I pointed, and Neil looked relieved.

250

By the time we'd got our pints, it was already nearly four thirty.

'You'd better drink up,' I said, 'if you're going to make it out of here by half four.'

'Well, I may have to leave my pint here if I do,' he said. 'There's no way round it really, if the System says I have to.'

'What system? I don't follow.'

'Here, I'll show you.'

He reached into his satchel and took out a ring binder and a calculator. He typed something in, and smiled slightly.

'It's OK,' he said, 'it was an even number.' He opened up the binder and quickly but neatly wrote something down.

'That's good, I guess.'

'Well, yes, it is. If it were an odd number then I'd have to find the corresponding activity and go out and do it.'

'Would you really?'

'Yes. That's the System. I generate a number at random between one and two hundred on the calculator. If it's an even number, I can carry on with whatever I'm doing. But if it's an odd number I've got to consult the table. Look.' He tapped on the calculator again. 'Now, I've just got ninety-one, which is an odd number. So if that had been the number I got just a minute ago, then I'd have had to look at the table.' He riffled through the binder until he found the page he was looking for. It looked like some sort of chart he'd coloured in with pencils. He ran his finger along one line of it. 'OK, ninety-one is . . . go swimming.'

'Neil, I know you can't swim.'

'Yes, but if I'd got ninety-one, I'd have to go out and learn, either in a swimming pool if it was open, or in a river if it wasn't.'

'That sounds very dangerous.'

'Yes, it would be.'

251

'And, uh, how often do you have to do this?'

'Every three hours.'

'And I suppose you'd have to stop at night, though.'

'No, not at all. If I'm asleep an alarm wakes me up and I have to do the numbers. Then I can work out if I can go back to sleep or if I have to get up and do something.'

'Neil,' I said, shaking my head, 'what's the fucking point?'

'Well, on a practical level, this is my piece for the degree show. I've been documenting it and I've filled a space with that. But if what you mean is, what's the philosophical reasoning behind it, it's this. I want to demonstrate the difference between a life lived and a life maintained. When I generate an even number, I have freedom to do whatever I choose, determined by what I genuinely believe to be moral and what I believe to have value. When I generate an odd number, however, I am a slave. I make the choice to give up the freedom to make further choices and hand it over to the System. I am not truly living, and am merely maintaining my existence, within the boundaries that the System dictates. And I would propose that in doing so, I am simulating the way in which many people in our society currently exist.'

'What do you mean?' I asked. I didn't like the way this was going.

'Well, take you as an example.' I knew it. 'I'm presuming you have a job, friends, maybe a girlfriend or a partner.'

'Yeah, what's wrong with that?'

'Nothing, if you can actually defend the reasons why you have these things. That's in relation to values that really matter to you. For instance, why do you have a job?'

'Because I have to pay bills, of course.'

'Fair point,' said Neil. 'But why do you have the job you have?

252

Do you enjoy it? Does it further any particular cause you strongly believe in?'

'No, not at all, and I don't enjoy it. It doesn't even pay very well. But it's just something to keep things ticking over while we try and get the band off the ground.'

I resented being interrogated in this way, it was like a low-key version of the sort of stuff he inflicted on people in the old English class, but I needed someone to ask me these things. These were questions that I'd built my life around avoiding having to answer, but now was the time, I knew.

'And is the band getting off the ground?'

'Well, we're gigging.'

'Touring? Record contract?'

'Well, no, but we're not quite ready for that yet.'

'But you've been playing for four years. Why aren't you ready?'

'I don't know.'

'Why are you doing the job you're doing?'

'I don't know.'

'Do you like your friends?'

'Yes. Some of them.'

'Do you love your girlfriend?'

'You can't ask me that, Neil. Of course I do.' I didn't. Right then, I knew I didn't. I just hadn't found the energy to change her for a new one. Or deal with not having one at all. But it had not occurred to me to think about it until that moment. And then it was clear.

'But you see what I mean, don't you?' said Neil. 'We often do things without thinking about why we do them. Or choose not to think. Or pretend not to think. Anyway, that's the point of the work.'

I felt as if I'd just been caught naked, like in a dream. Meanwhile, Neil seemed oblivious to the intensity of the violation he'd just committed. The room seemed to be moving. I thought for a second I was going to faint. Then I thought I was going to cry. Everything was over. None of it had been worthwhile.

'I think I might be hungry,' I said. 'Can we order some food?'

'Yeah, sure,' said Neil, as if it hadn't occurred to him that anyone stuck on a train all day might reasonably want feeding.

I ordered a burger and chips. Neil went for the vegetarian option.

'Back to the old tofu, then, Neil?' I said. Neil had been a vegetarian for most of his teenage years. Then when he turned angry, he'd stopped. It had been quite a shock seeing him biting into a chicken drumstick in the college canteen.

'Yeah,' he said, 'unless the System tells me otherwise.'

Over food we discussed mundane things, music mostly. I was surprised to find I'd actually heard of a lot of the things Neil was mentioning. Gram Parsons, Gene Clark, Dennis Wilson, Van Dyke Parks, Townes Van Zandt. He talked briefly about his mum dying, but only in a matter-of-fact-way. Cancer. Same old story.

By the time we'd waited for and eaten our food, it had gone half five. We had to get moving for the exhibition. Neil led me through the old town, a grey place of creepy old buildings and depressing new ones, to the art school. The school was like a spaceship that had landed in the town. It was similar to our old college, but where that had been crazy, this was very sensible. Straight lines, everything white. Lots of glass.

There were already quite a few people gathering on the lawn. People's parents mostly. Everybody was dressed up except us. I had no idea you were meant to. Neil obviously didn't care. As we walked through the crowd, the odd student would nod at Neil, but no one really acted as if they knew him. Four years, and it seemed he hadn't made that much of an impression on anybody.

The exhibition didn't start until six, but Neil said we could walk on in anyway. I didn't really understand a lot of the stuff. No idea if it was any good or not. There were paintings, some that were just splodges of paint, and some that were paintings of things, but painted really badly. Then there were sculptures that were just welded metal, or loads of foam painted brown. One thing I remember was that someone had got loads of Kleenex boxes and put the health warnings from cigarette packets on them, only they'd changed the word 'smoking' to 'wanking', so they now read things like 'WANKING KILLS', or 'WANKING SERIOUSLY HARMS YOU AND OTHERS AROUND YOU', or 'WANKING CAUSES AGEING OF THE SKIN'. I knew what Thomas would say about it all: 'What a load of wank.' A few other things stick in my mind: a door wrapped in tinfoil, little models of people at a supermarket made out of dried fruit. Besides that it was just stuff like people taking photographs of their trainers and words on card and things.

We finally got to Neil's space. By this point the exhibition was officially open and there were various smartly dressed people milling around with glasses of red and white wine or orange juice in their hands. Neil's room was absolutely full of stuff. Shelves with rows and rows of folders full of paper, detailing exactly what the System had told him to do every three hours. Some of the activities were documented with photographs or ticket stubs, or cuttings from the *Radio Times* of what he'd watched on television. Along one wall were giant-size versions of the tables from his ring binder, this time arranged in a big star formation, very tastefully coloured, and neatly printed and laminated. I think everybody presumed you weren't meant to touch because no one was looking at the folders. Ignoramus that I am, it never occurred to me that might be the case, so I flicked through a whole load of them. Apparently Neil had tried his hand at various sports, such as hockey, paintballing and darts. Photos of him failing to play any of them competently accompanied the text. Also, he'd been to see most new releases in the cinema, but had rarely made it to the end of any of them. In fact, he'd obviously insisted on buying tickets for films that were only five minutes from the end. He'd been on train journeys to places he had no reason to go to, only to go back home as soon as he got there. He'd knitted. He'd licked a post box. For three hours. He'd bought a woman's hat. On more than one occasion, he'd stayed up to half past four in the morning watching the test card. Most worryingly, he'd stood staring through the gates of a primary school. For three solid hours. Perhaps the strangest of all were the photographs of him standing outside closed shops, churches and offices in the middle of the night, sometimes in the pouring rain, unable to get in to do whatever he was being commanded to do, but nevertheless going as far as he could.

'Neil,' I said, 'exactly how long have you been doing this?'

He didn't want to answer.

'Neil, how long?'

'Three years,' he said quietly. 'But this is the end of it all. At half past seven, I do the numbers for the last time. And then, at ten thirty, it's all over.'

'Well, thank fuck for that. Neil, this is insane.'

'Yes, yes it is! But that's the point! So's everything else!'

256

I didn't want to argue. I just wanted it to end so I could go home again. I'd agreed to stay at Neil's that night, but I'd be gone first thing in the morning. I didn't want to be around this at all.

Some of Neil's classmates asked him what grade he'd got. He said he didn't know.

'How do you find out?' I asked him.

'Oh, there's a board with it all posted up on it somewhere,' he said.

'Aren't you curious?'

'No, not really. I expect I'll find out eventually.'

The place was heaving now. People were finally following my example and picking up the folders. Some of them looked puzzled, a few old posh ladies snorted with disapproval and went on about the way 'anybody could do that' and how 'he was just trying to shock'. God knows what Neil must have been doing in some of the photos. Other people laughed, and some nodded their heads because they must have got it, whatever there was to get.

I looked at my watch. It was already nearly seven thirty. Neil got his calculator ready. Then, at half past seven precisely, he conjured up his last number. He walked over to his giant wall-mounted laminated chart. He ran his finger along and found the corresponding command.

'Oh no,' he said to himself. I couldn't hear him but I could see that was the shape his mouth was making, over and over again. Then he stopped.

He closed his eyes and bowed his head, tapping no doubt into reserves of courage. He opened his eyes, and spun around.

'Your art is shit!' he shouted at some poor earnest-looking student.

'You've slept with too many people for someone your age and you know it!' he said, glaring at a girl in a slinky outfit.

'You're too old to be here!' The target was some doddery old woman in tweed.

'You're too fat for your trousers!' A plump red-faced man shuffled and looked down awkwardly.

'Shut up, Neil,' someone said.

I looked at the chart until I found the place where Neil had run his finger. It said, 'Try to hurt the feelings of everybody you see.'

'You smell funny!'

'Your walk is effeminate, yet you're not gay!'

'The patches in your beard make you look pathetic!'

'You're a coward who doesn't have the guts to do things properly!'

It took me a second to realise he was talking to me.

In the meantime everybody was telling him to be quiet, some people were swearing, and somebody had grabbed his shoulder in an attempt to motion him outside. A few of the girls were crying, and so was the old lady. A big burly man with a grey-flecked beard walked in.

'Your teaching methods are self-indulgent and ultimately ineffective!'

'Come on, Neil, calm down,' said his tutor. He turned to a student and mumbled something about a man called Bob.

'You're not as popular as you think you are!'

'The theory behind your work is pretentious!'

Bob arrived. He was wearing a security jumper with patches on the elbows.

'You have undiagnosed learning difficulties!'

258

'All right, you, out!' said Bob.

As more and more people crowded in to see what was going on, Neil's workload grew proportionately.

'You'll never get gallery representation!'

'Your boyfriends leave you because you're possessive!'

'You're simply not good enough. Give up!'

'Right, that's it,' said Bob. He grabbed Neil in a bear hug from behind and lifted him off the ground and into the corridor.

'Stand back, please,' said Bob, as Neil's legs flailed about. He struggled to keep up with the sheer number of people he needed to insult as he was led down the corridor and to the doorway. I followed on behind.

Bob carried him through the door and dumped him on the lawn.

'And don't think about coming back in tonight!'

Bob stamped off.

'Have you finished, Neil?' I said.

'The lack of black or gay artists in your record collection says a lot about you!'

'Neil, you've already hurt my feelings! You don't need to do it again. Why can't this just stop now, please?'

'It can't. Not until ten thirty.'

'Christ. You'd better not live far from here.'

'Not really.'

'OK, we're going home. Just . . . look at the ground, OK?'

'I can't do that. It's against the System.'

I punched him hard in the back. 'I think you'll find you can,' I said.

Neil led me down the road to the room he rented in some old lady's house. We passed a few people on the way, but I grabbed the side of his head and forced it in the other direction. He managed to insult some poor man in shorts, telling him his knees were grotesque, but I just signalled that Neil had a screw loose. The man shook his head.

'Your cleaning is substandard!' Neil shouted at his landlady when she caught the corner of his eye. We were halfway up the stairs to his room at the time.

'What did you say, Neil? I'm sorry, I didn't catch that.' Thank fuck, she was deaf.

I looked at my watch. It had gone half eight. Less than two hours to go of this weirdness.

Neil's room was full of stuff, fantastically ordered. Everything had its place, the books, the records, tapes and CDs, his writing desk, his art things. It was all arranged alphabetically or thematically, and lined up with total precision. You'd think he'd used a spirit level or something. There were no posters or pictures on the wall. It was as if it hadn't occurred to him that there ought to be.

'You haven't done anything good since *Blackadder*!'

At first I tried to kill the time by putting the telly on, but Neil started shouting insults at everybody who appeared on it, so after about five minutes, I turned it off.

'Nobody loves you!'

I couldn't think who Neil might have been trying to insult now, as he was just lying on the bed. Then I saw that he had caught himself in the mirror.

'Nobody loves you,' he said again quietly. He started to cry.

I put my arm round his shoulders and held him to me while he sobbed. I couldn't bring myself to say anything.

After a while, he stopped. 'Why don't you put a record on?' he said.

'What do you want to hear?' I said.

'Don't mind, you choose.'

I flicked through his collection. There was a Morrissey album. *Bona Drag*, it was called. It had that song he'd told me about, all those years ago outside the school gates, 'Piccadilly Palare'.

I put it on. Wasn't nearly as bad as I thought it would be. Quite liked some of it. Nice guitars. His vocals weren't my sort of thing, but not bad.

We listened to that, and then a few other things. Roxy Music, the New York Dolls, David Bowie. Neil pointed out things in the lyrics and made connections between the bands, and had lots of little facts about everything, like how one David Bowie song was about an artist who nailed himself to the back of a Volkswagen. Neil said that this guy was his biggest artistic influence. Had been for years apparently, since before the talent show and everything.

As I went to turn over the Bowie album, I saw that it was nearly half past ten. Neil began to get restless. At ten twenty-eight, I could see him reach for his satchel. I put my hand on its latch.

'No, Neil, it's over.'

I took the satchel away from him and emptied the contents on the floor in a big heap. Probably the first heap this room had seen. Then I jumped up and down on the calculator until it was just shards of plastic and circuit board.

Neil laughed. So did I. It really was over now.

6

I slept on the floor. Neil gave me a pillow and blanket, and even though we'd swept up, I'd occasionally feel a fragment of calculator digging into me. I woke up properly at half nine. The sun had been trying to get through the curtains for hours, and finally a white beam hit my face. Neil was fast asleep. He breathed heavily, in, out. The first decent sleep he'd had in three years. I quietly got up, folded my blanket, grabbed my bag and left.

I slept some more on the train, although I kept on waking up, afraid I was going to miss my connection. But I thought a lot as well. By the time I was back in Sholeham it was late Saturday afternoon and I had made many plans in my head. I was going to get things the way they needed to be. I started with Caroline.

I wanted so much to end it there and then that I nearly just phoned her up as soon as I came in my door. But I knew doing it by phone would be cruel and I'd regret it later. So I just said I'd like to come round if that was OK. She was going out with her mates at eight, she hadn't thought I'd be back until much later, but I could pop round before if I liked. I got in my unreliable Vauxhall. I parked it outside the house she rented with two of her friends. I rang the doorbell, and she answered, and we went inside. She offered me a cup of tea and I said no and I had something to tell her. She asked what it was. I said it was over. She was silent. And then she cried. And she asked why.

I said I was going to go to London with the band and make it.

She said I was a fucking idiot and told me to get out.

I couldn't raise the band that Saturday evening, so I had no choice but to wait until morning. I didn't get much sleep that night, because voices telling me I'd made a terrible mistake kept on haranguing me, but the next morning I still felt that it was the right thing.

At nine o'clock I started phoning. Nobody was out of bed.

'We need a meeting,' I told them.

'Can't it wait until the next practice?' they all replied.

'No,' I said, 'it's really important. Something's come up that could make us.'

They all wanted to know what it was. I refused to tell them. I said they needed to hear it as a group. Finally I got everybody to agree to meet round Jase's.

I picked up Ben in the car. 'So what's this all about then?' he asked again.

'All I can say is, it's time for you to move out of your parents' house at last.'

He looked as if someone had told him he had to eat shit off a plate.

'Right, what's the wankering point of this?' said Thomas, as we met up in Jase's living room. He still hadn't learned to speak normally.

I sat backwards on my chair and faced the others. Looking at them, I could see the effect that wasted time had already had. Ben had a pot belly from all the takeaways he'd wolfed down while lying on the big puffy sofa at his parents'. Thomas's hairline was beginning to recede, his curly hair cut short now,

263

revealing the loss all the more. Even Jase, who had always been in excellent shape, was beginning to look a bit stocky.

'Guys, we're going to have to move to London.'

Their mouths dropped open.

'Why?' said Thomas, with a venom I hadn't heard for some years. He'd become quite sedate of late.

'Because we're achieving nothing here! We're playing the same venues to the same people. The people who need to hear us aren't hearing us. We need to be there, right at the heart of things, where the A&R men are. We need to be making a demo in a good-quality studio, and getting people to listen to it. Don't you get it? We're wasting our time. We've got to go out and make it happen!'

There was silence.

'I'm not moving to London,' said Jase.

'Why not?'

'I don't want to. Why would I? I'm happy where I am. I like my job, money's coming in and I've got a flat with my girlfriend. We're actually talking of trying for a baby next year. Why should I leave?'

'Because of the band!'

'I was only ever doing it for fun, Chris.'

'You fucking liar!' I screamed. 'You've always wanted it to work, right from the beginning.'

'I never said that.'

'Well, fuck you then. We can get a new drummer. London's full of them.'

'I'm not going to London.' This time it was Thomas who spoke.

'What? You've got nothing! You're the man who repairs the

vending machine in the office! You have got absolutely nothing to lose. You gave up the chance to do anything else for the band! What's the point of not seeing it through?'

'I'm not going to London,' he said simply.

'What about you, Ben?' I twisted my chair round to face him. 'Are you happy on the bins? Are you happy living with your parents? Does being a lazy slob really make you happy?'

He thought about it for a full half-minute. I knew he couldn't pull the girlfriend card on me because he hadn't had one since last year. He'd gone out for a bit with this girl called Claire, who was a lazy slob like him, and they used to spend all their time together lying in their own filth at his parents'. Then she got tired of being broke so she found someone with money to leech off. It tore him apart, I could tell, but he never expressed it except for his guitar solos, which got too angry for our West Coast harmony sound for a few weeks.

The silence pressed down on me as I became aware that my face must have turned very red.

'I'll go with you,' he said. It was barely audible.

'What?'

'I'll go with you.' He enunciated sarcastically.

'OK, fine, we'll do it. Us two. We're really going to do it!'

I stood up quickly. The chair went flying.

'Come on, Ben,' I said. 'We've got plans to make.'

Ben looked like he wanted to stay and drink Jase's beer, but I motioned for him to follow me.

We sat in the car. I was having trouble breathing.

'I can't go to London,' Ben said.

I felt as if I'd just been kicked in the throat.

'You are fucking kidding me.'

265

'No, I can't go to London. It's too big. I couldn't handle it.'

'You just said, not five minutes ago, that you would. So you're fucking wimping out on me too!' I slammed the dashboard. It fucking hurt.

'No, that's not what I'm saying. I just can't go to London, that's all.'

'So what are you saying, then?' I said through clenched teeth. I felt anger rise within me like it had never done before.

'We don't need to go to London. We can go to Brighton. Loads of people are moving there from London now. Loads of music people. The London scene's dead, now Britpop's over. We can do just as well in Brighton. It's smaller, better for us. We'd just disappear in London.'

He was right. We would.

'So you'll really do it then,' I said, 'you'll come to Brighton with me?'

'Yeah.'

'Are you sad this is all over?'

'Nah, not really. I always thought the songs were shit. Waste of my time playing my guitar over them.'

'You could have mentioned that sooner.'

'Yeah, s'pose.'

I started the car. I looked up for a second, and saw Thomas glowering out of the window. And then I drove off.

7

It was tough starting again in Brighton. We signed up with the local branch of my agency, and it found us both work, but it was intermittent at first, a bit here, a bit there. Also, Ben didn't come across very well because of his attitude, so they were reluctant to send him to some places. All we could afford was a studio flat, so we were both sleeping in the same room. It wasn't exactly sexy, and Ben's habits were appalling. I constantly had to have a go at him about leaving his dirty clothes lying about, and it's not as if he washed that often or anything. And getting him to do any household chores, you can forget it. He'd either not do them at all, however much I asked, or do them so badly I had to do them again myself anyway. You could go on at him about it until the cows came home, but he'd just sit on the second-hand sofa smoking a roll-up and shrug. He was a total slob. Never again. On the plus side, our poverty was reducing the size of his pot belly, now he couldn't afford a constant diet of takeaways, and he began to look a little more like a rock star again.

Getting a new band going was even harder than paying the rent. We'd place adverts in music shops and hold auditions in rehearsal rooms, which in itself would cost a bomb. We'd decided we were only going to go for people who were just right, good musicians with good attitudes, but the only people who turned up were either useless, or wankers, or bass players into jazz-funk.

Sometimes we'd answer ads ourselves. We were well aware that although we could both play and sing, neither of us had ever been much cop at writing songs, so we needed to hook up with people who could generate material. Problem was, there were very few bands looking for two guitarists. And whoever was writing the songs was generally playing rhythm guitar already. They just needed a lead. I marvelled at how long it was taking Ben to realise I was dead weight. He was a brilliant guitar player. He could have joined the best band in Brighton if he wanted. If he just got rid of me. But I don't think he wanted to. I was his final comfort zone. His parents were gone, the dole was gone, Sholeham was gone. There was just me left.

This went on for months. The work picked up in the autumn, so our finances got better, but every audition, every wanted ad answered, led nowhere. The flat began to get cold. The bills went up. This wasn't working.

Brighton was not our city. We could never seem to click into its rhythm. We'd been there before years ago, on a trip to the North Laines with the band to get some new stage-wear, but we'd been panicked by the bustle in the crowded narrow streets and all the narcissistic preening, and retreated to Top Man in the high street in fright. Now we were living here it was just the same. Everybody was a star, or looked like one. Everybody was doing something amazing, or acting like they were. We were nothing. We were going under. Soon those narrow streets would swallow us and bury us, and the carnival would go on above our forgotten heads.

It was a November night, and a mist had fallen. The mist was our failure, it seemed. We were leaving our too-cold flat to spend money we did not have on drinks we did not want. It was a noisy pub, where everybody shouted about how great they were over a punk jukebox. But we had to go there. It was a musicians' pub, a place to make contacts.

We walked in. We got about two feet inside before the heave of bodies stopped us going any further. So we just stood there for a while, waiting to summon up the willpower to push our way to the bar. Then I saw him. Sitting, nursing a pint alone in an alcove, was Bernie Chessington. His cheekbones were unmistakable. He'd been big a couple of years ago, at the height of Britpop. His band, Chessington's World of Dementia, had had a couple of hits, notably one called 'London Nights', which was an awful song about a cockney prostitute or something. But by '97, tastes had moved on. *Melody Maker* had slated their last album, saying, 'If you like this then you've never had sex and you smell of wee.' I'm not kidding, that was the review. And there he was, his hair longer, his face puffier and his nose redder. I'm not entirely sure he knew exactly where he was, but there he was. He was alone, and nobody was bothering him. In '98 nobody wanted to be reminded of '96. But despite this, and despite his dishevelled state, somehow you could tell he was a star, or had been once, an awareness that he was the most important person in the room, any room. It was all in the posture, the stillness. He didn't need to move. The world moved for him. Or used to.

'You know who that is, don't you?' said Ben, needlessly mumbling in my ear.

'Yeah, I do. Let's go and talk to him.'

'I don't think he wants to be bothered.'

'Well, if he doesn't, he can always say. Let's go.'

Ben grumbled something and followed me as I pushed through the crowd. About five minutes later we finally made it.

'Hi there,' I said, as his eyes tried to focus on the vague forms in front of him. 'Are you Bernie Chessington?'

'Yeah, I am,' his speech was slurred in some horrible approximation of Keith Richards, deliberately or not, I couldn't tell.

'Hi, I'm Chris. I'm a great fan of your work.' I wasn't, I hated it, but it would be no use telling him that. 'This is Ben.'

'Hi guys,' he said, waving.

'So, is it true that Chessington's World of Dementia have broken up, then?'

'Listen, Chessington was me. The band was whoever I chose to work with at any moment in time. But yeah, I'm not currently operating under that nom de plume.'

'So, do you live here now, then?'

'Thinking about it, thinking about it. London's just so . . .'

We waited for him to finish his sentence, until it became clear he never would.

'We've just moved down here, actually,' I said. 'We're trying to start a band.'

His eyebrows raised and his misty eyes widened. 'Really?'

'Yeah.'

'Then you might be just the sort of chaps I'm looking for. What instruments do you play?'

'I play rhythm guitar, Ben plays lead.'

'Excellent. Fantastic. Brilliant.' He reached in his pocket looking for something. He failed to find it.

'Would either of you gentlemen happen to have a pen?'

'Yeah, sure.' I handed him a biro and prayed it would work.

He tore off a side of a cigarette packet and wrote on the back.

'Can you get to this address for four o'clock tomorrow?'

'Yeah, no problem.' This was a lie. We both had work. We'd

270

have to call in sick. I could see Ben was about to make a fuss, but I kicked him in the leg to silence him.

'OK, if you can get to these rehearsal rooms with your instruments, we'll try out a few things. You never know, Chessington phase II could start tomorrow!'

We both shook his hand and left him to slip back into his fog.

'We've got to get back home now!' I said.

Back at the flat, we frantically tried to work out the chords to 'London Nights'. Neither of us could even remember how it went, other than the chorus of 'She's such a sight on those London nights, dirty in a miniskirt, glamour in the headlights.' Like I said, it was shit. But even though we hated it, just to have this opportunity open up was more exciting than anything we'd experienced since we started playing. Our hearts were thumping faster than they'd ever thumped before. This was it. It was going to happen for us, we just knew it. When everything seemed hopeless, our fortunes had turned around. We were on the verge of becoming professional and successful musicians.

After half an hour we gave up trying to remember it. We simply couldn't. 'Bollocks,' I said. 'OK, first thing tomorrow, we're pulling a sickie and we're going record shopping.'

And that's what we did. Nine o'clock, and we were at the nearest independent record shop in the North Laines. Not only did we buy both Chessington's World of Dementia albums, but all their singles, just in case Bernie wanted us to play some obscure B-sides. From nine thirty onwards, we listened to each song twice, frantically working out the chords, running through it once and moving on to the next one. Fortunately, they were not that hard, as they were all based on pretty much the same chord progressions. We'd got them all done by half two. For the next hour we played 'London

Nights' and the B-side to the last, unsuccessful single nearly ten times each. Then we headed for the rehearsal studio.

The mist of the night before had turned into pissing rain. It was an absolutely miserable day. But we were so excited, the rain barely registered in our minds as we walked down the steep street of seaside townhouses painted the colours of Neapolitan ice cream. We were going to play with a proper musician, someone who'd been on telly, sold some records. This was really going to happen.

By the time we got to the rehearsal rooms, we were soaked to the skin. We walked into the reception, dripping waterfalls onto the cigarette-burnt carpet. From a desk plastered in 'musicians wanted' and gig posters, a bald man with tattoos and piercings eyed us through the metal in his face.

'Hi, lads,' he said. 'What can I do you for?'

'Do you know which room we could find Bernie Chessington?' It felt amazing just to say the name of a successful musician out loud, with the implication we were associated with him. 'He'll be expecting us.'

'Hang on a minute,' he said. He looked in a book, running his finger down a column. 'No, sorry, Bernie hasn't booked a room for today.'

'Are you sure? I think he has.'

'No, nothing here, sorry. He came in here about a month ago, but we haven't heard from him since.'

I turned to Ben. His face was even glummer than normal. 'Why don't we wait? He might turn up.'

'S'pose.'

We waited an hour and a half in the reception room. No Bernie.

'He's not coming, is he?' said Ben, finally.

'No, I guess not.'

272

We sadly picked up our guitars and went outside into the pissing rain. It fell on my face and into my eyes and my mouth. I stood there not moving, letting the misery it so neatly represented fill my every available orifice.

'I give up,' I said. 'I've had enough.'

And we went back to our flat and, accepting an IOU, I sold my guitar to Ben.

8

That was two years ago. As soon as the contract was up on our flat, I got myself out of Brighton. I just couldn't hack it. I also couldn't face going back to Sholeham. My failure would have hung over me everywhere I went. So I moved up the coast to a little town called Southwick, just because it was quiet, and I could still get into Brighton if I needed to. The agency found me in a job in the area, working in the back room of a wholesalers. It was very similar to the warehouse we rehearsed in that one time with Spencer, and I was right, working in a place like that would do something to your soul. I was stuck with some old middle-aged guy who was really common and stank of fags and had tattoos and everything. He used to be a driver, but he'd been put in the back room because of his health. I think he thought I was some sort of idiot. We didn't get on that well. We just didn't understand what the other was trying to say half the time. Not only that, but he had a habit of illustrating the most mundane thing with a line from a song. Like he'd need a particular form and he'd go, 'I'll tell you what I want, what I really, really want. I really, really wanna G-11 form.' Or he'd sing something by Queen. There was a Queen song for every occasion. If we'd got an order out on time, he'd sing 'Weeee are the champeeons, my friiieends . . .' When he'd finished a bit of paperwork, it was 'And another one gone, and another one gone, another one bites the dust-ah!' The most inventive one was when he put the kettle on, he'd go, 'I want to make tea, I want to maaake teeeaa . . .'

I had a new girlfriend for a while called Julie, or Jools, as she insisted on being called. We met in a charity shop, thumbing through the records. She was a couple of years older than me. Not entirely sure what she saw in me, but we hit it off. Jools had quite a good job in marketing, and she'd take me to these parties where young men about the same age as me would all stand around in their designer glasses talking about their music collections. I could have joined in if I wanted to, but I really didn't. They'd just be going, 'Have you heard such and such?' and the other would go, 'Yeah I have, have you heard thingumabob?' And the first guy would go, 'No I haven't.' And then the other would say, 'You should check them out. If you like such-and-such, you'll love thingumabob.' And it would just go on and on like that, like kids swapping football cards in the playground or something. Or worse, us metaller kids back at school doing each other tapes and wanting them back by Monday. It meant as little to me as the bloke at work singing his Queen songs.

But then music didn't really mean anything to me any more. I'd still listen to it and buy it out of force of habit, but I wasn't hearing it, not really. It was just noise. And in all honesty, even though I had a credible collection, with loads of things like Dylan, the Clash, the Stones, Pixies, Mercury Rev and everything, I'd come to the hard realisation that absolutely none of it had ever given me as much pleasure as Metallica, or Napalm Death, or even Stryper, all those years ago, back in the golden age. And I couldn't listen to those records any more – they're terrible, I think, now. But I'd spent years trying to rediscover that old thrill, and never quite finding it. It's gone. It's gone for good. A lot of the time I prefer quiet.

I was thinking about doing a course so I could teach guitar in a community college or something, but what would be the point? Lead more young kids up the garden path, have their hearts broken? Nah, fuck it. Fuck music. Music's shit.

I broke up with Jools a while back. My heart wasn't in it really, and, besides, I hated her friends. Then the agency said the wholesalers didn't want me any more. Said I wasn't bonding well with the other staff, which I suppose means the tattoo Queen-man didn't like me, seeing as he was the only other person in the room. Fair enough, I didn't like him. The agency hasn't been that helpful in finding me anything else since then, and I haven't been pushing them that much.

I'm on the dole. Thanks to music, I don't have the experience I need to get a job worth having, or half the qualifications. I don't have any friends here, and I'm not bothered about having any. Occasionally my mum phones me, then puts me on to my dad, and occasionally I phone my sister, but that's about it. I just want to be left alone, to be honest with you.

Of course, that's not true really; I want out of this desperately. I can't believe I've let myself get in this situation. It's not me at all. I had to see the new century in by myself, watching the *Hootenanny*. It wouldn't be so bad, but they pre-record that programme months ahead, which really rubs it in. But starting again, new life, new job, new friends. It all seems such a risk.

I suppose I should say a bit about what's happened to everybody else. Thomas and Jase, I have no clue. I haven't seen either of them since the day I drove off from Jase's flat all that time ago. Maybe Thomas is still fixing the vending machines. Would be pretty funny if he was, to be honest. Jase probably owns the garage by now. Married his bird and had seven kids and now lives in a mansion.

Ben came out good in the end. He joined a Brighton band called The Blow-Up, who are doing quite well for themselves. A couple of singles out on their own label, national tours, some good support slots and a bit of radio play. He phones occasionally to say when they're playing locally, but I've never quite got round to going. I suppose I should. They've got a TV spot coming up on late-night telly and he's going to play my old guitar on it apparently. Yeah, I should definitely see them next time they play round here.

And then there's Neil. Of course, there was that box the other day. Well, not really a box, more a bloody crate. Must have got my address off my mum or dad, I should imagine. The return address was somewhere in Newcastle. What the fuck's he doing up there? I opened it up, and inside were not only hundreds of records, tapes and CDs, but a load of books, and a lot of Neil's art, going back years, even to his coursework for A-level and GCSE, and even before that. It was like a whole chunk of his life, in one crate. Haven't a clue what I'm going to do with it all, it's just sitting in a corner of the flat at the moment. I've looked through it a bit, and there's some pretty crazy stuff in there. Can't really throw it away. I guess I'm stuck with it.

There was a note. It read:

Hi Chris
Hope this box finds you well. I've been having a bit of a clear-out and thought you might enjoy some of these things. Feel free to distribute amongst friends.
 Best
 Neil

That's it. That's all it said. What the fuck am I meant to make of that? But it got me thinking. Maybe it means he's OK. Because people who are OK have clear-outs, whereas people with problems hold on to stuff. That's why they have problems, most of the time, because they can't let go.

So maybe it's time for me to let go of what happened to Neil. I'll be honest, when I started telling this, I was all ready to beat myself up over what we did and what I didn't stop from happening. And sure, I've done that. But that's not all there is to it. Yes, I recognise that. And I know I should have allowed myself to explore what it was he was showing me. That door in me he opened at the talent show, that was his gift to me, and I did nothing with it. Not until it was too late, anyway. But Neil, he could fuck things up for himself without anybody's help. I mean, did any of that mad shit make him happy? Look, I fucked up, don't get me wrong. But I did OK too, some of the time, at some things. And I gave him a hell of a lot more time and attention than anybody else did over the years, even when he was obviously trying to mess with my head. Perhaps the problem was Neil was so busy trying to open doors in other people, he forgot to allow them to open doors in him. Maybe there was stuff we could have taught him, if he'd have let us. I don't know, maybe Neil's a mystery I'll never solve.

Still, there was something in the box that I thought might be a clue. First thing I found when I opened it. It was some artwork he did, years ago, for GCSE probably. I think I remember it, vaguely. It was essentially an Andy Warhol thing, rows of photocopies of a photograph, all in different colours, with the image getting darker and darker with each one. But it's only looking at it now that I can see the first image, before it gets too dark to make out properly, is an old family photo. Neil's family. You can make out a little Neil, very little, and his mum, who doesn't look mad in it, and . . . his dad. His dad's there, in the photo. Just some bloke in a seventies diamond-pattern jumper, losing his hair, smiling at the camera, waiting to go.

Does it mean anything? The image being obscured, the happy family disappearing, everything becoming dark. Is this what lies at the centre of Neil, looking right back at me? Or does it mean nothing, other than some stuff about reproduction and democratic art that Neil got out of some library book.

Time to stop That's it. Here I am. Just me. And my regrets. More and more, I think what I did to Caroline was fucking stupid. But I know, time to let go. Start again.

Look what else I found in the box. All those tapes of that programme Neil used to tape off the radio back when we were at school full of all the music that seemed so weird back then. Now I can see it's mostly just things like Syd Barrett, Echo and the Bunnymen and the Chocolate Watchband. I've got a lot of this stuff myself now. And here, on the tape marked 6 July 1992, is 'Flying Saucer Rock 'n' Roll' by Billy Lee Riley. The name sounds familiar. Rockabilly, I think, Sun Records. Finally, I can find out what this thing sounds like. Whatever the fuck it was we were meant to be playing, or not playing, at band practice in Neil's front room, all that time ago.

I open the cassette case. And I snap it shut again. I don't want to hear it. I can imagine it instead. And in my head, I hear it, almost. No, it's not that I hear it, I feel it. In the silence, I feel it, and it's like hearing Metallica for the first time, with Barry warning me that it was evil, and me not caring. He was right. It is. It all is. Music can control your soul. The sledgehammer wasn't such a bad idea. But you don't have to destroy something to stop it from taking you over. You just have to know who you are. And against that, it will be defenceless. I know who I am. I'm the man who was a boy, who had it all and lost it, who didn't believe enough and then believed too much. But now I've worked out where belief ends and insanity begins, I think. I hope Neil has too. And now it's time to start again.